On the Edge

Aadi Sahu

ISBN
Paperback 979-8-89906-638-2
Hardcase 979-8-89929-335-1

Ilustrator - Arya Deleon

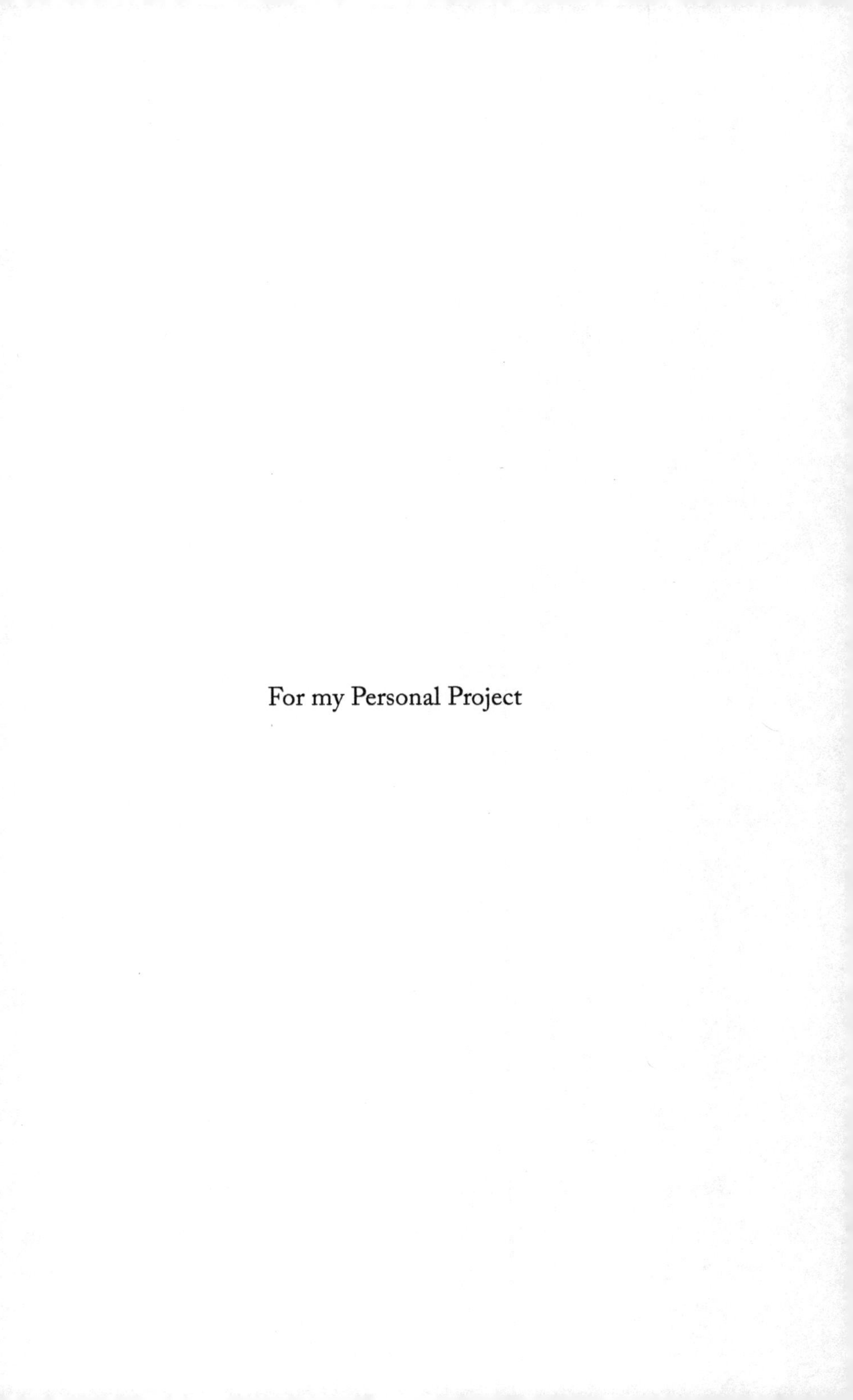

For my Personal Project

I would like to dedicate this book to everyone that has contributed to my growth—not necessarily as a writer, but as an individual.

To my incredible parents: your love, support, and limitless faith in me have molded everything that I am. You've always been my rock, and I'm forever in debt to the sacrifices you've made so that I can fulfill my aspirations.

To my teachers: thanks for your passion, your patience, and your love of learning. You taught me the power of curiosity, and you encouraged me to think that knowledge is not merely something we pursue—but something we give.

To my grandparents and to my brother: your encouragement did not always take the form of words, but in the small, unremarkable gestures of love that sustained me. You taught me that family is a steady presence, even when everything else in life seems uncertain.

All of you have played a role in this. Without your guidance, strength, and love, there would be no book. From the depths of my soul—thank you.

CONTENTS

AUTHOR INTRODUCTION

Hi! I'm a 15-year-old student at Kodaikanal International School, originally from San Francisco, California. I've always been drawn to stories—not just reading them, but imagining my own worlds and characters. Writing has been a quiet passion of mine for as long as I can remember.

During my tenth grade, I finally decided to take the leap and try something I'd always dreamed of: writing a novel. With no prior experience, I simply carved out time between classes and homework, letting my ideas grow into something real. It took many late nights and long hours, but it finally got finished.

I've been inspired by authors like Roald Dahl and J.D. Salinger—writers who know how to mix imagination with truth. Their work taught me that stories don't always have to make sense, rather have a purpose. That's what I've tried to do with mine.

This book is the beginning of my journey, and with your support, it may not be the end. I'm so excited to share my first project with you, and I hope you can help me improve for the better!

Chapter 1

HOME

I stand looking at the streets this cold morning. From my apartment, I can see everything—the baker kneading dough in the warm glow of his shop, the scent of fresh bread barely reaching my window. The aroma mingles with the sharp, acrid smell of coal smoke rising from the chimneys. Nazi officers, stern and unyielding, patrol the streets with an air of authority that chills more than the brisk wind. Their jackboots strike the cobblestones with a rhythmic, ominous thud. Austria makes me question my place in this world. The gray skies and thick air give the scene a dramatic, oppressive atmosphere. The perpetual fog and daunting military presence make me doubt the belief that we truly are the greatest nation.

As I smoke my cigarette, the smoke curling around my fingers, a flame burns in my heart for a better world. The Führer promises such a future, but I find it hard to believe him. He wants to eradicate the Jews. While I don't care much for them, the idea of exterminating an entire race will never make him sound like a man of reason. I watch a Jewish family hurry down the street, their faces etched with fear and uncertainty. The father glances nervously over his shoulder, clutching his child's hand tightly. My heart aches with a mixture of pity and guilt. An image comes into my head, the Führer stands tall in his crisp, pressed uniform, his voice booming with conviction as he addresses the crowds. But his piercing blue eyes seem to hold a hint of madness, a glint of something dark and sinister lurking beneath the surface. The fear in the Jewish family's eyes is palpable as they rush down the street, their faces etched with worry and uncertainty. The father's grip on his child's hand is tight as if trying to protect them from an invisible threat. A name is barely visible on a small boy's back, a name that could mark him for death in this dangerous time.

I see the Führer's propaganda posters plastered on every street corner, his face stern and commanding. The red and black Nazi flags flutter in the wind. The Führer stands tall and proud, his dark eyes filled with a burning determination. His words are both mesmerizing and chilling as they reach the ears of his followers. The streets are lined with propaganda posters, showcasing the strong leader. Meanwhile, the Jewish family scurries by, their faces etched with despair and terror as they try to hide from the looming threat of destruction. I see my name on the back of the young child who hides under his father. I break into a cold sweat. That's my name, is it not? I look again and I see nothing but the family going away. It may just be my imagination, but a profession like mine will make it real in a second.

I take a deep drag on my cigarette, feeling the smoke fill my lungs and momentarily distract me from my thoughts. The gray morning light filters through the window, casting long shadows across my sparsely furnished room. A small table, two chairs, and a single bed are all I possess. There are only a few faded photographs of my family on the wall, but every face wears a smile; it is in meticulous care. But beneath that, I dig deeper: the unspoken tensions that must have been in there, even when she was younger. The smiles are almost like photographs, faded over time; they feel almost "put on" to keep up an illusion of unity or happiness that perhaps never truly was. I cannot help but wonder how much of our memories are shaped through these so-called planned moments, and how much is left out with having disappeared or fallen under the surface of those heart-warming smiles. The pictures and mementos that once stood for connection now appear to be fragments of something more fragile and faintly cast a shadow over my sense of self. My father, a proud and honorable man, smiles at me from a picture taken before the war. He was drafted into the Weltkrieg, The Great War, and The War to End All War when I was just a child, and I can still recall the relief I felt each time his letters arrived. But those letters stopped one day, and the silence was unbearable. We were made of honor, but his death had none.

As I stand here, I wonder what he would think of the world we live in today. Would he be proud of me, or would he be ashamed of what we have become? I long for a day when I can be proud to call myself a German, in a Greater German Reich. The Führer's vision for the future feels like a twisted nightmare, one that I am forced to participate in against my will, but hopefully a nightmare for Germany's enemies.

I crush the cigarette beneath my heel and turn away from the window. The streets of Vienna hold no answers for me, only more questions. I yearn for a sense of purpose, a reason to believe in something greater than myself. The air is thick with the smell of coal and burning wood, a reminder of the approaching winter. But there is also a sickly sweet scent of burning flesh that fills the air, a sign of the atrocities on my heel. The Führer's promise of a "better" future reeks of lies and deceit, and a hint of fear and desperation from the Jewish family hurrying by. The acrid smell of hatred and prejudice also hangs in the air. The bitterness of the cigarette lingers on my tongue, a small comfort amid the chaos and uncertainty. Bitterness and guilt flood the mouth.

The streets are filled with the scent of fear, desperation, and smoke from burning books and buildings. Bitterness. The smell of oppression lingers in the air, mixing with the sickly sweet odor of propaganda and false promises. But as long as the fog of war and hatred hang over us, I fear that day will never come. The lingering feeling now passes as I toss the remaining embers.

The world is being burned so that the chosen ones will rise and rebuild, unlike ever before. This forces us, the ones selected, to be all tight-knit as if puppets to one man's ideals, any excerpt from him then becomes law, and disregarding the card for his faith makes you a failed martyr.

It falls on the neighbor's plant. A bright, tall, and luscious green plant, she took great care of all her plants, maybe as a way of recreation. Now, I see a blackened outline where I've made a hole. It doesn't matter to me, though. Why care when you can't do anything anyway? As long as I know that I am fine, I will be, if god was as kind as the father said he was, the Jews would have already been saved. Why would I try to be a philosophical hack, the madman running around the streets? All unkempt and dirty either ranting about the lack of a god, or the fact that we all must be virtuous to reach a better place. It doesn't matter, time is the one constant thing, and instead of trying to outpace it, I will do what I must to survive. I won't ever let myself be degraded to the likes of Nietzsche or Marx; they all have or will die, and their impact is just letting more people throw their lives away. Must I live with the burdens of those who fail? As one watches the innocent being persecuted and hunted.

I go to light another cigarette only to see my pack empty. I really must stop. I mutter under my breath as if anyone were near me. The sun was falling beneath the rural-urbanized construction of Vienna. I hope that we don't become like the gray jungle. I look at the grotesque amalgamation my apartment has become. I thought having two houses would be easy, but it has become an utter headache. My clothes are sporadically spread everywhere, the kitchen is always spotless, and a feeling of asylum rather than comfort. I intended to think it was one of those utopias: one bloodless, one orderly life with everything held in place. But life isn't tidy. I have a floor full of clothes flung across the room. Folded. Socks in a corner. Not where I'd like them to be, but there. Jackets strewn across the rack are a pain to travel with. My shoes, just some plain loafers, of course, standing in front of the door, but I am too weak to put them together neatly, so they lay amok.

And yet, the kitchen is spotless. Gleaming countertops and dishes are always washed and put away. It stands at odds with the rest of the space, like some monument to order in a sea of sameness. It's unsettling for that reason as if the kitchen's false sense of perfection laughs at the rest of the apartment's squalor. This place, rather than comforting me, feels like an asylum. The walls are too clean, too bare, and the emptiness, rather than being soothing, presses in on all sides. It feels like the space around me has become indifferent and estranged, only existing in the background while I play out my life against this backdrop.

Maybe I transfer my frustration to this white prison, to these rooms. Honestly, none of it should matter. What do wall clothes or spotless kitchens mean in the grand scheme? All I need, truly, is a pen and paper. To write is my necessity. For one thing only will cut through the noise, which is that I might make sense out of the mess that is life and mold it into something that makes sense for me; let the walls be pale white and bare, furniture few, and the bed half-folded, perpetually - I can live with that. Let me live as I feel, in the mess or in the quiet.

Some chaotic work of art.

Certainly not my first.

Chapter 2

KRISTALLNACHT

November 9, 1938, Berlin, Germany

I wake up to the sounds of disruption and distortion on the streets. It's early morning, and my sleep itself is as bright as the Berlin winters. Needless to say, I should inquire about this matter before I have to write about it today at work. As I got out of bed, I heard the screaming of Jews and Nazis alike, but in the moment they were all the same. The *constant* noise made me start to get the same feeling of annoyance one does with a baby who won't stop complaining. As if every day, people woke me up only to hear their complaints about the world that day, I couldn't tell them to be quiet as my interest wasn't even a concept in their hearts.

I step out to see the broken glass on the floor, faint traces of blood, and the dark red contrast on the black background of Berlin. The violence that erupted overnight left a stark and haunting aftermath, with evidence of the pogrom *visible* everywhere. All the people who had inhabited the city only hours ago were now left with an uncertain fate of life or death. Smoke still rose from the remains of synagogues that had been set ablaze, and the atmosphere was heavy with fear and uncertainty among the people. I heard the citizens outside jeering at one another, trying to weed out the rest of the "infestation" as they deemed. I was now out of bed and started my morning routine. Starting with a shower, I always avoid the water from coming to my hair, the *last* thing I want is to fall sick. It's not as if I leave it dirty, but I make sure that I won't be drenched. After about two minutes, I change into a plain and tattered beige suit with a yellow shirt, and crispy blue pants that are tearing at the seams. Still hearing the incessant noise, I start to grow sympathy for the Jews, not as if I ever thought they deserved such a fate, but though I've been taught that we as Germans are above Jews, such a dictation isn't just. I go down to my apartment, the room's in a mess, a mess of paper and clothes all alloyed together on the ground. My gray walls are all sparsely decorated with only a few pictures of me and my family; otherwise, I only have a portrait of my first story in the paper, August 26, 1937. A German plane bombed the small city of Guernica and somehow I was chosen to write the story for the public. I don't know why, but the management didn't realize that I was new, the pressure was so immense from the corporate office that I hadn't even grown accustomed to, had started going from too substantial to even see, and at that moment it was only me, all the rest of the slow office dwellers were behind me. Their lives do not *matter* as regardless of what I do, I realized, behind the dull, yet colorful office-suit exteriors, I never did or will matter to them, only I can help myself. In an hour, I told my superior, Max Amann, that I had finished. Interestingly, I think he was the reason that I had been able to get the opportunity. Max was a true Nazi and is a leader of the Völkischer Beobachter, though he doesn't heed the employees as much as he should.

Max Amann was a stocky, robust man with a somewhat imposing presence. Standing at about average height, he had a solid build, reflecting his military background. His face was often serious, with sharp, determined features, including a square jaw and a stern expression. He sported a short, tidy haircut, and his appearance fit the disciplined, authoritarian image that was common among Nazi officials. Amann was known to be a hard-nosed, pragmatic figure with little tolerance for dissent or deviation from the Nazi line. He was loyal to the party and Hitler, shaping much of his emotional disposition. Amann was emotionally detached in his role, driven by his commitment to Nazi ideology rather than personal sentiment. He was not known for warmth or empathy but was instead focused on efficiency, discipline, and control. Mentally, Max Amann was sharp, organized, and ruthless regarding business and propaganda. As the head of the Nazi publishing empire, he demonstrated a keen ability to manage large-scale operations, ensuring that the Völkischer Beobachter became a well-oiled propaganda machine. His mindset was thoroughly aligned with Nazi ideology, and he had no qualms about suppressing or censoring anything that contradicted the party's views. He was pragmatic in his approach to propaganda, understanding its power in shaping public opinion and maintaining control over the media. However, his intellectual breadth was narrowly focused on furthering Nazi objectives rather than broader cultural or philosophical exploration.

When I wrote it down, I didn't know what I wanted to be, just something that would please this Nazi idealist, and so I turned a tragedy into a story of German heroism. It was a moment that made me realize the true merit that this job would take on me.

As I go down the stairs of my apartment, the cold wind of Berlin hits me instantly. I see the tattered and dirty streets of the previous night and all the soldiers cleaning up their mess. On the drive to the office, I saw many of the masses who still suffer despite the Führers' talk of a "better world." I still see the same mistakes of an old world hidden behind this veil.

When I enter my office, I see countless other writers working tirelessly all night trying to please what the party wants them to write, so that the public stays calm. Before I even say a word, I must be sure to pay my respects to the Führer.

"Heil!"

Everyone makes sure to say this before anything else; sometimes, it's the only time you'll hear certain voices. In a sad way, this is the only real connection we will ever have with each other, his gaze making everyone feel watched as we work. Despite being a newspaper, we had the least amount of free speech, and opinions were fictionalized to let us serve a narrative among the Nazi public. I immediately started writing about Kristallnacht and how we Germans were saved from near death by the Jews by the graces of our rule. I made up lies about the Führer's greatness and the parasitic nature of the Jews. The Nazi soldiers who were often stationed around the office were spouting about the previous night's escapades, and some even making jokes about how the families were suffering. As I was sitting in my office looking at the typewriter, I felt a wave of disgust toward not only myself but the whole system that I needed to be a part of. I knew what I was doing, maybe my right as a citizen, but it still never felt right. I stopped halfway through the project, looking into the abyss that was my yellow-walled office. I began to realize why I despised the color as I always associated it with the lies I published. I always kept it very sparsely decorated, with the only photos being up were that of my previous works and one photo of my father.

My father was very tall and strong with his defined face and dark brown hair. He was always optimistic and had a large smile that was indistinguishable. His tall figure was opposite to my thin and frail build; only the height passed in the gene pool. I carried the resemblance of my mother, who had died in childbirth. My father always believed my looks to be a gift, considering it was the last real part of my mother still left.

He was the man I probably admired most, and I always felt a twang of regret whenever I looked at his photo as I knew it wasn't right that he was gone. He was drafted in the First World War when I was a young child, and I always felt relieved when his letters came. The essence of my ever-fleeting youth was caught in those few paragraphs on the letter. He was also the reason I even chose to pursue English. My father always wanted me to learn English and study abroad, so in his letters, he tried teaching me a few words and phrases he had picked up from other soldiers in the war. He said his dream was to send me to Oxford so that, in his words,

"You could conquer the world with an Englishman's education!"

He would say this in a tone so bright you would think that he could lead a country. His hope truly made me think that I had that in me, but alas, I still think his corpse rolls seeing what I've become today. The sad part was that at a certain point, he had accepted death and wrote many letters in a drawer that he had left for when he would be gone. My father knew how dangerous the war was and the possibility of him dying. In these letters, he wrote what he believed would be his last word to me; in every single one, it was a mix of hope and inspiration. He talked about the world as if I hadn't seen a grain of sand on the beach, always telling stories about his time in Belgium and France. How the world was so diverse and colorful that even seeing someone who didn't speak your language was an adventure. My father always spoke so highly of the European cultures, how they all flourished despite their differences, and he always told me that I should try to experience this as well.

The memories of my father flooded my mind, and for a moment, I was transported back to our small home in the German countryside. The smell of my mother's cooking, the sound of my father's deep laughter, it all felt so vivid and real. He had always been a beacon of light, guiding me with his wisdom and unwavering optimism. In a way, it helps that he doesn't see the way our country has become; life sometimes works like that.

But now, as I sat in my dingy office in Berlin, surrounded by propaganda and deceit, I couldn't help but feel a profound disillusionment. The stories I was expected to write felt like lies coated in sugar, meant to deceive the public and perpetuate the twisted narrative of the regime. The walls of my office were covered in propaganda posters, and bold red and black lettering urging citizens to join the cause. The desk in front of me was cluttered with papers, each one containing a message I was expected to spread to the masses. But all I saw were lies, coated in flowery language and false promises of prosperity. My unfinished article in the morning lay abandoned on the desk, a reminder of the truth I was trying to hide. Adorned with posters and banners, each bearing the bold image of a strong, blonde-haired man with piercing blue eyes. The air was heavy with the lingering scent of printer's ink and cigarette smoke, a constant reminder of who I worked for. My desk was cluttered with books and papers, but among the chaos, one unfinished article on Kristallnacht lay untouched, a glaring reminder of my duties.

I again glanced at the unfinished article lying on my desk. How could I continue to paint a false picture of salvation and prosperity when I knew the harsh realities faced by those suffering under Nazi rule? The weight of guilt and shame pressed down on me like a suffocating blanket. I now remember one letter he wrote me before he died, where he went into detail about a small town in France he went to during a ceasefire on Christmas Eve. He said that despite the war being so close, you could feel the love in the air, people who would advance, so I would keep thinking he was alive. Now, those letters are the only reason I motivate myself to work. I wanted to try and still achieve what my father thought I could.

After thinking about that, I went out for a smoke break. As I walked through the corridor, bathed in the same hideous yellow light that seemed to seep into every corner of our office, I saw my coworker Karl. Karl was a thin, lanky man standing about a foot taller than me. His face was shadowed by a thin outline of facial hair that seemed to accentuate his gaunt features. Like many others, Karl was enamored by Hitler and his grand promises of a prosperous future. However, he harbored a simmering resentment toward the Jews.

"Ja, it's a shame the Jews may die," he said, his voice carrying a cold indifference, "but the greatest horizon requires a storm to be recognized."

No one he told this to ever truly understood what he meant, only that he supported the party, and for most, that was enough. He accompanied me outside, and as we descended the floors of our drab office building, we found ourselves on the desolate stone tiles of Berlin. The cityscape was a grim tableau of wartime austerity, the buildings around us casting long, oppressive shadows in the dim afternoon light. The smoke lights were the only flames in the city, yet they were still as cold as the soldiers who inhabited it. Karl took a minute to get his lighter out, smothered in his coat pocket, between scraps of notes and an odd pastry.

"Klaus, I heard you journal in your free time, yes?"

Karl said in a dark tone that made me understand something was different from normal, as if his words were a trap waiting to spring.

"I do find myself scrapbooking occasionally, don't you? I find it to be a relaxing experience in times like these."

I tried being as light in tone as possible, trying to seem oblivious to Karl's suave attitude.

"Scrapbooking " is an odd term; books are made of tree scraps, are they not? The English are always making words that hold no true meaning or value. I find their people quite similar."

Karl's expression remained unchanged while he was speaking, as cold and dark as always, his beard outline becoming hidden in the cigarette smoke. It's a very conflicting feeling seeing people saying radical phrases that in most other places would get them persecuted or in some sort of trouble to be normal in the land of the party. Karl certainly isn't a bad person, but harbors a slight hatred for those he doesn't see as a proper German. Like most other people in this office, I know nothing about him. I don't think anyone knows anything about each other except for whatever we let come onto the surface; everyone is either too prideful or fearful to connect. We are only connected by the essence of survival, a problem hoped to have been solved in our modern day.

He leaned forward a little, his voice steady but full of conviction.

'The Spanish, the Italians, the Portuguese. They are not in the same league if you'll pardon my saying so. They've got their thing, to be sure, but there's something in our culture and history that makes us different. Look at what we've done and the strength we've shown, now, would you? Today, we stood up and made our point. Not many can do that, you see?'

His tone was even, as if he seriously believed in every word that came out of his mouth. Not what I would have thought. I didn't agree with it at all, but when he lets something like that drop as if it's nothing, you can't help but think: does he see things that way? And why is he saying something so bluntly? Is this a patriotic trust or a trap meant to weed out those who don't follow?

No matter, I nodded my head, it's a quiet solace and an unfortunate part of the Nazi regime. Everyone is less than a certain extent, even those who are thought to be at the pinnacle of society will still believe themselves to be worse than someone else. The reason people are like this is the simple human characteristic of jealousy and finding any way to degrade someone will make you feel better. The Nazis encourage this; any abnormality that someone sees in another can be reported, and so you can bully your way through the rest. In my English journaling, I have kept my secret from most in my life for this reason, exactly as if someone even catches a glance at my inner thoughts, I may as well live in Poland. Karl's line of questioning scares me at certain points, as I know that he is not interrogating me, but still at any moment, no one I know will protect me if I truly need it.

Maybe I'm just overthinking it.

Karl's cigarette was half finished now, but he swiftly took it out and threw it on the desolate and empty floor, stomping out its only light. He turned his head back to me, his face now darker in the absence of the cigarette light. He then made an odd motion to signal me to come back. I still had a sizable portion of my smoke left, but I decided that being alone wasn't worth it, especially if I became subject to later discussions with people like Karl. As we ascended the stairs of the building, I got flashed with the name of the newspaper *"Völkischer Beobachter"*. This name may be in some people's limelight and others' nightmares. For me, it's the latter. Karl has been working at this publication for a couple of years now, and he still looks as if he found it; funnily enough, he's my age. It doesn't matter though as we get back into the yellow-stained office. I walk down the hall toward my cubicle and see it covered in tacky and sticky wallpaper. Sitting down at my typewriter, I see the draft of my article, one where before I couldn't fathom finishing. But like most things these days, I have no choice.

Chapter 3

POTSDAM

December 23, 1938, Potsdam, Germany

Today is a special day as I have been tasked with interviewing the Nazi soldiers stationed in the town of Potsdam, not far by car from Berlin. I'm required to interview them in a way that shows the German people how great the people of Potsdam are, whether they are or not, but as long as I live in the Fatherland, I will serve it.

I left around 6:00 this morning so that I would be able to draft the article by evening. I stopped by the local bakery, which stood out as it was the only building with a semblance of life in the depressing city. I walked into the warm building and was greeted by the baker,

Brotlieb Kuchenmeister is probably the kindest guy I know. He also makes very nice pastries. He's built more like a bodybuilder than a baker, and despite being a Great War veteran, he still harbors great kindness toward everyone he sees.

"Hello Abel!"

He boasted at the top of his lungs as I had come in quite early today. His mustache and dark blonde hair ruffled as he spoke.

"Would you like some pastries? Here, take some before work."

I was surprised by his act of kindness and profusely requested that he take my money. Kuchemeister refused, and I reluctantly backed down because I knew he was just being kind, a rarity nowadays.

"Thanks"

I felt glad that Kuchemiester was happy; he deserved every bit of it. He had always felt bad for me as he knew I had lost my father in the war, so he looked out for me and tried treating me like a son sometimes. After I had thanked him, I left to go into my car and head over to Potsdam. My Volkswagen Beetle had been with me for quite a while and was one of the biggest conveniences in my life; it helped make the daft city of Berlin much more tolerable, and even with age, the nice green of the original paint still shone through. I arrived in my car around 7:00 in the morning and headed to the army station. As I came into the heart of Potsdam, I admired the lush and beautiful forest all around the city. The beautiful and very foreign-like architecture, as if it was from another time when Romans and Turks used to live, made it a popular tourist spot; the people as well were much warmer to me than the city folk of Berlin. I came and met the army captain outside the barracks because they didn't find it necessary for me to come inside. I saw the large and bleak-looking tan building and its hideously discolored red roof, which looked very bizarre compared to the intricate and regal Potsdam architecture. The captain, named Filch Bert, was a very proud man; his pride was said to make up for his height, in which he was around half a foot shorter than me and a full foot shorter than his soldiers. Filch's face was that of a mutt, with his eyes being hard to find in the mess of battle scars, dirt, and facial hair. The soldiers themselves were very rash and immature, constantly playing games and fooling around while I was conducting the interview. Filch glared at them every few minutes, which seemed to shut them down completely, though. His demeanor gave Filch an aura that made me see why he was a general. After finishing the interview with Filch, I went aside to ask if I could see the inside of the barracks, which Filch denied.

"I'm sorry, dear reporter, but we can't allow anyone in these forges. They are for members of the Third Reich only. If you want to go down a new life pathway, I could show you how these are. For now, though, you'd best stick to your limits."

The condescending tone in his voice showed a glimpse of Filch's true view of reporters. I bid him farewell, but then two young Nazi soldiers ambushed me.

"Hans, is this the reporter?" one of them said. He was very tall with bright, pale skin, blue eyes, and delicate blond hair, very Aryan. He looked a bit too childish to be a soldier, yet too mature to act as he was. He was wearing the standard Nazi uniform, but it didn't have the same imposition it should have had; the collar was shaggy and tattered, unwashed, and had undoubtedly been through many training routines. The greenish-brown uniform also showed similar age, though it may have been a product of the boy's overall unkemptness rather than the stress of war; then again, maybe both. The red, white, and black swastika on the boy's arm was still spotless, even though it's the most delicate part of the uniform. An oddity, he didn't seem like the typical soldier.

"Of course, he is Gefreiter, he's the one, Filch was bullshitting too just now, didn't you see?" the other exclaimed. This one was equally tall but more manly looking, with dark brown hair and a carefree aura. Yet again, a similarly tattered uniform, but this time with *holes* near the ends of his pants and sleeves. The swastika was again spotless on this boy's uniform… not typical at all.

"Makes sense, normally Filch would just tell you to go back to Frankfurt, or wherever you're from… Wait, where are you from?"

I was taken aback by these two and their immaturity, but I thought they could tell me something interesting, so I decided to humor them.

"I am Klaus Abel from the Völkischer Beobachter, Berlin, and I don't think your superior would appreciate how you speak of him. I work directly for the party and don't mind calling him on you." I tried saying this seriously, but the boys quickly picked up on the sarcasm.

"Well, Mister Abel from Völkischer Beobachter," the boy said this in a very television-like tone. "I, Hans Becker, am the aunt of Hitler and will tell him directly that what you write is as bad as the breath of Filch himself."

The way Hans presented himself, he looked like an anti-Nazi cartoon. I tried to contain my laughter, but the pair knew they had cracked me. So I decided to ask them more about their captain, and this time the other one, Gefreiter, spoke up.

"Filch is probably the most deceiving Nazi you'll see, he looks like a senile old man, but it turns out that he's one of the most cunning and strict guys in the army. Most soldiers don't even wake up without his permission," Gefreiter spoke as if he had seen the worst of Filch. Hans was now staring into the distance, looking at the vague figures of the people walking throughout the town. Every now and then, he waved at an ongoing citizen. These boys seemed to care about this little town of theirs. A boy then ran up and started yelling at me.

"Sir, sir! Could you take a photo with me and the soldiers, please!"

The brashness of this boy took me aback, but soon the two young men sprang up.

"Yes, Mr Abel, you'd better!" Han grew a smirk on his face.

"Here, take my camera," Gefreiter said, passing a large industrial type.

I took the photo, and the boy quickly ran off, feeling a little less tense after the whole ordeal.

"Klaus Abel from Völkischer Beobachter, you should include Gefreiter and me in your article. It'll anger Filch, and we can show our parents. I'm sure they'll be happy with us."

I thought for a moment and gave them a stern look. Their unwavering smiles and optimism moved me so much that I felt compelled to do it.

"I will do it, soldier, on one condition."

"What is that?" they said in unison.

"When you come to Berlin, bring your best uniforms. We'll ensure Filch sees just how sharp and disciplined his worst soldiers can be, even when he's not watching!" We all laughed, and I made sure I kept my end of the deal.

After I got back in the afternoon, I wanted to finish the article then and there. It was a very rare occasion when I became interested in my writing, and I felt invigorated to finish it by evening, if only for Hans and Gefreiter.

Volkischer Beobachter

01 JAN 2025

Exclusive Interview: Insights from the Soldiers of Potsdam

By KLAUS ABEL

Potsdam, Germany As winter settles over Potsdam, the air is thick with anticipation and preparation. Amid the chilling December air, I had the rare opportunity to speak with several Wehrmacht soldiers stationed in this historic city. These conversations provided an intimate glimpse into the lives and thoughts of those serving the Fatherland during these critical times. General Bert General Filch Bert, a war-seasoned leader known for his strict discipline and strategic prowess, oversees the operations at the Potsdam military station. His presence commands respect, and soldiers speak of him in hushed tones, acknowledging his role in keeping the troops in check. "General Bert is a force to be reckoned with," remarked Obergefreiter Hans Becker, his tone respectful. "He ensures that we adhere to the highest standards of discipline and readiness. His leadership is instrumental in maintaining order and focus among the troops." Besides Becker, Gefreiter Karl Schreiber nodded in agreement. "General Bert's experience is invaluable. He instills a sense of pride and duty in all of us. We know that under his command, we are part of a formidable force ready to face any challenge." General Bert's Influence General Bert's influence extends beyond the training grounds. His leadership style emphasizes preparedness and attention to detail, traits that have become the hallmark of the soldiers under his command. "General Bert keeps us on our toes," added Becker with a wry smile. "His unexpected inspections and drills ensure that we are always ready for action. It's tough, but it makes us better soldiers." As the interview concluded, General Bert's presence lingered, a reminder of the discipline and dedication that defines the soldiers stationed in Potsdam. Under his watchful eye, they stand ready to uphold their duty to the Reich. Meeting the Soldiers At the heart of Potsdam, in the shadow of the grand military academies, I met Obergefreiter Hans Becker, a seasoned soldier with a steely gaze and a deep sense of duty. Becker, like many of his comrades, speaks with a sense of unwavering loyalty to the Reich. "We are preparing ourselves for whatever the Führer demands of us," Becker stated confidently. "Our training is rigorous, but it is necessary for the strength of Germany. We believe in our mission and our leader." Beside Becker stood Gefreiter Karl Schreiber, a younger soldier whose eyes reflected both determination and the weight of the path he had chosen. Schreiber spoke of the camaraderie and the intense training they undergo daily. "The bond we share as soldiers is unbreakable," Schreiber explained. "We support each other through the toughest drills and exercises. It's this unity that will make us victorious in any challenge we face." Life in Potsdam Potsdam, known for its palaces and historical significance, now hums with the energy of military activity. Soldiers march through the streets, their presence a constant reminder of the Reich's growing power. Despite the militaristic atmosphere, the city retains its charm, and locals go about their daily lives, proud of their city's role in strengthening Germany. Obergefreiter Becker took a moment to reflect on life in Potsdam. "This city holds a special place in our hearts. It is a symbol of our heritage and strength. We draw inspiration from its history as we prepare for the future." Germany won't stop As the interview concluded, I asked the soldiers about their thoughts on the coming year. There was a palpable sense of readiness and a hint of what lies ahead. "We are prepared for any eventuality," Becker asserted. "We have faith in our leaders and in our purpose. Whatever comes, we will face it with the courage and strength that defines us as German soldiers." Gefreiter Schreiber added, "Our training here in Potsdam has prepared us well. We are ready to defend our nation and uphold its honor." Reflections As I left the barracks, the words of these soldiers lingered in my mind. In Potsdam, the spirit of determination and duty is evident in every step they take. This city, steeped in history, now stands as a testament to the resilience and resolve of its soldiers. As Germany moves forward into uncertain times, the soldiers of Potsdam remain steadfast, their hearts and minds dedicated to their cause. It is a resolve that will undoubtedly shape the course of history. I was shocked when I received praise from my bosses about the article, they stated that it was magnificently received and showed the good German people the power of the party. "Well, the benefit of the party is the best for me. After all, this is why we work, no?"

Reuters

International Moose Count Underway

By BOB O'BOBSTON

The UN-sponsored International Moose Census got off to a flying

I finished the draft and sent it to the office, and the next day I found it published on Christmas Eve.

I was shocked when my bosses praised the article. They stated that it was magnificently received and showed the good German people the party's power.

"Well, the benefit of the party is the best for me. After all, this is why we work, isn't it?"

I said this in a tone of deliberate celebration, and I even got the whole day off, which was extremely rare for this occasion. As I went home in my Beetle, I wasn't feeling very well; after all, I had just convinced thousands of Germans to support a cause I didn't even believe in. But it didn't matter much; I needed to survive like everyone else.

Money is a necessity after all.

Chapter 4

CHRISTMAS

24th December 1938, Vienna, Austria

Ihave gone back to my hometown of Austria to celebrate the holidays. Even though my father is dead, I still go to visit my aunt and uncle for the holidays. I owe it to them, especially after they raised me in my late teenage years. I didn't want to be too burdened and decided to apply to boarding schools so that I wouldn't be too obtrusive in their lives. I eventually went to Salem Castle School. Even though these people were my technical parents, I never was able to forge a connection because of my hubris.

As I entered the city, I was met with the memories of my childhood, the amazing places and sights of the city, and the refreshing but urbanized smell of the place, which made me feel free but ubiquitous within myself. Though as I passed, I knew Vienna's snow-covered streets were filled with nostalgia and sorrow. The city I had once known as a place of culture and peace was now under the oppressive shadow of Nazi occupation. The majestic buildings and festive decorations couldn't mask the grim reality that had settled over the Austrian capital since the Anschluss in March.

With its grand palaces and vibrant cultural scene, Vienna had been transformed. The swastika banners hanging from historic buildings, the presence of German soldiers, and the pervasive atmosphere of fear and suspicion were stark reminders of the new order.

Approaching Aunt Helga and Uncle Franz's house near the Belvedere Palace, I took a moment to appreciate the serene beauty of the palace grounds, now dusted with snow. I had always loved visiting this part of Vienna, a place that symbolized the city's rich history and artistic heritage. But today, the beauty felt hollow, overshadowed by the iron grip of the Nazi regime.

I looked up at the house, surprised at how big it was compared to the cramped city apartments I was used to; even my Austrian apartment was much bigger than that in Berlin. The white walls and numerous windows, as well as the arched triangular roof, made me wonder why I didn't want to live here.

I knocked on the familiar wooden door, and Aunt Helga soon opened it. The war had clearly taken a toll on her, and her once clean and happy face had been dragged out and withered by the direction our country was taking. She had also lost almost all her weight, looking as frail as a veil, which showed the deeper problems she faced but never opened up about.

The air was filled with the comforting scent of cinnamon and apples, mixed with the rich aroma of butter and vanilla. It was a sweet and homely smell that brought back memories of happier times. The air was filled with the comforting scent of freshly baked Apfelstrudel, warm and inviting. The aroma wrapped around me like a hug, filling me with the nostalgia of family gatherings and happier times. The comforting aroma of freshly baked Apfelstrudel wafted through the air, a mix of warm apples, cinnamon, and sugar. It was a scent that always reminded me of home and family gatherings.

"Klaus! Come in, come in," she greeted, enveloping me in a hug.

Uncle Franz appeared in the hallway, his face weathered and tired from years of hardship and struggle. Deep lines etched his face, and his eyes looked distant, as if carrying the world's weight on his shoulders. Despite this, his smile lit up the room, and his eyes sparkled with a familiar warmth. He stood tall and lanky, though his constant slouch made him seem more minor and more approachable. Uncle Franz appeared in the doorway, his tall frame slouched and tired, yet his face lit up with joy at the sight of me. He wore a worn-out shirt and pants, indicative of the struggles they had been facing. Uncle Franz's face lit up with a warm smile as he appeared in the hallway. His face was lined with worry and exhaustion, permanent etches of the war visible on his skin. Despite being taller than me, his constant slouch gave me the feeling that we were on the same level, both weighed down by the events of the world around us.

"Good to see you, Klaus. It's been too long," Franz said, clapping me on the back.

Inside, the apartment was a cozy refuge from the harsh winter outside. The Christmas tree, adorned with traditional ornaments and candles, stood proudly in the corner of the living room. It was a scene straight out of my childhood memories, a stark contrast to the bleakness outside. I was reminded of the last Christmas I had here. I had just been accepted into boarding school, and my aunt and uncle were pleased to see that I was trying to move on with my life, even though I had a high enjoyment of the whole ordeal. They were ecstatic to hear that I was coming back for Christmas, as the last time I was still a child and they had also just gone through a war. It seemed as though we could be a family if we allowed ourselves to be such a thing.

As I entered, I saw the house looking the same as I left, with all of Aunt Helga's knitted creations scattered around the house, only more abundant than before. Aunt Helga took me to the living room as Uncle Franz insisted on taking my luggage up for me, which I gave a major pushback on, but I knew that he would not change his mind. My Aunt Helga started bothering me all about the reporting jobs and general Berlin living.

"The job is hard, is it not?" she said worriedly. "I hope Berlin life is not worse than this, although if it is, I hope you come back here and stop living in your sad apartment."

Aunt Helga always teased me about such things, and it made me think if I should. Most of the years I had in Austria were formative, and I never really remember my childhood here. My formal years were spent in Germany, and I felt that sometime throughout that I was more of a German than an Austrian. That epiphany was always odd as I had been raised Austrian and identified as that all my life, even though my mother's side was all German. This always led me to try to hide this side of my family, especially since I never had a chance to connect with my mother's side after her death. The aroma of roasted chicken and freshly baked bread filled the room as we gathered around the table. I couldn't help but feel a sense of unease, knowing that my work was being compared to a man who symbolized such power and destruction. As Uncle Franz came down, he started complaining about his back and praising me. We began our meal, and Uncle Franz raised his glass of wine and toasted to my success.

"To our talented writer, may your words continue to captivate the hearts of many," he said proudly.

"Maybe you will become the speaker of the Führer someday."

I forced a smile in return, grateful for their support but burdened by their expectations. Aunt Helga reached out and placed a comforting hand on mine, her eyes filled with warmth and encouragement. It was the only time I felt that I had made someone I care about feel good from my work, and though it was only my aunt, I still felt immense gratitude to her.

"You have a gift, dear boy. Let your words be your legacy, not the shadows of the past," she whispered.

Her words stirred something within me, a glimmer of hope that perhaps I could use my talent for good. And as we sat together at that table, surrounded by love and acceptance, I thought I could do good for others even if it meant hardship. So, I now wanted to strive to recapture this feeling I had not felt in a long time.

The next morning, on Christmas Day, I awoke to the sun shining through my window, casting its rays of warm light across my face. As I descended the stairs, the living room was a stunning display of Christmas decorations. The tree was adorned with delicate ornaments, and the walls were draped with evergreen garlands and mistletoe. The red and green lights added a festive glow to the room. Pine and cinnamon filled the air, a comforting reminder of

Christmas. The sweet scent of pine filled the air, mingling with the warm and soothing smell of cinnamon and spices from the Christmas treats my aunt had baked for us. It was a familiar scent that brought back cherished memories of past holidays spent with my family. The room was filled with pine and cinnamon, a familiar and comforting smell that brought memories of past Christmases to mind. The fireplace added a hint of woodsmoke to the air, creating a cozy atmosphere. I opened my eyes to see a gorgeous Christmas sky, its gentle rays illuminating the room and putting a warm glow over everything, as the morning light slowly crept into the space. I was astounded to see the living room as I descended the stairs. It was decked out with festive decorations and sparkling lights, with a nativity scene featuring Mother Mary and her infant son, Jesus. Evergreens and traditional mistletoe gave the space a natural touch and made it feel warm and inviting. A joyful ambiance was generated by the red and green lights scattered over the space, which merged with the sunshine to provide a stunning color combination.

The sun's golden rays filled the room, casting a warm and comforting glow over everything. The Christmas tree stood tall in the corner, adorned with sparkling lights and shimmering ornaments. The fireplace was burned and empty with remnants of the night before. The room was a colorful explosion of reds and greens, with mistletoe and evergreens scattered throughout. I wondered if it would be worth it to try again. The thought nagged at me as I took in Christmas morning's familiar sights and smells. Despite the warmth and love surrounding me, there was a lingering sense of doubt and insecurity. I couldn't shake the feeling that I was meant for something more, something greater than just reporting on stories of the past.

I went out to smoke, a habit I had admitted to quitting to Aunt Helga and Uncle Franz in boarding school, months after I had gotten into the habit. As much as quitting seems like the right option, I can never do it. I looked out at the horizon coming over the quaint house. I wander off a bit when I'm not in my imagination and step over the newsletter sitting on the porch. A small amount of smoke fell on it, and the previous night's snow left the cover wet and unreadable. I thought it best to bring it in after coming back. The outside of the home was incredible with chalet-style houses, their wooden facades adorned with colorful flower boxes overflowing with vibrant geraniums and petunias.

The streets were narrow and winding, lined with cobblestones that seemed to hold centuries of history within their grooves. Tall, slender trees stood sentinel along the sidewalks, their leaves a rich tapestry of green that danced in the gentle breeze. The sound of birds chirping filled the air, harmonizing with the distant murmur of a babbling brook. I walked past well-tended gardens, each one a testament to the meticulous care of their owners. Roses, daisies, and lavender created a patchwork of colors and fragrances that delighted the senses. In the distance, the majestic hills loomed, their snow-capped peaks contrasting sharply with the lush valley below. It was a view I had almost forgotten—breathtaking in its grandeur and serenity. On the way back, I noticed the newspaper had been removed from its place, and the porch was slightly less wet. I knew both of them were awake. I opened the door and saw both Uncle Franz and Aunt Helga at the table.

As I sat down at the breakfast table with Aunt Helga and Uncle Franz, the silence hung heavily in the air. It starkly contrasted with the usual lively chatter that filled the room during the previous evening. My aunt and uncle hesitated to broach the subject that had been weighing on their minds since my arrival.

Finally, Aunt Helga cleared her throat and fixed me with a steady gaze.

"Klaus, there's something we need to discuss," she began, her voice tinged with concern.

I felt a knot form in my stomach, bracing myself for what was to come. I don't understand why, but whenever questions are phrased in such an open-ended way, I always interpret it as me being in some trouble. I started to close my fists and breathe much less, taking my jacket off, and drinking a glass of water. Was it the smoke? Did I somehow insult them? Maybe I'm just overthinking it, but I couldn't shake the feeling—the feeling that I was a problem.

As she approached, all these thoughts were convulsing in my head. A world of lies that I believed myself to have built, crashing on my head. What did I even do to deserve this? A writer getting jousted by the truth.

"When will you find yourself a wife?" she asked in a manner of such innocence it begged little to no concern, yet my stress had yet to dissipate. A wife, now? Was she mad or simply just prodding me? I chuckled nervously, avoiding her gaze by staring into the water glass in my hands. "A wife, Aunt Helga? That seems a bit out of the question, don't you think so?"

She raised an eyebrow, her expression teetering between amusement and exasperation. "Sudden? Klaus, you're not getting any younger. A man with your charm can surely find a nice girl or two," she said with intense honesty.

"You shouldn't still be wandering around aimlessly; how will you survive as you get older without somebody to rely on?"

Wandering? That stung more than I cared to admit. My work wasn't aimless. Writing might not have seemed like the most important profession, but it was my life; it sustained me. Yet not my purpose.

"I'll have you, and I'm not exactly wandering."

I replied, trying to sound lighthearted, although my tone betrayed a hint of defensiveness.

"Besides, marriage isn't something you just jump into. It's… complicated," my thoughts wandered off into the ocean in my head.

"Complicated is exactly why you shouldn't wait. The longer you put it off, the less chance."

I sighed, fixing the glass, which was lying on its side. This wasn't just about finding a wife. It was about settling down, proving that I could be responsible in the way she thought mattered most.

"Look," I said, leaning forward, "I appreciate your concern, truly. But marriage isn't on my radar right now. I have my work, my writing—"

"Your writing won't keep you warm at night, Klaus," she interrupted, her tone sharper now. "And it won't carry on your family."

There it was—the real heart of the matter. The family. I'd heard this speech a hundred times before, but it never got easier to stomach.

"I understand, Aunt Helga," I said, standing up, hoping to end the discussion.

"I'll do what you feel is right to help me improve."

She didn't look convinced, but she nodded, her lips pressing into a thin line. "I just don't want you to regret waiting too long; you focus too much on your job and not on the world around you. As you fixate on the mountains, you're forgetting to stay on the road ahead of you," she said softly, and for a moment, I glimpsed something more profound in her eyes—worry, maybe even fear.

As I left the room, her words echoed in my mind. I wasn't sure if the time would ever feel right.

Chapter 5

THE ADVISERS, MINISTERS, AND THE KING

30 January 1939, Berlin, Germany

I woke to the blaring alarm of my phone, ringing. It took me a minute to even get out of bed before I accepted the call. On the phone is Max Amann screaming. "Klaus, you have 10 minutes to get here; otherwise, I'll have you!" With that, he hung up, and I was still confused. However, I didn't have a wish to be on Amann's chopping block, so I rushed over. It's been a while since I've come to the office. After Christmas, I took an extended holiday, as Aunt Helga told me. I tried becoming more "whole", or whatever she wanted me to be. Life has been going slowly; after a while, I even stopped journaling and wanted to find a new way to pass the time. As always, cleaning left me with a sterile view of my abode.

When I entered the office, I panicked. All the papers were flying everywhere, reporters were frantically rushing to see what's next, and every other pending task was all but forgotten. The fuehrers were coming to make a speech today, and the country was intent on knowing what he would say. I am staring at the yellow wall that had recently lost its green allure that I was starting to warm up to, as if the Führer were to come, it would be necessary to show that the country's best news station was also the cleanest. My chair was slumping downwards, and my coat was edging the floor when suddenly my door burst open. Immediately, all the portraits on the wall started shaking, and one even fell. It was an old picture of me and my friend Juan, whom I had met in Spain. The photo was taken with a Kodak camera that I had specially imported from the United States in the previous year. It was a Kodak Bullet, and the bright silver linings and black build gave it much durability. I always had the camera slung around my shoulder in its rustic leather case that was starting to wear with time. Juan was a tall man, nearly 6'3", and had light brown skin as well as well-defined muscles that were surely built up from war. He always wore a young smile and a very well-adjusted beard. In the photo, he was wearing the typical suit of the Spanish soldiers with bright blue pants and a darker hue for his vest, with the glaring white buttons. His gun, what I assume to be a musket, was very pronounced when he met anyone; even in the photo, it seemed that he was an accessory to his weapon.

Despite the tough exterior, he was a very optimistic man who was fighting in the Spanish War in hopes that he could help his family. I wrote my story there early in my career, but something about him compelled me to stay longer. I turned a one week excursion into a month-long escapade and made great friends in Spain. This moment made me truly understand a different part of humanity. I don't know where Juan is, but I still have an address I could mail to.

I was now sullen as this photo was lying broken on the floor, and there would be no one to clean it for the rest of the day. Suddenly, I heard.

"Sorry, Mr Abel! Something major has come up!"

I glare up with my eyes half-open and see a spry young man with a cap too big and pants too short for him, his shirt slightly withered and torn. I suddenly realize that this is the paperboy, Alexander Becker, who frequented the office enough for everyone to have a slight idea of who he was. The boy was poor but had the ethics of a horse, and it helped that he was very charming. He had the typical short, crew-cut, blonde hair and brown eyes. He was physically very skinny but had decent height, yet seemed to lack presence. His face was never without a smile, and a bag more full of papers than you thought possible. I immediately soften my face and open my eyes a little more.

"What is it that made you rush in such a frantic manner, Mr. Becker?"

"Sir, you are called directly by Mr Amann to report on the Führer's speech. You must be at the Kroll Opera House in no less than an hour!"

With that, the boy fled to receive his paycheck and pray for the latest papers to be released. I sat still for a moment, frozen and didn't even believe that the last minute had passed. I looked at my desk full of papers that would never be published, and ink that would soon dry. I then let my desk fall to the floor as my feet became flooded in an ocean of my mistakes. Why must I report on this speech? Surely, someone like Amann could find somebody else.

I collected myself, raised my back by an inch, and then headed down the hallway to the stairs. While passing the identical yellow-walled office, I saw the intricate poster of the Führer and the German military. The white background featured protruding red details, some of tanks and others of planes, and next to them all was his face. An unforgettable imprint that casts a shadow over the nation.

I rush down the stairs and see the bustling streets, police monitoring every bit of traffic, and cars speeding. The array of colors was blinding. I then look to see my car, a Mercedes-Benz 770 issued by the paper, because it would seem rude to appear to such a great man in the car of a commoner. It's a masterpiece, an automobile to behold by its presence and luxury. It's a grand car with a sweeping silhouette, touching length, commanding attention at first glance. The body is sleekly sculpted with lines running in a very harmonious flow from front to back, imbuing it with an air of elegance.

The front is largely dominated by a bold chromed grille, with the three-pointed star sitting proudly at its center. Even though they have big and expressive eyes that almost seem to watch the world going on around them, their headlights are fairly typical for their size. Immensely huge fenders wrap around the wheels, enhancing its robust stance. You first notice the paint job - deep, rich, and shiny black or dark blue, glistening in the light. The finish is perfect, a mirror reflection of everything else around it. You get the feeling it's substantial, heavy, and businesslike.

As you go inside, you are surrounded by luxury. Soft but sturdy leather envelops you like sinking into a soft couch and asks you to sit back and relax. The leather smell and the warmth of oiled wood can be such strong scents that it feels like you are smothered in luxury. The dashboard features considerable amounts of glinting chrome detail and is very elegantly designed.

The enormous steering wheel has a solid feel in the palms of your hands, with a smooth, polished surface that invites you to take charge. Inside, as you settle back into the rear seat, you can stretch out considerable leg space to breathe. And there is a luxury only a few cars have accomplished in their elaborately crafted creations.

The engine roared to life with a smooth, deep rumble that resonated, hinting at power waiting to be unleashed. Its size gives you a commanding view of the road ahead; it makes you feel powerful and secure. More importantly, it positively sets the stage for a dramatic impact.

As I was fawning over the car and the smooth black silhouette, I suddenly got pushed over, my camera and paper all falling to the ground. As I lay and saw my hands bruised, but no blood. Before I could even get up, I suddenly got pulled right back to where I was standing. I rashly turned to see what was behind me and felt the foreboding presence, which could only be of one man.

"The Führer is coming just so I could interview him. Everyone knows that he's attracted to my aura."

Lukas Falkenstein, otherwise known as "The Atlas", is the boldest man I know and the best man I've worked with. He simply doesn't care for anything other than having fun and survival. He is probably the most renowned journalist we have, seeing every corner of the world. It's incredible how young he is, only around 30. Despite that, he can act as immature as a teenager. His immature demeanor is carried over in his looks as well, with a strong build and prominent chest, and a face that can only be described as serene, with a slight smile that suggests both confidence and tranquility, almost as if chiseled in stone. His eyes are bright blue, and his hair is always unkempt and shaggy. The seeming lack of care, but incredible experience, gave him quite a reputation within the city and with the ladies. Though never married, he still managed to keep a house in central Berlin, though he rarely frequented.

Lukas then enters the car but gets his fine leather jacket stuck on the inner lock while gesturing to me to get in. I started laughing as he was stuck mid-bow trying to imitate that of a Japanese woman while yelling at me to go in. As he claimed, he wrenched his jacket out of the door and went into the driver's seat.

"Hey, Klaus, you're as dull as a sober stone in the desert right now, but I bet a little buzz will have you as lively as ever!"

I then asked,

"How will you fix your jacket? It looks quite expensive."

"Hey, don't worry about it! I've got a few of these from Peru, so you can totally keep them if you want. I get that you never leave Berlin, but just remember, the world is like a story waiting for you to experience it. Sometimes, you have to let things go as life intends."

I stay silent as I know that Lukas never ran out of things to say, but that he always spoke the truth. He truly wanted what was best for his friends. He started the car, and he continued as we got on the road.

"You know, most people are always searching for something—some deeper meaning, a purpose, or maybe even a god. They try to change the world because they see it as broken. But honestly, from what I've seen, it feels like they're just trying to make sense of themselves. If gods were real and watching over us, do you think someone like the Führer would be up there, giving speeches about saving the 'master race'? It just doesn't add up."

Look, Klaus, I'm not trying to step on your beliefs. I just get that life's a mess right now, for all of us. And, well... that's okay. We just gotta live, let life come by, don't try searching for conflict, as I've seen it trouble is something that will always chase you."

I nodded silently. Lukas usually stayed very lighthearted, but today felt different; maybe it was just the tense atmosphere finally getting to Lukas, or maybe he saw something wrong in me that I have yet to see in myself. He kept jabbering about menial things such as his coffee being too sweet and biscuit too dry, but his words were consistently repeated in my head, everything outside fading away. The streets were the consistent gray mess that I always saw, but now, more posters than ever are all the same as those I saw in the office. Heavy military was bombarding the sights, and it all felt blurry after a while. I asked Lukas for a lighter; his head tilted toward me, with a sad look on his face.

"Do you still smoke?"

"I'm trying to quit," I started to put the box back in my pocket.

"Don't worry, just let me have one first."

I gave him the pack and then saw my smokes all hovering out of the window. While annoyed, I understood what Lukas was trying to do. I looked ahead at the road and decided that it would be best to rest my eyes for a minute. I glanced at my watch and saw that it was only noon.

"How long is left until we reach? Only about 20 minutes. Don't worry about time; we're already three hours too early. "Should we get lunch before we go?" Lukas's eyes wandered all over the steering wheel, his mind split between driving and food.

"The traffic is moving like a sloth, it's better we get there and decide." I turned back to the road, and as I did, I then heard a bang.

My body jolted sideways, and I hit Lukas. Suddenly, I hear the car horns blaring, and Lukas is prying the other cars that hit us out of the seatbelt. The crowd of people now covering the car, I swiftly try to get out but get cut by a lock mechanism that pried out. I then look at the disheveled beetle on my left, my mind screaming to move, but my body refusing to comply. I got pulled out by Lukas, who was much less scathed and only suffered a minor blow to the side. I was bleeding from both my legs and arms, still unable to move my body. I slowly got limped out by Lukas, who started screaming at the driver who hit us.

"You idiot! Do you know what you have just done? He'll be lucky to limp again, let alone live as he did before!"

I was now lying down on the side of the road, the only sensation I felt was that of my hand on the cold and rigid pavement. Lukas was still yelling at the driver, but I couldn't make out what he was saying, only hearing vague sounds and motions. Everything started becoming blurred, my eyes started to feel heavy, and I suddenly saw black.

When I awake, I'm greeted by the view of a bustling café, tables packed, and constant yelling from the waitress for orders in all directions. I also see the figure of Lukas eating what looks like an assorted platter of salad and meats, sausages, cold cuts, and grilled vegetables, an order I've only seen on a person like Lukas.

He then looked up at me and motioned the waitress over to me. She frantically rushed over and started yelling.

"Oi, sleepyhead! Just what makes it so that you require me to take your order, better than the screaming lot, are we?"

"It's nothing like that, just…" I noticed her name tag said Bertha, and she had a small lapel of the swastika.

"I couldn't be less bothered. Now what is it? I'll only give you 5 seconds."

I felt so lightheaded I didn't even register what she said, luckily Lukas was never short of a story, or charm.

"Madam, if you were to give me a minute, I will tell you the stories of a place called Vietnam, where food is cheaper than the rubbish we throw, and the people are nicer than those of a German child on a summer morning. A world where the French have transformed a beautiful land into one of forever peace."

"Well, that seems all fine, good sir, but just tell me what you want."

"If you insist, get my friend your finest sandwich of any type."

As she walked off, I heard her yelling at the chef to create the "Special" whatever that was. In all the excitement, I had forgotten what I was supposed to be doing in the first place. I then asked Lukas for the time, my voice unable to convey the stress I felt. Lukas was unfazed though; he boldly proclaimed

"We have two hours to freshen you up and make you proper. Just be sure that your head is still attached to your shoulders. I don't mind driving you home if you want?"

A slight chuckle indicated his attempt at a joke, but I knew that it would be impossible for me to leave now, if at all, just to spite the driver. I look out and see the Kroll Opera House, a captivating sight, especially the main facade which is grand from all angles. The primary entrance of the structure is accentuated with large vertical structures presumed to be columns, at the top of which is a well-carved engraved triangular region containing figures and depictions from folklore, enhancing the illustration of civilization. The pale stone finish of the building sparkles in the sun; ornamental plasters provide depth and beauty to the building. To top it all, a large dome is prominently situated in the middle of the structure, providing a contrasting profile to the dominant tower of the Kroll Opera House views in Berlin. Wide stairs lead toward the decorated double doors, which welcome guests into this place of luxury and culture where the Kroll Opera House stands as more than just another building, a work of art in the city's center. The heavy military that encases itself with only symbolism for the party protruding about this elegant venue was also that of pure fear. The waitress then came back, in her hand a massive sandwich full of assorted vegetables and nothing else: lettuce, tomatoes, carrots, and more. It seemed like the market just fell between two slices of bread. Lukas was laughing off his chair, his amusement so infectious, now at least half the café was watching us.

"You now will eat like the Führer, to think like him!"

I felt more annoyed than anything as it seemed useless to resist his jokes. I was going to ask for a different order but decided that it would be futile to resist. I just looked at my watch again; it's a custom-built watch from Switzerland, gifted to me by Lukas, who always likes to get people gifts from abroad. The sleek gold finish, with this warm glow, feels timeless. It's slim, maybe 8 millimeters, and when you hold it, it feels delicate, almost weightless, but solid. The dial is this beautiful, creamy ivory color, with small, graceful numbers in a simple font. The hands are golden too, in this fine leaf shape, and they just glide over the face precisely. The strap is genuine leather, deep brown, smooth to the touch but sturdy, and it's thin enough to keep the whole watch looking sleek. Over time, the leather has picked up a bit of a patina, like it's aged with character, giving it this vintage charm. The buckle matches the gold of the case, tying the whole thing together. The watch gave me a feeling of security and that time would be in my hands. I see that the time is 2:00 PM.

"Only two hours?" I was still fixated on the watch as I saw every second tick down and the dial circle around the frame.

"You know I'm quick, Klaus, and we weren't too far off anyway," Lukas said, now starting to get back into a more manageable state.

"I'm just glad we still have time." I had just finished my plate of food, and the adrenaline started to hit me.

"Time for you to stop looking like shit, now wash up before you begin to appear like a beggar," Lukas had now come to pick me out of my seat and walk me over to the washroom.

Inside was quite standard with a dull green and faded white atmosphere. The sink was somewhere in between that, a translucent yellow. I turned the water on, finding it oddly warm to my touch. As I vigorously rubbed the water along my face, I started to notice the imperfections in the cracked mirror, a new cut right below the eye socket. I didn't feel it before, but it was quite apparent.

My beard slightly undone, and hair went from greasy to wet, all shabby along the sides, and after pulling back, definitely too long to be professional. My eyes looked swollen and darker than ever, and I felt like a black porcelain cup, about to shatter on the floor.

My cuffs started to soak, and I kept applying the water in hopes of polishing my look. After 10 minutes of trying, I still couldn't salvage my appearance. As I left the washroom, I found Lukas's arm firm around my shoulders, holding me upright as we headed toward the Opera House.

"Don't worry, buddy. Sometimes in life, we may get set back down to what seems like our worst, but that's how we appreciate our best!"

I wondered why he decided to say what he did, but at that moment, it was as if he had transformed from the Lukas I knew into the "Atlas" shown to everyone else.

Yet my side burned with each movement, a fierce pain and pulsing ache that refused to dull, no matter how much I willed it away. I could feel Lukas's urgency pressing into me, pulling me along.

"Hold on, Klaus," he muttered, his voice low and strained. His grip was ironclad, a silent command not to falter.

"Just a few more steps. You're not stopping now," Lukas, while overdramatic, was probably right. I haven't been able to concentrate since the morning ordeal, and now might be one of the most important days of my life.

A few more steps. It sounded simple, a trifling request. I thought as if I might be able to hold onto normality, but suddenly

I collapsed, a crippling pain fell on my chest, everything. But each one jarred my bruised ribs and turned my insides to flame. Every instinct told me to stop, press a hand against my side, and force out a breath, but Lukas's relentless pace kept me in motion. His focus was unnerving, as if he would physically carry me inside if I refused to go any further.

Through my haze of pain, I could see others streaming up the broad staircase leading to the doors, some of them pausing to cast curious glances at us. We must have looked like an odd pair—me limping, face pale and covered in dust, and Lukas half-carrying me, eyes set forward like a man possessed. The smell of fuel still clung to us, sharp and unshakable, and I was sure it marked us out as we blended with the crowd.

"Don't look at anyone, just keep going," Lukas murmured, his voice firm yet quiet. His words were simple enough, but the pressure in his grip told me everything. We couldn't afford the scrutiny; any delay would be disastrous. I fought to keep my gaze down, forcing each step forward as the mass of people thickened, all pushing toward the heavy wooden doors.

The sound of the crowd was a strange comfort—a hum of voices, scattered laughter, the scratch of coats and leather against one another as we jostled forward. Each voice felt distant, muffled by the insistent, dull throb in my head, like I was underwater, struggling to surface. I could barely think straight, the pain splintering my focus. Only Lukas's hand on my shoulder kept me from giving in to the urge to stop right there and then, to collapse against the cool stone walls and let myself drift away from the agony searing my ribs.

Lukas paused at the base of the steps, his fingers tightening on my shoulder, his jaw set as he surveyed the entrance. The guards there watched the crowd with hawkish eyes, scanning each face and person stepping up to the doors. For a brief moment, I wondered if we'd make it, if they'd sense something off about us. But Lukas's hand dug into my shoulder, anchoring me back to the task, back to reality.

"Remember, you're just here for the speech," he whispered to me, low and steady. "Nothing else. We walk in, we report, and the story will be on every German doorstep by day."

I nodded, though every nerve in my body screamed in protest. Another sharp, blinding pulse of pain shot through my side, and I bit down, my jaw tightening to keep from crying out. The door was only a few steps away now, each one feeling like a mile, and I could barely feel my legs, numb under the weight of the effort.

Lukas guided me through the doorway, nodding at the guard with a curt smile that was almost charming, almost too casual. I kept my eyes down, forcing myself to look only at the floor as we entered. The murmur of voices echoed around us, the heavy interior of the Reichstag pressing in like a fortress, its vaulted ceilings somehow both grand and oppressive. The smell of polished wood and lingering smoke filled my nose, mingling with the sharper tang of blood at the back of my throat.

Inside, the voices rose in anticipation, an eager hum waiting to be unleashed. I could barely concentrate on any of it, my vision blurring as I fought to stay on my feet. Lukas kept me steady, guiding me through the crowd with ease, his focus laser-sharp, unwavering. The pulse of pain in my ribs had dulled to a relentless throb, a background noise in the chaotic symphony of my mind.

"Almost there," he whispered, leading me to a place in the back, tucked into a shadowy corner. We could see the podium and the gathering crowd from here without drawing too much attention.

I slumped against the wall, careful to keep my face composed, the pounding in my side now just a dull ache under the haze of exhaustion. Lukas's gaze flicked around the room, his jaw set with quiet determination as he scanned the crowd, never truly relaxing. I knew now that we weren't friends anymore for the next few hours, rather comrades.

The sides were completely covered by soldiers at all corners, standing uniformly, with their eyes all glaring at different corners of the room. I see other eager reporters all around me rushing to see if they can get an interview with the Führer himself. All the guards have rigid faces and sharp features that hint at discipline and severity. All eyes are piercing, possibly light-colored, with a cold, dispassionate gaze that seems almost calculating, bearing the standard-issue dark gray or black SS uniform, with a high-collared jacket bearing the distinct double-lightning SS insignia on one side and his rank insignia on the other shoulder. The belt is strapped tightly around his waist, supporting a holstered Luger pistol, the leather grip torn from use. The polished leather boots rise to his knees, spotless and sharply gleaming.

Their posture is straight, almost stiff, as though perpetually standing at attention, shoulders squared and hands often clasped behind their back. All movements with a sense of purpose and precision, an unspoken authority in every glance and gesture.

Despite the rigid exterior, hints of unease or tension in expression, as if constantly aware of the scrutiny from their superiors or the gravity of their duty.

Brushing off the desperate reporters like flies, I'm amazed by these men's restraint. I would be much more passive, ignoring these reporters rather than egging them on. Circulating are some of the party's most notable members, some I've been acquainted with, others unknown, but their chests all boast their accomplishments. Among them, I see one whose presence outshines all the rest, drawing the room's focus as if by gravity, Draco Selva. His very name commands a silence, with subtle nods of recognition from those around him. They say he has two jackets overflowing with accolades, and yet not a single ribbon on his chest seems out of place.

Selva is no ordinary general; he was one of the key minds behind the brutal battlefields of Verdun, where he helped Falkenhayn shift the course of history. His calculated strategies left an indelible mark on that bloody campaign, and rumors still swirl about his cold, methodical approach. I can feel a distinct memory in recounting that he was one of the first men I ever had the privilege to interview, a privilege extended only because he found my persistence "amusing," as he put it, his face betraying the faintest hint of a smirk. This quality has seemed to diminish over the years, as an interview is now hardly a challenge to find.

Yet, even after all these years, I remember that moment vividly. His voice was sharp and low, every word deliberate. Selva was not a man to waste time on small talk; each sentence was as exacting as his commands on the field. His eyes flicked to mine, locked with an intensity that seemed to intrigue me more than the gloating of his peers.

Even now, as I observe him here, surrounded by his peers, his posture conveys a mastery that needs no affirmation. Suddenly, I saw him coming up to me, ignoring whatever his men were saying, even though it never seemed that he was interested in their conversation. I got looks of disgruntlement from the people around, and one man even started to try pulling Selva back, but got calmly brushed back. Selva's large body was only a factor of his presence. He had dark blonde hair, soft blue eyes, and his muscles were bigger than those of two men each. Despite that, he still held the record for the fastest sprint in the military, constantly outpacing some of the fittest soldiers. His cupid-esque face, peak physical shape, accomplishment, and defiant respect for all those around lent to why so many were desperate to be in his "inner circle". Yet the ironic thing is I don't believe him to be conceited enough to indulge in such behavior. Draco approached me, and as I looked up at him, I saw a smile creep along his face.

Suddenly, everyone around started looking at the two of us. Murmurs were rumbling across the ground, and even many soldiers diverted their focus onto us rather than the event. Draco hadn't noticed the sudden change and quickly pulled me to his side. His enormous strength crushed me, and I almost collapsed halfway onto the floor. Selva's grip was firm but careful as he steadied me before I could lose balance. His voice, smooth yet edged with a commanding tone, filled the space between us, somehow intimate amidst the eyes fixed on us. He then said quite calmly.

"Seems like this crowd never tires of a little theater, doesn't it?" he murmured, his lips barely moving, the amusement in his voice just a whisper beneath his breath. His piercing blue eyes met mine for a moment. I glimpsed the familiar spark that had always intrigued me, a glint of curiosity mixed with cold, calculating prowess.

Around us, the murmurs grew, a ripple through the onlookers, a subtle tide of fascination and perhaps even envy. More of the high-ranking officials glanced our way, their expressions a mixture of awe and disdain, as if unsure whether to admire Selva's disregard for the formality or scorn his casual ease in this regimented space. But Selva remained unfazed, holding an unbreakable command over the room. Even as his voice fell to a low tone meant only for me, it carried with it an undercurrent of authority.

"You look as if you've been to hell and back, my friend," he continued, a glimmer of something resembling sympathy beneath his disciplined exterior. "Tell me, would you be here tonight if not for your occupational passion?"

"I... I suppose I could be interested. For the country, right? For everything we believe in..." My voice trailed off, as though trying to convince himself more than Draco. The words felt hollow, clinging to a sense of duty that he wasn't sure he could grasp. I took a steadying breath, managing a small, wary smile.

"This is the hope of the citizens, " the soldier said. You... are just like us, someone who will be dead at any moment, to help the citizens who by themselves may be useless, though they are the reason we fight."

"Well, we're not always there to fight, we help so that somebody will always come by in our moments of weakness."

I replied, feeling the weight of his scrutiny but standing firm under it. For all his decorated accolades and the weight of his rank, Draco Selva made anyone feel seen, even when wrong, drawn into his orbit by sheer force of character. Selva chuckled, a rare sound that seemed almost alien in the echoing formality of the room.

"Still chasing stories that rattle the bones, are you?" His smile faded slightly, a reflective edge crossing his face. The sudden change of topic was something that I was glad to see. I believe we both got answers in our own way.

"Not as exciting as what you probably see, but I manage," I now was able to push a grin that Draco returned.

"Good. The truth can slip through fingers that don't dare to tighten their grip."

As he released me, he took a moment to scan the room, his expression hardening once more as he looked over the crowd. His posture straightened, and he became once again the figure of polished authority, the general who bore the weight of his deeds and wore his scars well hidden. He leaned in closer, his voice dropping to a near-inaudible murmur.

"This gathering is the kind of theater I have no patience for. Remember that we gather to strive for greatness, which will always come pain. You, my friend, must not bear with pain; you must kill the pain, and to do that, you must either show all your emotions on your face or hide them where even you can't find them." He pulled back and gave me one last look, the faintest of nods, and with that, he came with me to leave me in my seat.

And just as quickly, he returned to his place among the others, leaving me with a sense that I had witnessed the unguarded Selva, a rare glimpse behind the iron-cast exterior he showed the world.

Through the haze, I became aware of the silence settling over the room, the crowd's murmur ebbing away as a figure approached the podium. Lukas came back from the crowd, dropping his hand to my shoulder, his eyes fixed ahead, his face expressionless but intense. I forced myself to focus, to ignore the searing pain in my side and the fatigue clawing at me, to stay present in this moment, knowing that our entire mission rested on what would happen next. Lukas pulls his head forward and takes us to our seats, embroidered on them I see Völkischer Beobachter, the leather seats losing class, and as we go to sit down amidst the noise of all in attendance, I feel the relief of my pains washing away in the seats. As I take in the beauty of the Kroll Opera House, I see rows upon rows of seats stretch toward the stage, their leather worn thin, creased from countless evenings of loyal attendance. Embroidered in faded gold thread on each person's arm was a symbol of the cause. The walls, red and black a reminder of the Reich's propaganda machinery permeating even the fabric of this grand hall. The seats, though elegant in design, carry the faint mustiness of old leather, mingling with a faint, metallic tang that lingers in the air.

As I sink back, the relief in my aching limbs intensifies, and for a fleeting moment, I forget the pain that gnaws at me from the crash. I turn my gaze upward, drawn to the grandeur surrounding us. A monumental space, an imposing blend of Baroque extravagance and Teutonic austerity. High above, a series of massive, arching vaults intersect, their plasterwork rich with swirling motifs: feathered eagles, twisted laurel wreaths, and abstracted shields of the Reich; each flourish seemingly designed to instill reverence, or perhaps submission, in its occupants. The plaster's gold accents reflect the chandelier's glow, an almost divine halo as if consecrated for some grander purpose.

Chandeliers hang from iron chains anchored into the ceiling, each chandelier a complex lattice of crystal prisms that cascade downward, catching the dim light and scattering it in subdued splinters of amber. They lend an otherworldly glimmer to the room, softening the otherwise stern lines of the architecture but unable to fully erase the underlying sense of looming power. The air beneath them feels thick, with an undercurrent of tension that vibrates just below the surface. Feelings of stress, anxiety, and relief, a collective breath held in anticipation.

My eyes shift to the walls, where towering columns stretch toward the ceiling, their marble surfaces polished to a mirror-like sheen. Each column is crowned with intricate carvings. In one corner, finely etched oak leaves and iron crosses interwoven with serpentine patterns, symbols of both traditional strength and rigid order. Flanking the stage, enormous banners unfurl, their deep crimson hues marked by stark black and white insignia, catching the faint currents of air and giving the illusion of a heartbeat. Now, the bolded decorations on the sides become invisible to the crowd.

Around me, the audience murmurs in low, restrained tones, a symphony of hushed conversations interwoven with the occasional staccato of boot heels tapping against the floor as men shift their weight, adjusting uniforms. Some avert their eyes, so as not to insult the presence of those who stand behind the curtain. Others notice each other's polished medals glinting on chests, silver and iron decorations worn with pride, though no one dares to admire them openly. Faces are set, expressions hardened; some seem to revel in the grandeur, while others look weary, their eyes flitting about as if wary of unseen gazes.

Just then, the house lights dim further, signaling the start of the evening's address. Shadows deepen across the room, casting a somber cast over the faces in attendance. I grip the armrests of my seat, their leather cool and smooth under my hands. Magnificence surrounds me, yet there's a collective edge in the air, a sensation of beauty carefully staged to cloak. The room seems to pulse with an unseen rhythm, the walls vibrating faintly, almost as if they are witnessing the proclamation.

The stands started to get full startlingly fast, and my fatigue as well. Sitting in the chair, I began to phase in and out of consciousness before Lukas awakened me.

"Idiot! Get your notebook out and start listening, he's here."

Before I could even ask a question, I bore witness to the most important man of our times come out from behind, Adolf Hitler.

All my pains, which cursed me, seemed to wither away in fear. His imposing image was that of a portrait, and even without speaking, the buzzing auditorium was as silent as a morgue. The man seemed smaller in person than in the posters looming over every street corner. There was a sharpness about him; a strangled, almost feverish intensity that seemed to ripple through him, every movement tightly wound, deliberate. His eyes were pale and piercing, as if he looked at everyone and no one simultaneously, holding a light that was neither warmth nor compassion but rather something colder, like the glint of steel, a blade sharpened to a fine, deadly edge. Darting over the crowd with an unsettling swiftness, as though weighing each face, each whisper, like one might assess the worth of metal under a jeweler's glass.

The man's voice, however, started almost conversationally, drawing you in like the beginning of a storm before swelling to a crescendo that filled the room. His words pound against you like waves, holding the crowd like a puppeteer with taut strings. He knew precisely when to raise his hand, when to pause, and when to let the silence hang in the air like a threat.

But behind the rhetoric, I sensed something else. No warmth, no trace of humanity or kindness in his gaze. His gestures, his gaze, and even his moments of stillness radiated an air of cold calculation, a machine-like precision that kept everyone around him on edge. He was no ordinary man; he was a living symbol.

In that moment, I realized it wasn't admiration that held the room captive, it was innate fear, an instinctive recognition that this was a man who could, with just one gesture, set the world alight.

I wrote down everything I heard feverishly, but even with his suave tone, I couldn't comprehend my opinions. Instead, I was left in awe of his great wisdom. I looked over at Lukas to see what he had written down, but I only saw a blank piece of paper.

He had never been one for notes, but it surprised me that he refused at least to give any statements in such a crucial place, yet I saw complete engagement in his eyes. A man who didn't even care what he ate in the morning was now fully engrossed in the speech, disregarding the job he was sent to do.

Is this the grasp of the Führer...

Every person around us seemed to have perfect timing, applauding when he paused, and all stopping at the movement of his hand; no one made a sound unless ordered to. A perfect script for the rise of the German people.

At the end of the speech, no one was out of their seats with thunderous applause, yet no commotion. Everyone agreed; the speech gave heed to the party's advancement, and the decline many non-conformists heralded on the streets was nothing more than delusion. The speech spoke for those too misconstrued to entitle themselves to an opinion of their own. Amidst all the noise, I still felt like the speech went by quickly. I checked the time and around two hours had passed, yet I felt as if only ten minutes had passed, and I could recall each moment of the speech.

Walking out of the hall, I felt the fleeting warmth of the sun fade from under the skylines, the walls transitioning from gray to a dark navy hue, cars of all kinds scattering around, and the words spoken never escaping me. The world felt as if it was expanding all around me, yet I was becoming more closed in. The pains of the day rolled off with the rain, as the stress started to dissipate.

Lukas clapped me on the back ecstatically and went off on his usual tangent.

"The speech of the century, right at the cusp of the new year! Wonderful it is! Why Klaus, you too seemed so focused on his words, not even a page is written."

That's right, I just realized that I had barely a page of notes written, and now a story is expected to be produced. My amazement started to fill with dread, and the pain creeping up around my back.

A story of this magnitude, within the hour, it should be done. Lukas, upon sensing the severity, hailed a taxi straight off the curb, a miracle considering the amount of crowd.

"Völkischer Beobachter" said Lukas, looking at the onslaught of a crowd starting to slump in the bright leather seat. The car seemed to be fully furnished and brand new, and smelled of the fumes of oil and factory, hitting me as I started to settle in.

The taxi driver looked quite ecstatic, with his perpetual smile and chipper attitude apparent at first glance. Lukas was in a similar mood, and the black car started to feel warm inside despite the cold, harsh weather we were facing all but a minute ago.

In his usual way, Lukas started to quickly acclimate himself to the space, emptying all his notebooks, camera, and other items in his pockets all over the car. As I began to pick up after him quickly, he started to strike up a conversation with the driver.

'Nice car, get a lot of people coming in?' Lukas asked with a feverish flair.

"I find enough strangers like yourself. Men wander with direction but no purpose. I fancy that people like yourself will always have a job to fulfill, but never feel that satisfaction of completion." The man said in a tone still full of joy. Lukas's interest seemed to peak, a testament to his relaxed, passive lifestyle. It appeared that this was meant to be.

The taxi driver let out a small laugh, his eyes twinkling in the rear-view mirror as he considered Lukas's words.

"Ah, that sounds like the musings of a man who's known a lot of searching. Tell me, how many roads have you walked only to end up right where you began?" Lukas hesitated, his gaze slipping to the city streets beyond the window, lit up in blurred streaks of gray.

"Maybe enough to know that going in circles is part of the journey," he replied, his voice a bit more guarded.

"Sometimes, a man's got to test every path. I think that's... common enough, don't you?"

The driver nodded thoughtfully, slowing down at a red light.

"It's common, sure. But I'd argue that those who don't look so hard find what they're after. You might surprise yourself, friend. Maybe fulfillment is what catches up to you when you're not looking."

The car then stopped at the light. The taxi driver looked back, his glee ever-present, and face clean-shaven. Eyes, a dark brown and sharp facial feature all became more apparent as the car came to a halt. Lukas didn't respond immediately, a small frown etching his brow. The words lingered, somehow heavier than he'd expected from the taxi man. However, it seemed that a spark of excitement arose in Lukas's mind even throughout the ever-growing fear. As the light turned green, Lukas turned his attention back to the driver, a newfound curiosity in his expression.

"What about you?" he asked. "You seem to have all the answers, but you're driving people around in circles every night. Don't you feel as if more is waiting for you in the world? There are lands many times larger than ours, yet you still have traversed this place more than anyone else. This city—you know from bottom to top, every street, road, and even person. Why stay?"

The driver grinned, the corners of his eyes crinkling. "Maybe once I did. Maybe I was more inclined to let life come to me—like it did tonight." He glanced at Lukas in the mirror, his eyes sharp, as if seeing right through him.

"You might find, good sir, that if you slow down enough, life will hand you what you need..."

There was a beat of silence as Lukas digested this, the city's buzz washing over us. In that quiet, Lukas wondered if the driver knew more about him than he'd let on—or if he'd just seen enough lost souls in the backseat to know exactly what he was dealing with.

"Fulfillment is something that can never come; it must be given. Only then will you appreciate it. I don't need to journey for a purpose, as it cannot be found, only experienced." Lukas still had a gaze of indecision, hoping that the taxi driver would validate his claims, rather than challenge them.

The driver, looking ahead, seemingly content with the interaction, kept up his radiant energy. Lukas was about to ready himself with another quip before the driver said to me,

"So you, my friend with the big camera and coat. What is it that you desire, what makes you want to live? Certainly, you would want to do something else in life, rather than try to avoid the rain in Berlin..."

His voice trailed off in a sense of intrigue rather than the unease set precedent by Lukas, who himself was directing his attention toward the outside traffic. However, it was evident that he was intent on hearing the conversation.

"I am just a man intent on finding out the truth of our world, in a time where history will change. I must do my best to be part of that change," I said with a clear indecision in my voice; the driver also noticed this.

"Do what you will, my friend—the Kings will not make history, rather it's his Advisers, Ministers, and all else who surround him who will control the world he precedes. Do you control, or will you be lost under a King's foot?" His tone, while serious, never lost the jovial quality present before. In fact, it seemed to increase, as did a slight spore of agitation."

"A King will always be fit to overthrow, but so are those who will flock to help him. I don't tie myself to any such leader, rather I allow myself to be safe and free." I tried to keep up a tone of confidence, which seemed to be fading away as I saw myself eating my words up. The driver, noticing this, kept up his speech.

"The King must be in place, so that he will fall, all the greats will lose something. I just hope our King doesn't fall too soon..." His voice trailed off. I felt the compulsion to answer immediately. It was as if I was being goaded into debating with the driver.

"A King will not always fall, maybe the empire on which he stands, but his ideals will live on. One can't say the same for his courtiers; they all will be forgotten in history unless they prove themselves prominent. For such instances, we must be ready to accept that failure is the greatest tool of success." The driver looked at me with a twinkle in his eye, becoming larger than ever.

"Maybe so strange, maybe so." With that, the car came to a halt. I looked over to see the omnipotent building that is the Völkischer Beobachter. I looked to see the protruding black-smoke-colored exterior—Lukas was rummaging through his wallet looking for the cash to give the driver.

"How much?" he said,

"No need to pay you two, just don't forget about me," he said joyfully. Lukas simply refused to accept this exclamation.

"That is simply irrefutable, my friend, take this!" With that, handing his whole wallet to the taxi driver. The driver simply threw the wallet out of the window, and as Lukas went to rush onto the street to pick it up, the taxi swiftly went away. Lukas was befuddled on the roadside. As I went to pick him off the road, I saw Lukas's conviction in his face, a fire ignited by a passion that seemed to be reignited in him. I only had one thing left to say.

"Did you get his name?"

Chapter 6

THE MARTYR

February 10, 1939, Berlin, Germany

It's been two weeks since the speech—since that seismic moment when the world seemed to tip on its axis and spill its contents into chaos. After that day, everything changed. Lukas left the station almost immediately, claiming he needed to go on some grand adventure of self-discovery. Whatever he saw or felt in that room must have struck a chord deep within him, something I couldn't grasp or perhaps something I was too afraid to confront.

The office hasn't changed, though. It's as cold and indifferent as ever, filled with the relentless clatter of typewriters and the murmur of voices talking about anything but what truly matters. The air feels heavier now, though, weighed down by a growing sense of dread that seeps through every crack in the plastered walls. I sit at my desk, slaving away under the harsh glow of a single flickering lamp, the keys beneath my fingers sticky with ink and sweat. Every click feels like a nail being driven into my psyche.

I've been back for a month, but it might as well have been a lifetime. Not one person greeted me when I returned. No "welcome

73

back," no casual nod of acknowledgment. It was as though I'd become a ghost, drifting unnoticed through the corridors I once knew so well. The people around me seem hollow, their faces etched with the same tired expressions of resignation I see in the mirror every morning.

And the work—oh, the work. It's torturous. Day after day, I churn out stories, weaving words about people torn from their homes, families separated, lives obliterated. Every name I type is a life now marked for persecution, each keystroke another reminder of how powerless I am in this machine. My fingers tremble, but I cannot stop. To stop would be to disappear entirely, to abandon what little I have left.

Outside the office windows, the world seems to collapse further with each passing hour. The streets are lined with propaganda posters, their bold letters screaming messages I can't read anymore. Soldiers march in perfect formation, their boots pounding the cobblestones like a heartbeat that doesn't belong to me. People glance over their shoulders before speaking, their voices hushed, their eyes darting nervously. Even the sky seems oppressive, a thick layer of smoke and ash blotting out the sun, leaving everything cloaked in perpetual gray. No longer does it feel good to be on the side I stand on; the whole system I have grown to depend on is no more than a fictitious *fallacy* upheld by those who will reap the essence of joy and hope from the bottom for only *them* to thrive. This is all my life is, a method for someone else to thrive.

Suddenly, Herrmann enters my room. A regular at the office, he has become more of a senior manager for our office, as Amann controls the whole station. He barely fits through the door, as his military-ready muscles get in the way of the skinny doorframe, and as he came in, he started berating me over my office.

"Why is this a mess, Klaus! Our top reporter, and you can't even organize your paperwork! You also have *three* dustbins, yet they're still all overflowing." Hermann was truly a nice guy, but he was starting to grow stern and less of a friend as the pressure started to close in.

"Klaus, it's been like this for too long. You're constantly slacking and moping around the hallways. And for what? Your life is better than most. Just thinking about what happens outside makes me doubly grateful!" Herrman was a very optimistic, but it seemed that something else was getting him to act this way, mostly a verbal lashing from a boss. But still, this seemingly uncharacteristic attack managed to annoy me.

"Sir... if my morale is bad, I'll leave, but consider that replacements are hard to find. With everybody having their skeletons come out of the closet, it's asking for trouble on your part. And I do contribute; just give me my own time." This sudden boldness when I spoke was much different from what happened to me normally. Herrman seemed to notice this, too, and habitually recoiled, a tactic grown through years of gnarly interviews.

"Klaus, don't give me that. You've gotten more leeway than anyone else in this office."

"Look, I know you're trying, but we all need encouragement. It's just that you should set an example for the rest of the office." Though his words were heartfelt, I gave back the same cold stare I saw peering through his eyes. A *facade,* put on so that I feel important enough to want to waste away my life at this dull building, stressing over stories that, after print, hold *no* meaning to anyone. Whether or not I'm here doesn't matter; it's only the work I produce.

"Maybe Klaus, you should take a break," Herrmann said with a tired expression, reading that *he* was fed up.

"But I just came back, why another break?" I tried to be modest but didn't want to waste the opportunity. Less work might make me happier, and maybe I could pick up Aunt Helga's advice again. I went over to hand Herrmann my paperwork, but he just brushed it aside, stating,

"Give me the work when it is ready, not when you are tired of it." Still irritated, I didn't respond. I kept my head down and slipped through the office door. The office was the same as ever, trapped in stagnation, a relic that refused to move forward. The walls, marred by the endless cycle of propaganda posters plastered over each other. The newest ones were sharp and vivid, their red and black pronounced and loud, while the remnants of older posters peeked through in peeling corners, their muted colors whispering of times not so long ago.

I brushed past the bullpen, our paper's so-called "heart"—a chaotic, inefficient mess. Desks, all scattered haphazardly across the room, each one buried under mountains of papers, cigarette butts, and half-empty coffee cups, stains etched into cabinets. The smell permeated into an indescribable aroma that was impossible to remove, no matter the amount of cologne used.

The writers and editors were just as disorderly. Jonas Koch, a wiry man with a permanent scowl etched into his sharp features, sat on the edge of his desk. Flicking through a stack of papers, his pen scratching half-hearted corrections across a page before tossing it aside. Though being a senior editor, it was clear that his position was a result of luck rather than skill. His edits are mostly so bad that they have ruined articles. One time I yelled at him for this, calling him a neanderthal, a word not known by him, but after that, he hasn't spoken to me since.

Across the bullpen, Janet Baier leaned back in her chair, her feet propped on the desk as she doodled aimlessly in the margins of a newspaper. Her shirt had a coffee stain she hadn't bothered to clean. She was laughing—not at anything funny—just mumbling to herself. Next to her, Calvin and Peter were in a heated argument over some trivial topic, their voices rising. With his thick glasses and perpetually ink-stained fingers, Calvin gestured wildly as Peter rolled his eyes and lit another cigarette, blowing the smoke directly into Calvin's face.

Everywhere I looked, people were doing anything but their jobs. Jonas threw a wad of crumpled paper across the room, narrowly missing Peter's head before landing on his desk with a soft thud. A typewriter dinged intermittently, though its owner, Frank Herrman, was nowhere to be seen, probably still messing around in my office. It was a circus disguised as a newsroom, where everyone seemed to be avoiding the inevitable weight of their roles.

And yet, despite their inefficiency, this was the foundation of our publication. This was where stories were born—or at least, where they were supposed to be. But as I pushed through the chaos, a space that only barely functioned because it had to, not because anyone cared enough to make it thrive.

Walking outside, I view the great "Völkischer Beobachter" sign. I tried to hail a taxi but had no luck. I decided I wouldn't go to my decrepit apartment; rather, I preferred to wander around and see what I'm told to have missed. The tall buildings that enclosed me from the sky were as gray as ever. The streets were restless. People moving in small clusters, voices dimming as they approach each other, their faces shadowed by hats and scarves. A couple hurried past me, clutching their coats tightly, their expressions etched in uncertainty. A man leaned against a lamppost, lighting a cigarette with a slight tremble in his fingers, eyes closed, yet they yielded a slight twitch. Somewhere in the distance, the faint sounds of rupture could be heard, screams becoming more commonplace, fear all but expected, and distrust among each other encouraged. The joyful banter of civilians started to vanish in the air.

I passed a café, its windows fogged from the heat inside. Through the glass, I could see the faint outlines of patrons—silhouettes hunched over steaming cups, their conversations too muffled to make out. The servers distinctly scream across the restaurant, clearly audible from the outside. I felt like going in, but after what happened with Lukas, I was pretty comfortable avoiding such places for a while.

The further I walked, the more the city seemed to close in on me. Posters covered nearly every surface, their slogans screaming in bold, oppressive fonts. "Unity Through Strength," one read, its words framed by the stark imagery of raised fists. The phrase always reminds me of Zorro. Another declared, "The Future is Ours," beneath a sharp, angular symbol that had become inescapable. The atmosphere, becoming thicker, bearing the color of the posters, thicker than the paper used, made me start to feel a choking sensation.

I turned down a narrower street, the crooked cobblestones twisting under my shoes. Here, the city's pulse felt different—quieter, darker. A street vendor was packing up his cart, his face worn and weathered under the light of a gas lamp. He nodded briefly in my direction but said nothing. As he moved on, I felt I should return to the main street. Despite it not being too late, only about afternoon, I still felt an overwhelming sense of darkness.

As I got back on the main street, I fell back into that feeling of suffocation present, yet I also began to notice the whispers of a world that seemed to have eluded me. The delicate smell of freshly baked bread wafts from a bakery. The faint laughter of children muffled from a window above. The creak of a bicycle as a delivery boy sped past, with a half-attached satchel slung across his chest. These were the pieces of life I had supposedly missed, the fleeting moments of normalcy that still managed to persist in the cracks of a fractured world.

But even in this wandering, I couldn't shake the feeling of being watched. Every glance over my shoulder revealed empty streets and shadowed windows; the sensation lingered, heavy and oppressive. It was as though the city had eyes, its faceless structures bearing witness to my aimless journey.

I kept walking, unsure of where I was going, unsure of what I was searching for. All I knew was that I couldn't go back—not to the apartment or office. The city stretched out before me, endless and indifferent, and for the first time in a long time, I allowed myself to drift within it, untethered. I still felt watched, and that feeling grew. I turned back and looked out to see no one, and just then I was approached by a voice, "Hello, Sir!" I looked back to see a girl looking at me, at a glance, she was about my age, and a half-inch shorter. With blue eyes and blond hair, she was the pinnacle of what the regime desired. Her voice was innocent and sweet, seemingly unaltered by the presence of the regime.

"What is it?" I asked, trying to remember who she was. I was certain that I didn't know who she was. I glanced around me and saw nobody near, but the feeling of being watched still loomed. The girl stood there, unbothered by the emptiness around us, her hands clasped neatly in front of her. She was dressed, in a pale blue coat, and her demeanor exuded a strange mix of confidence and naivety. "Oh, I'm sorry if I startled you," she said, her voice carrying a lilt that felt out of place. "You just looked…" Her gaze met mine, unwavering and curious, and I felt a strange unease settle in my chest. There was something almost too perfect, like she'd stepped out of one of those propaganda posters.

"I'm not lost," I replied curtly, still trying to make sense of her sudden appearance. My eyes darted around the street again. But there was no one. The street was as empty as before, save for the faint glow of a lamppost a few paces away. "Do I know you?"

She shook her head, a soft smile tugging at the corners of her lips. "No, but I know you. You work for the Völkischer Beobachter, don't you?" Her tone was still light, like she had just started something as innocuous as the weather. My stomach churned.

"How do you know that?" I demanded, my voice sharper than I intended. The girl didn't flinch. "I read your articles," she said simply. "How you write about the people, about the stories the regime doesn't want anyone to hear—it's... fascinating." Her words struck. I felt a tension that wasn't very present in my everyday life. I felt my breath catch, I got a sense of excitement from her that couldn't be replicated. My articles? The ones that passed through layers of censorship, stripped of their truths and reshaped into a narrative that lost all semblance of truth? It makes sense that she may have read my articles, but to know my truth as a person, why I've never let that show in print. Interviews I've done, but few, and never recorded, only put on pages. Never did I think someone would confront me like this in the open. I certainly was glad that nobody could hear us.

"I think you've made a mistake," I said, my voice lower now, laced with a warning. "I don't know what you're talking about."

Her smile faltered for the first time, and her gaze softened.

"You don't have to be afraid," she said, stepping closer. "I'm not going to tell anyone. Klaus, tell me what it is you seek?"

The air between us started to morph, the silence deafening. Her words hung in the air, heavy with implications I didn't know about. "Who are you?" I asked, my voice barely above a whisper. She hesitated momentarily, her eyes flicking to the shadows behind me as though checking for unseen listeners. When she finally spoke, her voice was lower, urgent.

"That's something you can learn later."

Her words somehow sent a chill down my spine. I didn't respond, my mind racing to piece together who she was, why she was here, and what this meant for me. She took another step closer, her presence both disarming and unsettling.

"You don't have to trust me," she continued, her voice softer now, almost a whisper. "But I think you'll want to hear what I say. Come, we have a little sunlight." As she rushed, I knew she was an optimist if she still believed that there was sunlight in a city as decrepit.

As I followed, I was in two minds, as on one hand she seemed to be telling a complete truth about herself, yet I knew less than before I met her. To me, she is nothing more than a stranger, yet her insistence on my presence enamors me. It's baffling the power that a little information about a person can have on others. No matter as we embarked down the bleak streets, I overheard the stomping of soldiers' boots and could feel the ever-present fear lurking in each apartment. Children were being heralded indoors, and scared housewives were closing the windows; the lack of stability is starting to show. Still in the distance, the lady was fluttering without a care, her presence being something that reminded those of the days when my worries didn't matter. "Hurry up!" she exclaimed, while I started to slow down, she sped up. As she said that, I began to feel heavy, my pockets weighing me down, and my foot stuck into the uneven cobblestone, as I started to fall over to my side. My camera hit the ground, and all the papers in my satchel lay across the sidewalk, swept away in the wind.

"Damn it," I muttered, kneeling to gather the scattered documents.

My journal fell out as well. The woman noticed this; she dashed, her pale coat a blur, as she darted after a stray page.

As all my belongings fell, I swiftly collected some left scraps of paper, as well as my notebook. As I began to collect myself, she went to hand me the journal, but her sense of curiosity got the best of her. Before she gave it to me, she started to look through the journal. Her fingers brushed the cover, and curiosity lit up her face. Before I could stop her, she opened it, her brow furrowing as she scanned the pages.

"Hey—" I began, reaching for it, but her voice cut through my protest.

"No need to hide anything, I'm only here to see what the legendary Klaus Abel, the 'Propaganda Paria,' keeps hidden, it's a privilege." I wanted to speak but no words would come out; the name, while silly, was now becoming something I was known as, only a tool for my government. She flipped through the pages, weaving past me as I tried to seize it from her hands. We started to move forward as I lunged and attempted to get my journal back; she could foil my attempts with fluid ease without ever looking up from the book. Her gaze was intently focused on the book, her eyes darting from right to left, feverishly going through the pages. Her eyebrows were raised in confusion, and her speed seemed uncanny. I could feel my energy draining as I stumbled after her, my heart pounding from a mix of exertion and sheer frustration. After she got about halfway through the book, I was almost out of energy; as I stopped, she seemed to tire as well. Her fingers stilled on a page, her eyes scanning the words with awe. Then, as I stood there, catching my breath and bracing for whatever came next, she finally closed the journal. As she came to give me back the journal, she muttered.

"Why do you write in English?" she asked with a sense of authority. Why write in the speech of our enemies, especially since you are so keen on harming them? I suggest journaling in

Hebrew next." Her voice stayed calm, even though she was furious. She couldn't be caught saying this in public. I wanted to quell the situation, but it was of no use.

"Well, I write in English because I was taught to; it just feels more natural, I guess." I wanted to sound as sincere as possible, but I was confused by the habit. It was natural from when I was a boy, so much so that I never found it odd. I turned back to the lady and saw her expression. Her face expressed betrayal, but her eyes felt softer as if she trusted me more.

"Now tell me, did you understand what I wrote?" I asked in a tongue-in-cheek sort of way.

"Not really, but I know that whatever it said was rubbish. I mean, why use a journal if you already write all day? Klaus, you most certainly confuse me."

'What confuses me is that you are forcing me to follow you, yet I still don't know why,' I became agitated as I spoke.

"I just wanted to see how long it would take to see the true side of you. I guess now I've seen enough." Her smile faltered, and her expression shifted to something more serious. "I just wanted to see how long it would take for the real you to show," she said, her tone measured, almost contemplative. "I guess now I've seen enough."

Narrowing my eyes at her, my frustration mounting. "What's that supposed to mean?"

"It means you've been wearing masks for so long that you've forgotten what your face looks like," she replied, steady and unflinching. "But I saw glimpses of it. In your journal, in your words, in the way you speak. You're not what you want people to think you are."

I opened my mouth to respond, but no words came out. Her statement struck a nerve.

"And that," she continued, softer now, "is why I need you."

"Need me? What *for*?"

"To write Klaus, to show us what we're missing, you have only pushed an agenda not made by you, and therefore by your own conscience, allowing these opinions to become yours. I need you to speak for us." Suddenly, I felt a feeling that was not very familiar to me.

Hitting all at once, a tangled mess I couldn't fix, leaving my chest tight and my breath uneven. There was now a cold, twisting ache deep in my stomach, carving its way through me. Yet, beneath it all, a strange, unwelcome energy simmered, quickening my pulse in a way that made me writhe in discomfort.

Something bitter settled on my tongue, heavy and sour, as if every word I wanted to speak needed to be inspected. My thoughts tangled and crashed into one another, leaving my head pounding and my shoulders heavy. I tried to roll them back, tried to shake off the weight, but it clung to me—awkward, constricting, impossible to ignore.

Every step felt unsteady like the ground beneath me had shifted. My fingers curled into fists at my sides, as though holding on to anything might stop the world from spinning. There was a pressure building inside me, something unfamiliar, like a mantle I hadn't asked to carry but couldn't set down. With that, I could respond, no, I had to say something, otherwise what would I do? Must I live a life as uncertain as this?

And so I ran. As I ran, her voice followed me, sharp but fading, like the echo of a bell. I couldn't make out the words—not entirely—but her tone clung to me.

Chapter 7

SS

March 13, 1939, Berlin, Germany

My footsteps had fallen unevenly on the cobblestones, the jarring sound hitting against the heavy silence of the streets. I thought I heard her again—closer this time—but when I glanced back, there was nothing. For a moment, I slowed, a brief moment of relief. My hand brushed against my satchel, somewhat lighter than before, the rough fabric catching onto my skin. I turned a corner and my building loomed ahead, a gray mass rising out of the dark. The door creaked as I pushed it open, the sound startling. When I reached my apartment, I laid all my items on my couch; all the furniture was still, my clothes were all properly in the closet, and the dishes were all clean, as expected by now. Yet it didn't feel right, something was off-putting my senses in a way unnatural. I was still experiencing that stress that I was unable to cope with then. The couch, now a mess, I decided to check the time: 6:43 PM. It had been a month. All this excitement hasn't left my mind.

No matter what, I still can't get over that night. Who was she? Was I right, or did I make the biggest mistake of my life?

Still, on the couch, I looked up at my apartment's bleak, stained brown wall; nevertheless, I was subjected to the noise of the traffic outside, while less frequently a complete annoyance. It took me a good while until I was able to pick myself off the couch and trudged over to the kitchen where I opened my pantries to see that it was empty. The countertops were spotless, but that also meant I would have to get more food. While the hunger became more intense as I contemplated the decision. The local bakery was soon to close, but I was sure that I could go there, most grocers now fled due to the regime.

Heading down my apartment floor, I could hear the cohorts of people being hosted by my neighbors; it was always like this no matter the day. I could hear some call friends over for a cocktail party, while others made plans to escape. It was ironic considering that they went to great lengths to have these gatherings in secret, yet the walls are thin enough that we can all hear each other. I never cared much for it. As I went down the floors, the conversations all became muddled, all an endless chatter accumulating into a mess. I suddenly felt the urge to run again, but this time I didn't know why. The stairs twisted and tilted in ways that I felt disoriented. The feeling of pareidolia became so strong that I couldn't stand still. Suddenly, I could feel all the energy in my body dissipating onto the floor. Everything that was driving me forward lay barren, and as I hit the ground, I could feel the pain surge through my body.

Unable to get up, I just allowed myself to rest on the cold and decrepit carpet floor, my chest throbbing with pain, without the adrenaline rushing through my veins. I don't think I would even be able to stay cognizant. I still had a flight of stairs to go, and my hunger only kept growing, but after checking the time,

I saw that I had only around ten minutes left before the baker closed. Begrudgingly, I hoisted myself up by the banister rails of the stairs and kept a tight grip on them until I reached the front of my apartment. There I saw the light of the bakery. I headed along the streets and quickly went into the shop; the smell of fresh bread being thrown out and dough being prepared for the next morning gave the bakery a great sense of warmth. The clatter of pans and the hum of the oven filled the room, blending into the warm glow of the space. Alongside, Mr Kuchenmeister was always pleased to see me.

"Ah, Klaus, testing to see when I close now?" he said in a joking manner.

"I guess so, and I'm now going to test my appetite, give me whatever can be considered a meal." While ravished, I kept my composure. Kuchenmeister was a dear friend after all.

"Well, let's see, how about something off the menu? It's different, but I think you will enjoy it," Kuchenmeister said in his ever-present joyful tone.

"As long as it's savory, why not?"

A sudden smile then spread across Kuchenmeister's face,

"Savory, you say? I've got just the thing." Kuchenmeister's smirk deepened as he started to grab ingredients from the cooler. His movements were deliberate, the kind of efficiency that comes only with decades of practice. I leaned against the counter, the ache in my legs easing slightly as I took in the surroundings. The shelves were nearly empty now, save for a few loaves of bread and some pastries that had grown stale under the glass case. Yet the place still felt alive, brimming with pride.

"You've had a long day, haven't you?" Kuchenmeister called out, still facing the back.

"You could say that," I replied, my voice heavy and raspy.

"I can tell," he said, his tone softening. "You're dragging yourself in here like a ghost. Whatever it is you're chasing, it'll wait. But you need to eat first. I'll bet you forgot to eat all day, didn't you?"

"I had some salad in the morning." An obvious lie that I muttered out for no conceivable reason.

"Salad, ha, what a joke! I know of toddlers who can make better lies than you, Klaus. Tell me, how do you work at a news station if you can't even make up stories on the spot?"

Before I could answer, he emerged with a plate, steam curling upwards in delicate tendrils. On it was a dish I didn't recognize—something simple. A thick slice of rye bread topped with what looked like braised cabbage, onions, and a layer of spiced sausage. "Try this," Kuchenmeister said, setting the plate before me.

"It's an old family recipe. A meal for when there's no time to waste but still a need to feel whole." His voice now becomes mellow, and he has a sense of care similar only to that of a parent. I hesitated, the aroma pulling me in before I could overthink it. The first bite hit me like a balm, the sharp tang melding with the smoky richness. It couldn't be just food.

Kuchenmeister watched me intently, leaning against the counter. "You see? Sometimes the simplest things remind us of who we are."

"I don't even know who that is anymore," I muttered, the words slipping out unbidden.

His expression didn't change, but something in his gaze sharpened as if he was weighing my words carefully. "Maybe you don't need to know right now."

I didn't respond, instead taking another bite. Kuchenmeister's words still lingered in the air, slowly becoming heavy and unsettling.

"Thanks," I said finally, standing to leave. Kuchenmeister nodded, his smirk returning, though it started to soften.

"The road's always clearer after a good meal, Klaus. Don't forget that."

I stepped out into the night, the chill biting at my face. My energy started to come back as I walked across the road again; this time, the noise of traffic was back, but it wasn't as piercing as before. The bakery's glow faded as I walked away, replaced by the dim, flickering lights of the street lamps. Somewhere in the distance, boots stomped against the cobblestones, the sound of order and chaos colliding. My pace quickened, though I couldn't tell why.

As I approached my building, the slick stone gate loomed ahead, its surface glistening faintly under the weak glow of a streetlamp. The gate had always been unremarkable and stoic, blending into the tired facade of the building, but tonight, something about it caught my attention. For the first time, I noticed the angels carved into the sides of the entranceway—delicate, intricate figures etched deep within the stone. Their faces, serene yet unsettling, seemed to follow me as I stepped closer. Though blank and unseeing, their eyes had an eerie weight to them, as if they weren't blind at all but observing with an omniscient detachment. Each figure was positioned differently, some with their hands clasped in prayer, others holding scrolls or trumpets, their wings unfurling in graceful arcs. All the figures were different, yet they looked of the same kin. The craftsmanship was meticulous, every feather on their wings etched with immaculate detail, each fold of their robes flowing naturally into the stone. However, something about them made the tension in the air rise. No matter where I stood or how I shifted my gaze, the angels seemed to meet my eyes, their stone faces locked in a watchful, silent vigil. I couldn't tell if it was the way the shadows danced across their forms or the precise angles of their carving, but it felt as though their presence was alive. The damp stone made the details of their faces more pronounced—an odd curvature of the lips, a faint crease of their brows—giving them an uncanny expression. It wasn't quite benevolent, nor was it entirely foreboding. It was something in between.

I wondered how long they had stood there, silent and unyielding, watching every passerby with that same detached scrutiny? It was as if they had just appeared, and I couldn't unsee them.

I hesitated before stepping through the archway, the cold stone feeling closer now, pressing in around me. The angels' gaze trailed me as I passed beneath them. I looked back and although the gate was behind, I still couldn't shake the feeling of being watched. A pair of carved eyes held a kind of judgment I couldn't fully understand but couldn't shake. As I walked up, I saw another statue at the head of the handrail with a similar expression, yet posed as if it were running away from the gate, turned away up the stairs rather than poised at the gate. As I continued up the stairs, the thought still lingered in my mind. I couldn't shake off the image of the gate. For some reason, it was engraved in my mind that the statues were present even though I had never seen them before. Ascending the stairs, I could still hear all conversations present, but the voices were lowering, the dim light of the streets became harrowingly dark, and the stopping of the soldiers only became more pronounced.

When I reached my apartment, I saw that I had forgotten to unlock the door, a common mistake made by me, especially when in a rush. I always then checked for missing items but was quite sure nobody would steal, considering the amount of law enforcement on every corner. When going to my couch, I picked up a book from the side table, and piled it under a bunch of others, I just felt compelled to read it. The cover was simply brighter and more appealing; I felt a sense of duty to read it. The title was "Burmese Days" by George Orwell, a book I had been gifted by Lukas when he was in England. Texts other than German were generally confiscated, and I had built quite a backlog. I had one shelf entirely dedicated to all foreign books, from French cookbooks to Japanese Poetry. As I started, I became engrossed in the world of the book, and once I started, the time flew by fast.

At a specific time, I had forgotten about bed and had fallen asleep on the couch only to be woken up by a knock. The dull thud of a knock jolted me awake, the sound reverberating through the halls. Groggy and disoriented, I clumsily headed to the door while getting up. When I opened it, the sight before me drained the last vestiges of warmth from my body. A Nazi officer stood there, his figure looming in the dim hallway light. A deep green accented by the unmistakable blood-red armband wrapped around his sleeve. The stark black swastika emblazoned on it seemed to pulsate with authority.

His presence filled the doorway, a monolith of power, with an undertone of menace. The crisp lines of his uniform amplified the sharpness of his features, high cheekbones casting shadows under the unforgiving light. His eyes were the most unnerving—cold and calculating, like a predator sizing up its prey. They glinted faintly beneath the brim of his peaked cap, which was tilted just enough to obscure part of his face, making him seem both larger and more distant.

He said nothing at first, letting the silence stretch between us. His gaze raked over me, observing my features, his eyes darting all around, yet still focused intently on me—my unkempt hair, the wrinkled shirt I'd slept in, the dark circles under my eyes. My throat tightened, and I could feel my pulse quicken, a heavy thudding against my ribs. I gripped the edge of the doorframe to steady myself; I could feel the pain from my ribs swelling again.

"Good evening," he finally said, his voice low and smooth, the weight unwavering. It wasn't a greeting but a warning, and I could only hope I was in the wrong place.

"Can I help you?" I managed to stammer, though the words felt weak in the face of his overwhelming authority. He stepped forward, his polished boots clinking softly against the floor. Instinctively, I took a step back. The movement felt futile, like retreating from an oncoming storm. He reached into his coat and pulled out a folded piece of paper, holding it up casually. The shadow of the eagle insignia stamped at the top fell across my chest.

"Klaus Abel," he said, as though the name alone was an accusation. "I am SS-Obersturmführer Hans Landa. I make your acquaintance as I am informed you may have information about a traitor in Berlin." His words struck like a hammer, but I barely registered them. My gaze was fixed on his hand, gloved in smooth black leather, resting loosely on the holster at his hip. The mere presence of the weapon was enough to send a shiver down my spine.

"I... I don't understand," I could only mutter.

"You will," he replied, his tone detached. Without another word, he stepped aside, gesturing down the hallway with a tone of such intense impartiality that I could only feel anger. My feet felt rooted to the floor, my body caught between the instinct to flee and the paralyzing grip of fear.

"May I come in?" he said as a smile grew on his face, his tone becoming softer.

I didn't have a choice other than complying. "Why, of course."

"Klaus, your house is certainly well-kept. I'm surprised you can manage this all on your own," his voice still held a distinct lack of empathy.

"Well, I try to keep it clean. I'm glad you appreciate it. Here, have a seat. I'll get you a drink," I tried my best to stay calm.

"I'll just have water because as much as I would love to stay, I understand that you only recently had an accident, so I believe that it would be best to just get into business." His growing facade soon dropped. "Klaus, we are under the impression that a secret informer in Berlin is trying to steal classified information from high-ranking party members and that you are one of the targets." Words hitting me like a train, I stayed quiet.

"Furthermore, I believe she has already obtained the necessary information." The room now started to feel smaller, the air compressing in toward me, suffocating in its silence, broken only by the faint creak of my chair as I adjusted nervously. Landa sat across from me, his presence commanding. Though his expression carried a veneer of politeness, his eyes betrayed a sharp, predatory focus. His eyes became slimmer and less wondrous, instead intentful and knowing. He leaned back slightly, folding his gloved hands neatly on the table between us.

"Let us not waste time, Herr Abel," Landa said, his voice low and syrupy. He paused and grew a genuine smile, letting the weight of his words settle before continuing. "You see, I have quite the curiosity about the company you keep."

I swallowed hard, my throat suddenly dry. "Company?" My head went blank, words unable to escape and create a lie I could shield this away with. I could barely let out, "I haven't a clue what you are saying."

His lips curled. "Yes. You have been... observed. People talk, Herr Abel, even in small little whispers, and whispers... as you know, can reveal the most fascinating... truths." His gloved fingers tapped idly on the table's edge, the sound rhythmic, unnerving.

"I don't know what you're talking about," I repeated, my voice strained but steady. "Rumors are nothing but lies made by the weak and jealous. Why would I rashly give up all I have, all the party has given me for women I had just met?"

Landa's smile widened, though his eyes remained cold. "Perhaps not. Or perhaps you are simply a very good actor. And you just let too much slip." He reached into his coat and latched onto a small notebook, flipping it open with a theatrical flourish. "Names, places, dates—everything has a story, and I do love stories. Would you enamor me with one unable to be in print? Tell me about the famous English journal you keep with you at all times.

Or the exploit with the Spaniards that almost led to death among the party. See wherever you go, Klaus–"

"I didn't do anything! What could I have that an enemy of the state would want to know? Tell me!" I started to sweat, the pressure increasing, the feeling of before coming back.

"Don't be a Buffon Klaus, you know why, knowledge. The knowledge you possess is more valuable than anything, and failing to recognize that makes you no smarter than a roadside laborer. I have all that I need except the truth." He started to chuckle. His laugh was soft, almost patronizing, as if he'd already figured it out. "The truth," he mused, closing the notebook with a snap. "Do you know what I've learned about the truth, Herr Abel? It's slippery. Rarely does it stand on its own. It requires coaxing and shaping, often with a little force. Now I will get the truth no matter what, even if it means that you suffer along the way. As you said, rumors can all be lies made up by the poor and jealous, but you forgot one other type of person, the bold!" He slammed his fist against the table, his hair now a mess. He unlatched his notebook and put it on the table. The blood drained from my face as he slid the notebook toward me. Inside, scribbled in precise handwriting, were notes and addresses—names of colleagues, neighbors, and friends, some of whom I hadn't seen in months. My mind raced, trying to understand how he had gathered so much.

"How do you have all this?" I could no longer hide my fear. Hans was preying on my pain now.

He chuckled softly, leaning forward now, his face inches from mine. "Oh, Herr Abel, critical thinking is all that is necessary. It insults both of us. Shall I make it simpler for you? You work under me... and by that logic, I shall know everything about you. Just because you don't fight doesn't mean you're not a soldier in this battle."

He flipped to another page, revealing a photograph of the woman—my stomach dropped. "You know her, don't weave another intricate story," Landa said, his sharp tone cutting through the air like a blade. "Do not deny it. She has been most... elusive, but I suspect you are the key to finding her. Tell me, Herr Abel, where is she?"

"I don't know," I said quickly, too quickly.

Landa's smile grew, accompanied by a cold, hard stare. He let the silence stretch, the tension in the room growing unbearable. Then, in one swift motion, he stood, the chair scraping against the floor. "You don't know," he repeated, pacing, his boots clicking ominously against the hardwood. "Yet you were seen together only days ago. Strange, isn't it, how coincidences seem to pile up in times like these?" His hand started to bang against the wooden table.

"I also want to know where she is, but I left before she could even say her name! If you want to look for her–"

"You disappoint me, Herr Abel," Landa said, stopping abruptly and facing me. His voice was calm, but there was a steel edge to it now, a promise of consequences. "You see, I had hoped we might resolve this matter amicably. But perhaps I overestimated your willingness to cooperate. I shouldn't have trusted a journalist scum like you. Watching us die while you still complain about your office, while we have to see the blood of our brothers be split only because you couldn't handle the pressure." I stood there watching Landa slowly gaining a little distance from him. Then he kicked the table at me, the legs now on the floor and the dust filling the air.

"Why do you think there are so many of us? Why do you think fear is present wherever we go. They believe it's us, the soldiers, all running around every corner to make sure the filth who have infested our streets for years gets cleaned up. However, no matter how noble the task, the reporter will defame us. Make it seem like we are stationed just to waste time and instill fear in the public. Your kind is no better than those who we kill, and I would very much like to punish you however I see fit! Your streak of luck isn't over, though I am bound by rules and honor, unlike you, I must deal with you liberally." Hans then snapped his fingers and left the room, kicking one of the chairs on his way out. Before I could react, he gestured to the two officers intently watching the conversation. They stepped forward, their heavy boots echoing ominously.

"Take *him*," Landa ordered, his tone as casual as he entered. All anger expressed seething back into his heart. The officers grabbed me roughly, pulling me to my feet. I struggled, but their grip was unyielding. Landa watched with an almost amused expression, his head tilted slightly as if studying an animal caught in a trap. His fox-like gaze was studying my fear.

"Klaus Abel, you are hereby summoned for questioning," he said with a mocking bow.

"I do hope our next conversation will be more productive." As I was dragged out of the room, his cold and hollow laughter followed me, echoing in my mind long after the door slammed shut behind me. Suddenly, the reality of the situation crashed over me like a wave.

I was being arrested.

As they guided me out into the cold night, the officer's towering figure remained just ahead of me, his movements calculated and deliberate. The sound of his boots echoed against the walls. I tried to focus on anything else, but all I could feel was nothing.

The angels carved into the stone gate stared down at me as I passed beneath them. As I walked out, I saw the black car ahead. I looked back to see if any help was left; the only thing I could see was the cold stare of the angels. As I went onto the street, nobody else could see me, all engrossed in their lives full of fear and anguish; only then could I still see the angels' stare.

— • ⬤ • —

Chapter 8

THE WALL

April 5, 1939, Berlin, Germany

The walls are a cold, dark green that reverts into gray on the floor. I hear the pipes leaking, but I do not see it, as the sun's light is becoming a concept foreign to me rather than the common right I used to believe it was. Guards' boots running up and down the hallways, I can't even imagine where they run off to. The interior was quite shabby; I thought I would see colors in the end.

Is one's life limited, or is it just that they quit trying to live?

I find the Führer's plan for our nation hypocritical. I recognize the allure of strength and togetherness, of a Reich that would endure, but at what price? Our country's essence is being perverted by a man who promises glory but instead brings about disaster, and he is being consumed by hate, terror, and blind loyalty. In the shadow of this new Germany, my father's values—his sense of honor, responsibility, and pride—have faded into the past. I'm compelled to feel imprisoned.

Just then a guard comes, standing like a carven sentry, posture unyielding, carved in stone. The lines of his gray uniform were cuttingly sharp, seeming cut from the same fabric that framed his harsh visage, every seam pressed tight to hint at obsession: an obsession with control. A stark red swastika encircled the bicep of his left arm, jarringly pulsing with authority. His boots, polished to shine like a mirror, clomped on the floor at every deliberate step, a menacing thud.

His face was a mask of cold efficiency. High cheekbones cast deep shadows under his eyes, which were a pale, piercing blue, almost unnatural in their intensity. Those eyes seemed to see everything and nothing at once, scanning the room with an unnerving detachment. His jaw was set in a hard line, lips thin and almost bloodless, as though any hint of warmth had been drained from his features.

There was an air of suppressed violence around him, the way his gloved hands rested a few inches away from the holstered Luger by his side, fingers twitching slightly as if always ready to react. Insignia on his collar - the silver runes that glistened menacingly - showed that he was something more than just a soldier. He wore an aura of confidence around him that would come with completely the kind of guy who would change the lives of men and women just by giving them a flick of his wrist. Even standing, he was claustrophobic, a force that seemed to be pushing down on the room itself. When they landed on you, his eyes were like a spotlight, freezing you in place and removing any pretense of defiance. Every feature screamed inherent intimidation, a man who didn't need words to create conversation, a man whose very existence was a weapon of fear.

"Herr Abel," he stated in a tone of superiority, one has when feeling helpless. "The commander would like to know when you will divulge any information to him. Of course, he insists that you are free to remain within the confines of this prison for as long as you want."

"I'll take the latter, Herr Adler," my voice vexed. Despite his menacing appearance, Thomas Adler was a simple-minded lackey within Landa's circle. He rarely had a thought of his own and compensated for that by using the little authority wielded to push down those he felt like. Adler had come every day without fail to check in on me, his presence becoming an annoyance rather than instilling the fear of the party.

"Do you have children, Adler?" I started speaking without thinking.

"I have two sons, Herr Abel, but why does that concern you, a man without children, or even a family?" His eyes shifted toward me, thinning as they came down.

"Well, tell me, when we win the war, what will you tell them?" I started to grow a smile of mischief.

"Meaning?" Dropping the facade, he gave in to curiosity. I myself got too deep into the conversation.

"That their father was a failure to the German army, whose only job was to intimidate captured prisoners, behind bars!" Adler looked at me unfazed. I looked deep into his eyes, his stare becoming cold, an unwavering will surfacing on his face. My grin soon turned to a wilt, as I, with disheveled, greasy hair and tattered clothes, still believed that I was winning.

"If you insist, Herr Abel, I wonder how it is that for over a month you have lived in this cell. I couldn't imagine what must have happened to you. Your belongings are now with us, and soon we can do as we please with them. You may leave a free man, but penniless on the street. I do hope that you break tomorrow, Klaus…"

With that, he left, his detached tone made me feel even more isolated, and the guards were under strict orders not to let any visitors in. I had tried my best in the situation though, from cleaning the damp walls of the cell to fixing myself a proper bed with a little stitch work of the old mattresses. Adler now left me more confused than ever before, but I decided to put that aside. Luckily, I was needed for information; otherwise, I would have already been sent to the camps, at least that's what I've been told. I haven't been able to get any mail in my time here, and day by day I get drip-fed the news by overhearing the guards as they pass by my cell. Tidbits about run-away convicts, and how the militarization of our country is becoming stronger, or hearing about the massacre happening just a few kilometers away from us.

I had spent every day of the last month waiting for Adler to come, and now it felt stale to be rotting away in a jail cell such as this, with no sense of frivolity or passion. Rather, a bleak and cold wall was all I had.

There was something else, yet it wasn't tangible, my journal. Locked away in the office of the commanding officer, Fredrick Frank, almost all my immediate possessions were put in there and have never left. He was one of those men whose very presence dominated a room. It wasn't just his size that filled the space, though his broad shoulders and square jaw had already lent him an aura of unshakable authority. His voice carried a commanding weight, every word clipped and deliberate, like bullets fired with precision. He was a figure to be revered—or feared—by his men.

He was the kind of leader who led from the front. His uniform was always crisp, clean, and immaculate; his boots had a gloss reflecting his unrelenting expectations. In the field, he was remorseless: a strategist able to outmaneuver his enemies and push his troops to their limits. He could make even the bleakest situation into an opportunity, a quality that had both earned him admiration and resentment. His commands were sharp, unwavering, and with an iron will.

Beneath that facade of power, however, was something much more brittle: Frederick's ego. It was an unstated rule among his lieutenants that though his power was absolute, his pride was a landmine - one misstep and it would explode. He wasn't only asking for obedience but adoration, the kind that fed his insatiable need for validation. Any little thing against his leadership might transform his calculated composure into a storm of fury. He tended to overcompensate to hide his insecurity. The office in which my journal was kept - a place with maps, medals, and books in leather-bound covers - was more than a workspace; it was a shrine to his triumphs. The walls were lined with framed commendations, his desk a fortress of perfectly arranged documents and trophies. But the more he surrounded himself with reminders of his triumphs, the more fragile the inside seemed.

Frederick Frank was powerful, yes. His presence could still fill a room, break armies with his strategies alone. But his need to control, to be known, was his Achilles' heel. It was as if every decision was insufficient, every victory insufficient to fill the hollowness gnawing at him from inside. To cross him risked everything, but flattery bought time. It was good that I could stroke his ego easily. Hitting him with a "Looking slick, Fred!" or just talking badly about his men always gave him a smile. Either way, I was biding time until Frederick would give me more leniency, and by proxy, power.

I thought that any day I could get a taste of freedom from Frederick. With immense patience, I had laid out all the groundwork and woven my designs into the ordinary texture of life. Casual references to boredom were strewn in like breadcrumbs, always sufficiently laced with deference to make it seem like my discontent was not based on dissatisfaction but on an appetite for something better to serve. I painted writing as an outlet for discipline and productivity, a harmless pursuit that may even honor him in some abstract way.

Compliments flowed from my lips with the ease of a well-rehearsed script. I spoke of his tactical brilliance, of his decisive maneuvers in past battles that had turned the tide of conflict. Each word was chosen carefully, not too effusive to seem insincere, but enough to make his chest puff with pride. I watched as his posture straightened, his eyes gleaming with satisfaction at my praise. He loved talking about himself, his victories, and I provided him with a podium to do that.

Discussions about the book I claimed to be writing were another calculated step. I presented it as a tribute, a chronicle of his life and achievements, which would cement his legacy in the annals of history. "Your story deserves to be told," I would say, watching the corners of his mouth twitch upward in a self-satisfied smile.

"People need to understand the man behind the medals, the brilliance behind the victories." It wasn't difficult to see how much the idea appealed to him.

I knew Frederick's need for validation was insatiable, and I fed it in small, deliberate doses, like bait on a hook. He didn't see the strings I was pulling, the web I was weaving around his inflated sense of self. All I needed was for him to loosen his grip just slightly, to grant me enough freedom to maneuver. I talked myself into the fact that he'd drop his guard the following day, the one after, or the next, and allow me the chance to flee his shadow.

And days turned into weeks. I felt the weight of the charade growing on my shoulders, the seconds of the clock ticking at the back of my head - there it was: each one reminding me how necessary this gamble was and yet, how hazardous. And so if Frederick ever suspected me for even one moment, if he ever saw beyond the honey-coated words and the backhanding manipulations, swift and merciless would the consequences be. Still, I had no other option but to play along with the game.

Then the clock struck 12:00. I knew that it was time for Fredrick to come; his arrival always met with a thunderous entrance, but no applause. This immense tardiness was largely due to the terrible party habit he had gained due to the immense stress of the job. As a police captain, he could also slip by any monitoring from his superiors, leading him always to have a signature disheveled look. As he entered, he looked in a particularly bad mood, as if anything could make him crumble. He motioned for a guard to come over to him. I couldn't hear what he said, only that whatever it was sent the guard into a frenzy. The guard ran over to the keys, and then over to my cell. I perked up but didn't make any mention to Fredrick as I knew that to anger him would be detrimental. I only observed the guard, watching him go through the stages of grief as he came to unlock my cell. Before he did, he made the blunder of shouting at Fredrick.

"Are you sure, sir?" he exclaimed.

"Are you daft? Or do you simply want trouble? Do as I say or tomorrow you won't have anything to lose!" Frederick had a great deal of sorrow; this decision clearly wasn't his, so now I needed to know who it was. The guard who was now fumbling with the keys unlocked the cell gate with a great deal of struggle and looked over at Frederick with a similar gaze of fear. The commander went into his office, gesturing me over inside; here he let me sit down inside his office.

Frederick's office was a stark contrast to the man himself— imposing yet disorderly, a space that seemed to reflect both his need for control and the chaos brewing in his mind. The walls were lined with dark oak panels, their surface gleaming under the low, amber glow of the desk lamp. A large, ornate portrait of Adolf Hitler loomed behind his desk, its presence a silent, oppressive reminder of who truly held the power in Frederick's world.

The desk itself was massive, its polished mahogany surface cluttered with papers, folders, and a half-empty ashtray spilling fine gray dust. The ashtray's contents were a testament to his nerves, the sharp tang of stale smoke lingering in the air. A meticulously arranged array of pens and pencils sat on one side, a feeble attempt at organization amidst the disarray. On the other side, a worn leather-bound notebook lay open, its pages filled with tightly scrawled notes and diagrams. Behind the desk was a high-backed chair, its black leather cracked and worn from years of use. It looked like it had been dragged from another era, a throne for a man desperately clinging to authority. Nearby, a smaller chair—plain and utilitarian—stood for visitors like me, offering no comfort or reprieve. The room was heavy with an air of tension. A map of Europe stretched across one wall, pinned with markers and strings, the web of lines crossing countries and borders like veins through a body. Beside it, a cabinet with glass-fronted doors displayed a collection of medals and commendations, each gleaming under the light as if to validate Frederick's fragile sense of worth. Yet, for all its attempts at grandeur, there were cracks in the facade. The edges of the carpet were frayed, and the corners of the room were shadowed and dusty. A stack of papers had toppled onto the floor near a filing cabinet, left untouched as if he couldn't summon the energy to fix it. Even the air itself seemed heavy, a mix of leather, smoke, and something faintly metallic, like the scent of anxiety.

Frederick gestured to me toward the plain chair without a word, his own movements sharp and clipped. He sank into his chair behind the desk, the leather creaking under his weight. His hands moved to shuffle the papers before him, though his eyes never left me. I could feel his sorrow, his frustration simmering just beneath the surface.

"Why am I here?" I said. "This wasn't your intention, was it, Frederick?" The man looked at me and sighed, his eyes unable to meet mine.

"No," he said, his voice faltering.

"Then whose was it?" I kept my tone diplomatic, careful not to provoke him.

"I cannot be at liberty to say," he replied, his words quivering, as though speaking might summon whoever had issued the order.

"I don't want to ask again—"

'And you won't have to.'

The interruption came sharply, a voice so distinct and recognizable that it could belong to only one man.

"Lieutenant Selva!" Frederick now jumped from his chair, fast enough that it flung onto the floor. Although his appearance was still ghastly, his eyes lit up in the presence of Selva. A mix of awe and terror was strewn across the man's face. Draco's presence was extraordinary, now adorning an even larger suit with medals all over his body. He also sported a new trench coat that seemed custom-made due to his body's sheer mass. Draco eyed Frederick from top to bottom, his posture perfectly straight. Despite the intimidating presence, he brought an odd sense of warmth to the room, one that Frederick didn't seem to reciprocate.

"Have you set this man free?" Draco asked with an eerie calmness.

"Of course, Lieutenant Selva! Why wouldn't we disobey orders from an SS officer!" Frederick responded quickly, but it should have been better scripted.

"So you're saying that if anyone else asked, you would disobey them, harming not only a fellow German but a member of the Nazi party. Someone whose whole job is to reflect on your work, who has been imprisoned unjustly? Is that your version of justice, Herr Frank?" Draco's face remained, tone monotone, but his point was emphasized. Frederick himself started to look ill.

Frederick's voice trembled, betraying his attempt at composure. "Lieutenant Selva, I assure you, I had no intention to disrespect.

This... this wasn't my doing. I didn't even request this transfer." His eyes darted nervously.

"It was Hans Landa," he continued, the words spilling out too quickly. "Yes, Landa. He... he overpowered me, forced me to keep Herr Abel captive. If I hadn't complied, I'd be charged with treason myself." He started to back away, his arm ever so slightly extending outwards.

He paused, wiping his brow with a shaking hand. "In fact," he added, his voice tightening, "I tried my hardest to let Herr Abel go. Isn't that true, Klaus?" His gaze finally flicked to mine. I tried not to look, as I felt that I would smile if I did. Looking at the man, I spent months trying to please, quiver in fear just due to one's presence was too funny for me. It didn't bother me either, so I just briefly mentioned it.

"I guess you never did harm me..." Frederick, still panicking, made another gesture at me as if to tell me to go on, but I didn't feel compelled to for whatever it was worth. Draco took note of this and immediately started to walk out. While still maintaining distance, Frederick went out with us, but it seemed that Draco was much more ready with words than I was.

"Commander Frederick Frank, if I hear words of instances like this from you, I will not hesitate to make you live a sentence double than theirs. But for now, rest easy knowing that you can thrive another day." We left, and Frederick only watched as we left the office. When on the street Draco looked ahead at the cars on the street, very few were near us, mostly empty. I didn't know why he had released me, but he reached into his pocket and handed me some items, including my journal, my camera, and my satchel.

I didn't say anything as it seemed that Draco wasn't in the mood for small talk, considering how dismissive he was to Frederick.

"Wait," he said, "he will come soon."

"He?" I asked passively. Draco ignored me, but I heard the screeching of tires and the faint smell of burning rubber. Turning the corners was a dark black Volkswagen Beetle charging at full speed, almost hitting a trash bin on the way. The driver seemed insane, but Draco then walked over, holding his hand and giving a nudge of direction; the car came to an immediate stop. When it stopped, I saw the run-down state of it, with numerous scratches all over the doors and the headlights having lost the metallic shine so prominent. One of the lights had an odd inward curvature that didn't seem intentional. The back of the trunk door also had a hinge missing, yet it was still decently flush with the rest of the car. The driver, a dark man—looking a bit funny, sloppily rolled around the door, hanging onto for support, as he glanced over at Selva. His posture was in shambles, with his lower and upper back seeming as if they had been connected by tape, while he had a smile that could only be registered as that of a loony. Draco wasn't put off by it though; instead, he seemed to be happy within the presence of this driver, who was motioning us to come inside.

The interior was about as glamorous as the last, with cracked leather seats and dirt piled around the edges. The car was full of old papers that seemed too thin for the press, but not that of a notebook. As the driver went to adjust his rear-view mirror, I saw that some old propaganda papers had tied on it. His trunk was empty yet it reeked of an herb-like odor. It took a good minute of trying for the engine to turn on fully, and only then did Draco come in. His bulky body is almost too massive to fit us both comfortably.

The driver then reclined his seat back so far that he had to put my legs onto the car seat. The driver laughed the whole time, and Draco still hadn't said a word.

Draco shifted slightly, his expression unreadable as he finally folded his broad frame into the cramped car. The driver's demeanor seemed utterly unaffected by the tension, probably as he was lounging in the front.

"So... how is the family, Dracula?" the driver asked casually, his voice laced with a peculiar mix of humor and irreverence, very similar to that of Spanish origin.

Draco's lips twitched, but it wasn't a smile. "Good as always, Fring, my daughter is now learning how to read, and my son is about to go to college," he corrected, his tone was truthful, but not honest. "How's your family, all alive and well, I hope."

Fring let out a bark of laughter, tapping the steering wheel with a bony hand. "Alive, eh? That's a word I wouldn't even use for myself most days." He shot a sideways glance at me, his erratic grin widening. "And you, Herr Abel? Keeping Dracula here on his toes, are you? Mr Prisoner Celebrity?" I was amazed that he used my name; he said it so relaxed that it felt like I knew him from somewhere.

I blinked at the sudden address, unprepared for the attention. "I... suppose you could say that," I replied. My voice sounded far smaller than I intended. "I had no intention of bringing Lieutenant Sleva here; I'm just as shocked as you are."

"Nonsense, what are you saying? Either you have dirt on Vlad here, or you are just that great, because as long as I've known him,

Drac is quite shy to the public, right, Mr Reporter?" This "Fring" said, winking toward me.

"You have a way with names, Fring," Draco commented.

"Don't mention it... Lieutenant Selva!" making a slight jab at me.

"Fring" didn't seem to notice—or care about the discomfort I was showing. He smacked the dashboard, causing a faint puff of dust to rise. "Good man! We all need someone to keep us sharp. Especially him." He jerked a thumb toward Draco, who simply stared out the window. "You too can become like him, just stop having your kind of fun, *if you know what I mean (wink)* and embrace your inner darkness, no matter what!" His lighthearted demeanor started to etch a smile on my face.

The car sputtered as Fring tried to shift gears; his movements were jerky and imprecise. I wasn't sure whether the vehicle would hold together for much longer, and from the way Draco clenched his jaw tighter every time the engine groaned, I suspected he felt the same.

"So," Fring continued, his tone maddeningly cheerful, "We're off to somewhere important, I take it? Where can you do what you do best, Selva?"

Draco handed him a paper. It was as small as a flashcard, but it looked fresh; the ink that bled was still fresh. "No stops," Draco said, his tone still marginally more relaxed than I had ever seen him before.

"Fring" became much more relaxed now, cutting the chatter and focusing on the road, whistling discordantly as the car rattled along the uneven road. I glanced at Draco, but his face was a mask of calm intensity. Whatever he was holding back, it was clear it wasn't for my ears—or Fring's, for that matter.

"Fine," Fring said after a moment, throwing his hands up theatrically, though one remained precariously on the wheel. "Keep your secrets. Just don't expect me to drive this rust bucket straight into trouble without a little forewarning, eh? You should be glad that I have a family. Otherwise, I wouldn't give such tolerance to your cracks." I was starting to miss the silence. Draco turned his head and gave a blank look to Fring.

"You should give thanks to my family, otherwise you would still be in uniform," Draco snapped back.

"Fair play, but remember who saved whom first. Anyway, it's in the past. All I know is that I drive you… so there's no need to argue. But realize that no matter what, I will have a better house than you!" He started pointing at Draco, and Draco even chuckled, something unheard of.

"No kidding, but for now you'll drive where I tell you," Draco said at last. For the first time since stepping into the car, "Fring" looked momentarily subdued. But the expression didn't last, and soon his grin returned, though there was a flicker of something else behind his eyes—respect, perhaps, or maybe fear.

The rest of the ride passed in strained silence, punctuated only by the groans of the car and the occasional muttered curse from Fring. Whatever lay ahead, I could feel its weight pressing down on us, even if no one dared to speak of it. At this point, I had been through enough where I couldn't question what was happening; all I could do was hope to pull through. So before I knew it, all bunched up in a dirty car seat, I slept.

When I awoke, I saw that I was on my apartment sofa, clothes the same, but something felt off. The apartment was clean, but not by me; the clothes on the counter were folded lengthwise, and the pillows were scattered without meaning. The chair that Landa had broken was now replaced. Something had happened, and then I heard a man yell, "Klaus!" It was none other than Lukas Falkenstein in my apartment, and coming out from the kitchen was Draco Selva, sporting a casual blazer that made him seem uncanny.

"What are you doing here?" I asked weakly.

"To help you, of course. Why did you only get out of prison a day ago? Now, how will you survive?" Lukas went over to grab me a platter of eggs.

"Survive, I think I can manage that."

"Don't be so sure. You went from the propaganda master to a common criminal in the public's mind, and your internal reputation needs a little work now," Draco uttered from the back of the kitchen.

"My reputation? I thought all charges were cleared."

"For now, yes, Klaus, but Landa is still convinced that you are a conspirator in some sort of conspiracy. While the news isn't too keen on maintaining the pressure, you better hope to clear your name before Landa goes ballistic," Lukas blurted while walking around the room. His shirt was ripped and his pants were tattered; it looked like he came out of a forest.

"Well, that's a first. I guess I should ask what Landa accuses me of first, right?" I asked half-seriously, as though I didn't know it already.

"Sure, buddy," Lukas mumbled. "Look, here's the low-down: you messed up when you were interacting with some mystery woman, who Landa claims is an enemy of the state. I don't know if she's an informant, Jew, terrorist, or what; all that we know is that she's bad news. Now, Landa is keeping this close to his chest, not even Selva can get a word on him, but it seems that his plan is working. Media pressure may start coming despite the Beobachter's best efforts, because who doesn't love a good story? And soon you will be caught, Klaus, and who knows what will happen." He looked exasperated, even more stressed than me, because I could only wonder one thing,

"Why, why are you helping me?"

Draco straightened, brushing a speck of dust off his blazer, his face unreadable. When he finally spoke, his voice was steady, carrying a weight I hadn't expected.

"Well, you want to know why I'm helping you?" He met my gaze, his dark eyes unwavering. "It's not out of charity, Klaus. I've seen men like Landa before." Men of power, a hammer to use upon anyone who threatened, or was merely an inconvenience. The entirety of my life has been dedicated to the benefit of this regime. Seen all these years, the kind of damage it inflicts upon the human race, seen men broken not for sinning but because somebody needed a scapegoat.

His jaw clenched, and he looked away momentarily, as if fighting with something inside. "I'm helping you because, in you, I see the same trap I barely managed to escape once. There was a time when I believed the lies they told me—that loyalty would protect me, that if I just followed orders, I'd be safe. But it's never enough. There's always another enemy, another purge."

Draco's voice dropped lower, almost a whisper now. "You think you're just a man caught in a web of accusations, but this is bigger than you, Klaus. Landa's not just targeting you; he's sending a message. He wants to prove that no one is untouchable, that even someone with your reputation can be brought to heel. If he succeeds, it'll set a precedent. No one will be safe."

He took another step closer, his huge form casting an even longer shadow in the dimly lit room. "I'm helping you because if I don't, he wins. And if he wins, men like him will continue to twist this world into something even darker. I don't have illusions about what I am, or what I've done, but if I can stop this—if I can stop him—it's one small step toward balancing the scales."

There was no drama in his voice, no attempt to seek favor— only a grim determination, born of experience and regret. "So, no, Klaus," he concluded, his voice steady again. "I'm not doing this for you. I'm doing it because sometimes, even in a world this broken, there's a line you can't let them cross."

"Here's the plan," Draco began, his tone measured yet firm. "Lukas will return to the *Beobachter* and track down this woman at the center of all this chaos. Meanwhile, you can't stay here; it's too exposed. We'll move you somewhere you can blend in among the soldiers, where their loyalty ensures you'll be well-protected."

I blinked, struggling to process the gravity of his words. My life, already teetering on the edge, had just been thrust into yet another upheaval. The sheer absurdity of it all left me momentarily speechless. "Klaus, we may not see each other for a while, but stay safe and never speak of anything that happens. Try to journal less as well; that, too, has given you part of your reputation. Otherwise, we will stand still until further notice from Lukas."

"Where though"

Chapter 9

AN ACCIDENT

May 3, 1939, Prague, Czechoslovakia

Prague was nothing like the life I'd left behind. It was smaller, simpler, and suffocating in its stillness. The walls were an unremarkable shade of beige, their surfaces marked with faint cracks spidering out like maps to nowhere. A single window, set deep into the wall, overlooked the street below, its old wooden frame groaning every time I forced it open to let in the sharp, bracing air. Curtains hung limp on either side, a faded mustard yellow, their edges frayed and unraveling—like everything else in this place.

The furniture seemed to be a collection of cast-offs. The armchair in the corner, upholstered in a hideous green that could only be described as the color of despair, had a sunken seat that swallowed me whole whenever I sat down. The small round table by the window wobbled if I glanced at it too hard, its top cluttered with empty glasses and half-crumpled notes I'd scribbled in restless moments. One lamp in the room casts a faint, lopsided light that seemed to do more to deepen the shadows than dispel them.

The kitchen was hardly a kitchen at all. A narrow counter ran along one wall, stained and chipped from years of neglect. In the corner, an old gas stove occupied, its burners blackened and stubborn, half the time refusing to light. The fridge, humming louder than it had any right to, contained little more than a bottle of milk and a loaf of stale bread. I'd long since stopped trying to make it feel like home—it wasn't.

The floorboards creaked with every step, reminding me how old and fragile this building was. The ceilings were low enough to feel oppressive, as if they were slowly pressing down on me daily. And then there was the smell—a faint, lingering odor of damp wood and something metallic, like rust. While still maintaining the life I had at home, I still couldn't lie down comfortably. It seemed wrong to live like this, away from everyone.

At night, I could hear the city breathing through the walls. Distant voices drifted in from the street below, muffled and indistinct, mixing with the occasional screech of tram wheels and the hollow clatter of footsteps. Prague felt alive in a way the apartment never could—a cruel contrast to the stifling quiet that filled this space when I was alone. This was where I existed today, not living but waiting. Waiting for the next step, the next move, the next piece in this puzzle that had, somehow, become my life. Not a refuge, but a purgatory, from which time crawled, tramping me down into the echoing of my own thoughts.

Only being accentuated by the Germans who resided here. The beautiful culture-ridden streets are being torn by the soldiers who put up their own messages on the walls. The mix of pastel blues and reds becoming black and white. More conquering for us to boast about. The buildings, standing but deserted, the bright-yellow walls desecrated in gray ash. The rivers, once bluer than the sky, have become a reminder of the pain faced, now embellished in a red hue.

It's been close to a month since I left the prison, and yet I still feel trapped. Now I was Josef Svoboda. Despite the change in location, the eye of the father was still gazing upon me—no matter where. Despite the setbacks, I was still able to live an honest life. Draco had set me up in a condemned apartment, away from much suspicion, as he had a good relationship with the owner of the apartment. Due to the recent occupation as well, the Völkischer Beobachter hasn't reached Czechoslovakia yet, leading me to be much safer. The apartment housed only a few people, but I had only met two.

My landlord (whom I didn't pay), Ms. Tereza Veselá, is a short woman with a great deal of temper. Ms. Tereza Veselá was not a woman easily forgotten. She stood barely five feet tall, but she carried herself as if she were six. Her wiry frame moved with an energy that seemed to crackle in the air around her, and her voice, sharp and commanding, had the uncanny ability to cut through walls. Her age was impossible to pin down; her lined face and graying hair spoke of a life well-lived, but her fiery temper and relentless vigor betrayed no signs of slowing down. She had an air about her, as if she'd fought battles the rest of us couldn't begin to imagine, and somehow emerged victorious, if a bit scared.

Tereza owned the entire building, and she made sure everyone knew it. The clatter of her heels on the stairs was her herald of arrival, and woe to anyone in her path. She ran this little kingdom of hers with a mix of stern authority and begrudging care. She had no use for excuses, especially regarding rent. On the other hand, I'd once seen her leave a loaf of fresh bread outside an elderly tenant's door after an argument over late payments. Her temper was legendary, even among the most resilient of her tenants.

I had witnessed it firsthand on several occasions, usually involving some imagined slight—dust in the hallway, a loose banister, or the faint scent of tobacco trailing from my apartment. Her sharp tongue had a way of reducing even the most defiant to stammering apologies, though her tirades rarely lasted long. Tereza's anger burned fast and bright, like a match that quickly consumed itself, leaving behind only the faintest wisp of smoke. Despite her rough edges, something about her commanded respect or even admiration. She was fiercely independent—a widow who had no family to speak of—and yet she appeared to know everybody in Prague. Her contacts went as far as the grocer down the street and also the local police—a feat I suspected wasn't precisely coincidental, considering she knew so much more than she ever cared to remember about her tenants' personal lives.

Yet all the bluster aside, Tereza Veselá had a soft spot deep inside her tough exterior. She would never admit it, of course, but it was there—in the way she grudgingly tolerated my mounting debts, or the time she left a wool blanket outside my door when she noticed I hadn't been using the heater. Introduced to me by way of a shouting match on my first day in the apartment—"This isn't a hostel!" she had declared, wagging a finger in my face—Tereza had since become an unyielding fixture in my life.

If it wasn't for her, I probably would be loafing in alleys in the slums of Prague, and for that, I am ever grateful to her. The only other person I had met was my downstairs neighbor, Eva Horáková. Eva Horáková was the kind of girl who seemed to drift on the wind, like a feather caught in a gale. She was forever in motion, never exactly stopping. A whirlwind of ideas and emotions swirled inside her brain, and thoughts often rushed out faster than she could catch them in words and phrases. Everything about her was transient: her ambitions, her moods, even her appearance, which changed depending on whatever artistic whim had struck her that week. One day, her hair would be pinned back neatly, and the next, it would cascade in wild curls, dyed a color that matched her current "creative phase."

She described herself as a "seeker of inspiration," though what she was seeking or why remained elusive even to her. Her apartment reflected this constant pursuit—cluttered yet oddly charming, filled with half-finished paintings, stacks of books, jars of dried flowers, and an old typewriter she swore would one day produce a masterpiece. It hadn't yet, but that didn't stop her from declaring her imminent literary breakthrough to anyone willing to listen.

Eva didn't have goals; she had aspirations, loftier and more romantic. They rarely coalesced into anything tangible. She would decide one week she would be a poet and spend hours furiously scribbling away in a notebook before abandoning the notion of being a poet by the weekend in favor of learning how to play the violin. She frequently discussed "the muse," speaking as though it were some kind of actual being she visited regularly, looking at the world through nearly childlike wonder, taking meaning from things mundane, beauty in the imperfect.

When I met Eva initially, she was open toward me, and it seemed almost too invasive. She seemed entirely unbothered by social conventions, introducing herself with an exuberance that felt misplaced in the dingy stairwell where we crossed paths. Within minutes, she declared an "instant connection" between us, something she attributed to fate, serendipity, or some other intangible force. I was skeptical, but her enthusiasm was difficult to resist. Before I knew it, she had invited me into her world—or, more accurately, pulled me into it without waiting for an invitation.

Eva was as exasperating as she was endearing. Her flights of fancy often left her unreliable, and she habitually overstepped boundaries in her quest for "authentic experiences." Yet, there was an undeniable charm to her earnestness, a sincerity in her belief that the world was full of endless possibilities, if only one knew how to look. She lived as if every day might be a day of miracles, and though I used to find her exhausting on many occasions, I have also admired her relentless optimism in a city that's as gray and cold in its crumbling facades.

Eva had become a strange but persistent presence in my life in the short time she had known me. She was that sort of neighbor: one who would place a fresh loaf of baked bread outside your door just because the aroma reminded her of a dream she used to have or invite you to a spur-of-the-moment gathering in her apartment, packed with acquaintances from the café she stopped at for coffee every morning. I never understood her, but maybe that was the appeal—she was a contradiction, a burst of color in a world otherwise painted in shades of monotony. The only real issue I faced within my apartment, apart from the drag, was the Czech language; thankfully, German was somewhat known, otherwise I would have been no better than a duck trying to navigate the city. I have tried learning, but it was all for naught, as no matter what, I couldn't understand all the complications in the language. From the conjugations to the writing style, apparently, I was mixing it with Slovak as well. Despite the struggles, I managed to live.

This particular morning, while I was watching the sun rise over the silhouette-like city, I could hear the banging of Ms. Tereza; this early could only mean one thing,

"Josef! Your mail!" she yelled across the building. "Why do you get so many letters, child? I can't do this every day," she said in front of my doorstep. It was pretty ironic to me as she was the one who imposed this upon herself, yet always had a comment about the mail delivery.

"Well, Ms, I guess people from home miss me a lot." I boldfaced a lie I told as only one person dared to have contact with me now; he was just persistent.

"I see that your speaking has improved, I can understand half of what you say now," she said in a very proud voice. "Now sleep, child. I see the bags under your eyes only growing darker." With that, she went back down to her flat. Her heavy footsteps echoing throughout the floor, I went back into the decrepit hollow of my apartment. I had three letters in my hand: one set of bills, which were all good to ignore; a message from a friend for the tenant who lived here previously, a Novak Kučera. He seems like a good guy, getting so much mail, but I couldn't understand why I kept getting his mail.

The last letter I got was a surprise. A discreet letter with the name Josef Svoboda appeared, and it was sent from R. M. Djokovic, the false name we put under Lukas. I immediately locked the door and rushed into the furthest corner of the room. I had no reason, yet it felt necessary. Carefully, I picked a sliver of the creamy edge on the slightly discolored paper, ensuring I could get one clean tear.

In one swift movement, I could rip the letter clean, opening what I thought to be salvation.

To: Josef Svoboda

From: R. M. Djokovic

May 1, 1939

Dear Josef,

I hope you're tolerating these difficult circumstances quite well—or at least, as well as might be expected. The days no doubt weigh heavily upon you, like the heft of weights across your chest, but you should exercise patience. Time is wonderfully adept at shaping the darkest shadows into clarity, although this doesn't feel anywhere close to fast enough.

The spring in Prague must remind you of earlier times, yes? I imagine the blossoms on the Petrin Hill gardens mirror the blooms we once admired at Sanssouci, though perhaps they lack the same air of grandeur. Still, simplicity has its charms. Consider the view: soft pink petals cascading down, carrying the promise of change. A reminder that even the heaviest branches cannot hold their blossoms forever.

It keeps me busy, though, with the world changing daily. Now, the ink seems to run out more quickly in my pen than ever. There's some odd satisfaction in telling tales, isn't there? A quiet rebellion against the silence. Do you know if you've been following my advice to write scantily—to just write enough to preserve the essentials, like we left notes to each other on birch bark when we were lads? Those little whispers of memory served their purposes well, didn't they?

Regarding your situation, I want you to know that efforts are underway, though they require precision and subtlety. Think of the chess game you taught me in Dresden—the strategy lies in seeing several moves ahead, even if it means losing a piece in the short term. Do you remember the gambit? Sometimes a sacrifice is not an end but a beginning.

Keep your head out of the window. It must be airy, and walls can only hold what we let them. Open up the window at dusk and watch how the fading light puts a shadow on the rooftops. There is poetry in transitions. When day gives way to night, it promises another dawn.

I trust Tereza has been her usual formidable self. Be kind to her, Josef; she's likely more of an ally than she lets on. As for Eva, her world of colors and words may hold something for you too, perhaps a fleeting sense of freedom.

Lastly, Josef, remember that names are but labels. Who you are runs deeper than what people choose to call you. They might try to obscure the truth, to tarnish what they don't understand, but truth has a stubborn way of resurfacing. Think of the forest trails we used to navigate—how the underbrush seemed impassable until we found the hidden markers leading home. The path is there, even if the brambles obscure it.

Keep your head up, my friend. The burden you bear will ease, one letter, one step, at a time. Keep an eye out for the next play—it will come sooner than you think. And remember: patience is not inaction but measured waiting for the right moment to strike.

Yours faithfully,

R. M. Djokovic

I scoured the letter, reading each paragraph repeatedly, and hadn't mailed it once since I left, so long that I had almost forgotten about his alias. Sitting on the edge of the bed, I crumpled the letter, trembling in my hands.

The paper felt heavier than it should have in my hands, as though the weight of its words pressed through my fingers and into my chest. The faint, familiar curve of Lukas's handwriting brought both a pang of longing and a flicker of hope I dared not fully embrace.

I reread it, letting my eyes trace every line, lingering on every nuance, every deliberate choice. He had written to me before, but this-this was different. Beneath the surface of politeness and abstraction lay something else.

"A game unfinished is no game at all."

Chess. Lukas knew how much I hated leaving a game incomplete. Every move had meaning; every piece left on the board carried the weight of possibility. He wasn't talking about a game, though — he was talking about me, about Berlin. About the life I'd been forced to abandon.

I swallowed hard, the dryness in my throat nearly choking me. Could he mean what I thought he did? Could it be that he had found a way?

"The birch trees stand tall, unbending, even in foreign soil."

Foreign soil. Was this his way of acknowledging my exile here in Czechoslovakia? And the birches—those damned birches from the Tiergarten. My fingers tightened on the letter. It wasn't just a sentimental nod to home; it was a promise. A promise that my roots, my identity, had not been forgotten.

My pulse quickened as my eyes scanned the next lines.

"Some pieces belong only in their proper place. You know this."

Yes, I knew it all too well. I didn't belong here, hiding like a criminal. My place was in Berlin, no matter how much the city might have turned against me. And Lukas—god, Lukas knew that. This wasn't just reassurance; it was an assertion. A signal. He was telling me he hadn't given up.

I set the letter on the table, staring at it as though it might reveal something further if I looked long enough. The words blurred, but their meaning sharpened in my mind. Lukas had found a lead, a way to clear my name. The references and careful wording weren't for my benefit alone. He couldn't say it outright, not in a letter that might be intercepted, but it was there if I looked hard enough.

Relief surged, but it was tinged with a bitterness I couldn't shake. Hope was dangerous here. I'd learned that too well in the long weeks since I'd fled Berlin. Hope had a way of turning on you, of becoming a weapon in the hands of your enemies. But this-this felt different. And yet, beneath the flicker of hope, depression clung to me like a shadow. Even if Lukas had found something, would it be enough? Could I trust myself to believe in it? Or would this, too, slip through my fingers?

I folded the letter slowly, smoothing the edges as though the act could bring me closer to the city I missed with every fiber of my being. Lukas had made his move, and the pieces were in play. Now it was up to me.

Berlin felt impossibly far away, yet for the first time in months, it didn't feel unreachable. Depressed hope—that was all I had left. And for now, it would have to be enough. Though it may be, I still felt the need to get out in the world—be proactive, even if it would induce a little trouble. I couldn't take this life anymore. Going down the stairs, I felt rejuvenated by the movement, checking my watch. I saw it was only about 7:00 in the morning. As I headed down the streets, I could feel the warm morning air hit me, and the bliss of the sun was an unforeseen luxury living outside the amalgamation of Berlin. The pastel-like rooftops gave credence to why everyone seemed so happy. Walking down the streets felt so mundane; the buildings all closed in on each other, and they varied in color and shape. The vast variance is something both foreign and delightful to me.

That really became an impossible place to visit; only now, for the first time, did it seem as though there was not the long, unending journey ahead that I could bring it. All that is now left to me is depressed hope, and for the time being, that will have to be sufficient. Honestly, I really needed to be out there instead of just keeping a distance - there could be a little trouble sometimes in doing so, but that is how one gets to live life. I had enough of this life - the waiting, watching myself slowly unravel. Let movement happen, at least it will probably keep me grounded to something.

The warm morning air filled the outside as I stepped out; a gentle caress against the skin. This was not really the cold and soot-congested air of Berlin, laced by the faint tang of industry. This was lighter, cleaner, and something different - feeling somehow disconcerting. The sun was already casting its soft gold onto the streets without being asked. In Berlin, the morning rhymes decidedly more as a battle against the city: cold shadows thrown by the tall, imposing buildings, a faint clanging of trams, and the sound of hurried feet. Here, the light falls freely and unobstructed, unlike the towering structures that I used to know. I have wandered and allowed the streets to lead me.

The pastel-like rooftops stretched into the distance, their soft hues blending with the sky's blue. They were completely opposite from Berlin's iron-gray facades and sharp, geometric lines. There was a cheerfulness to them, with a quaintness lifting spirits that surrounded them. The people, the passers-by, moved slowly; their faces relaxed, as if such luxuries were offered in the city's pace.

The streets, how they looked, really changed. Though Germany still resided here, where every step became construed under it, it was also about unease. So much warmth above with the morning air, and those jaunty rooftops seemed like a cruel juxtaposition to the undercurrents of tension simmering just below the surface.

Moving around the city's streets, I saw all those indicators of Germany's reach all over. Gray-green soldiers stood at street corners, their presence intentional and unavoidable. They weren't standing, loomed, boots planted firmly on the ground as if staked. Occasionally, one would bark an order, their sharp voices slicing through the hum of the city. I saw a shopkeeper dart out of his store to adjust a German-printed poster on the wall - propaganda plastered carelessly over Prague's buildings' warm, colorful facades.

"Strength through unity," the bold letters declared above a stern eagle gripping a swastika. Beneath it was a Czech translation, though smaller, like an afterthought. The sight twisted my stomach.

These streets, with their quaint cobblestones and vibrant roofs, were no longer truly their own.

Below that, I came across a burned building, its blackened walls real evidence from the past. Windows shattered and wooden frames splintered, all of which counted for nothing. I guess it was better just to look away and pretend it wasn't there. But I couldn't ignore it. A lingering smell of smoke and acrid, clinging, like that of a ghost from the fire which had not melted. I tried to walk faster as two soldiers turned their heads in my direction. My coat felt too thin, my face too bare. Did I look German enough to pass unnoticed? I wasn't sure. The wrong word, the wrong glance, and it could all unravel. I wasn't really sure about it. He could say just one wrong word, or give a misdirected glance, and everything could unravel. I kept my eyes ahead, but it thudded in my ears.

A young woman emerged from an alley barely ahead of me, clasping a little stack of papers. Nervously scanning her surroundings, she adjusted her coat and blended into the masses. She wouldn't look back, but the tension in her shoulders said enough. She had seen the soldiers, too. There were all of these small, unspoken moments along the roads. A man shoved against a wall by a soldier as others hurry past, heads down, pretending they aren't seeing. A family quickly shutting their shutters when a patrol walks by. And the whispers—always whispers. Voices murmur in corners, words clipped and hurried, as if the air itself might betray them.

Every corner I turned felt like a gamble. Would there be another patrol? Another burned building? A checkpoint I couldn't avoid? My steps faltered near a square where a German flag hung prominently over what I assumed had once been a government building. The flag looked new; its crimson bright and garish against the pale stone. Beneath it, a group of officers stood talking; their laughter was sharp and unsettling. I glanced at them briefly before I moved on, though my heart raced with every step. I had heard stories about fugitives dragged from streets, accused of crimes they hadn't committed, or worse, crimes they had. The letter in my pocket suddenly felt heavy, like burning through the cloth, and I tightened my grip around it as if that would somehow keep it safe.

Passing a little café, I came across three sitting German soldiers outside, their rifles propped haphazardly against the table. They seemed at leisure, loud in their sneering laughter, as though this city were theirs by right. Nearby, an elderly man shuffled by, his back hunched further with each step. I was a fugitive in a city that wasn't truly free, and every step I took was a risk. But I couldn't stay hidden forever. Lukas's letter was proof of that. Berlin felt impossibly far away, yes, but if I stayed here, it might as well have been on another continent. I walked faster, blending into the crowd as best I could. The streets weren't mine, just as they weren't truly theirs. But for now, they would have to hold me. Just a little longer.

Walking by, I was still mesmerized by the flowing air, the breeze gently caressing my hair. It felt good to be free from the confines of work or daily life, an escape with the ever-knowing knowledge of those meant to protect, watching every corner for me, even if I may not be known yet. Soon, I will be discovered. Sooner, I will face my consequences. As I went, I started to feel the lack of presence from others. The more corners I turned, the more people stared, and the more I became odd-looking. I quickly went faster, but the feeling only started to grow. The cool breeze began to become a wave of heat.

I wanted to get away but it kept spiraling, the building no longer straight, but turning in on me. The vibrant colors all turn in on each other, not losing their presence, but multiplying. My legs felt weak, but I could not stop, my mind numb, but unable to process, my voice unable to scream. I was struck by a force I couldn't control, all that was left was waiting until it could stop, but it never did. I felt as if time wouldn't pass unless I kept going, but it was the last thing I wanted to do. I could hear the voices of others, figures forming within the spirals of colors.

Why are you here?

You don't deserve to live!

Turn yourself in!

I couldn't stop the onslaught, only able to wallow in silence as it all unfolded. I wanted to answer, but my throat closed up. The words were locked away, just out of reach. The voices clawed at the edges of my mind, their accusations weaving seamlessly around me. As the spiraling colors seemed to throb, their vibrant hues pulsated like a warning. Each step felt like trudging through quicksand, yet I couldn't stop. My legs moved not out of instinct, but out of fear. The air thickened, no longer the crisp morning breeze that had once kissed my skin, but a suffocating weight pressing against my chest. I blinked hard, trying to steady myself, to reclaim some semblance of control. Faces emerged from the swirling mass, half-formed and ghostly, their eyes like shards of ice.

I stumbled, nearly falling as my knees buckled. My mind screamed for clarity, for reason, but the hysteria drowned out all logic. I wasn't sure if these voices were real or just the product of my own unraveling thoughts. Each accusation struck like a lash, carving into me the weight of my guilt, my own fear. It couldn't be real!

I pressed forward, forcing my legs to carry me even as my vision blurred. The buildings around me seemed to mock my struggle, their once-beautiful forms twisting and contorting into grotesque shapes. The pastel hues of Prague now felt garish, a kaleidoscope of judgment. Then, faintly, cutting through the chaos, I heard another sound—something softer, steadier. My name.

"Klaus."

The word was barely a whisper, yet it pulled at me, anchoring me for just a moment. I whipped my head around, searching for the source, but the spirals of color and noise only swirled faster.

"Klaus," the voice repeated.

It wasn't angry or accusatory like the others. It carried a note of something unfamiliar in this storm of torment—kindness.

I stumbled to a stop, gasping for air, my vision slowly beginning to focus. The colors began to recede, the voices fading into a distant murmur. I was left standing in the middle of the street, drenched in sweat, my heart pounding like a drum. The buildings straightened, colors softened, and the streets regained their mundane quiet. I glanced around, but there was no one. Just strangers passing by, their faces neutral, indifferent. Had I imagined it? That voice?

Shaking, I leaned against a lamppost, trying to collect myself. The fear still lingered, a gnawing presence in the pit of my stomach.

But so did that voice. It felt like a hand reaching out through the chaos. Stumbling through the streets, in my delirium, I couldn't manage to think straight. I wandered around until a soldier stationed at the corner caught my attention. The soldier had drawn my attention even before he opened his mouth: a silhouette cut from the same mold as many fellows stationed around Prague.

He didn't have that initial glance; something about him was holding my attention. Perhaps the way he stood, rigid, but not quite so disciplined as a child playing soldier, peering down through the eye of a child from underneath. The uniform didn't fit—every button catching the faint morning light. It was as if he wore the ideals of the Reich more than a man whom he truly was - a hollow shell wrapped in authority."

His face, youthful though it was, bore the marks of premature disillusionment; the shadow that hung below his eyes spoke of long nights spent awake in vigilance or, as might well have been, of a conscience gnawing at him, though he would never concede it. His posture was such that he could not be omitted - eager to prove himself and rise above the muck of expendables his kind were in the grand design of conquest. A recruit, perhaps, brought fresh into this place, hoping that by enforcing control, he'd feel that he had some of his own.

His gaze was the thing that struck me strongest: the way he had looked at me when I fell into his line of sight. There was recognition there, not of me as a person, but as an idea. A German, but out of place. A kindred spirit, perhaps, but sullied by the fact I wasn't supposed to be here. His eyes flicked over me like a man trying to decide whether he'd discovered something worth reporting or a nuisance better left ignored.

It was a dangerous gaze - one that sought validation from the uniform he wore, one that measured every interaction against the ideals he thought he was meant to uphold. That was the game we played. I could see it before he even spoke. He wanted to feel strong, needed to feel like he had the upper hand. Yet something in the set of his jaw, in the subtle tremor of his fingers around the rifle stock, suggested a crack in his resolve. As I approached, I wasn't sure on which side of him I would face - the staunch believer ready to enforce order or the uncertain boy hiding beneath layers of propaganda. Either possibility, however, would have to put my own ability to walk the razor's edge between survival and exposure up against the test.

"Oi! You filthy drunkard, what are you doing acting like a buffoon in the streets?" I was not surprised by the accusation, but a little hurt nonetheless.

"Nothing, sir, just admiring the weather," I said, my words a little slurred.

"Knock it off, otherwise I won't show sympathy toward scum like you!" he shouted in half-decent Czech.

"Of course you won't?" I exclaimed in perfect German. The soldier took a step back, realizing that I was not who I seemed. I myself stepped back, as I knew that part of my cover had been blown. The soldier, now cautiously approaching me, asked simply.

"My good sir, why is it that you stay here, when you are in fact a good citizen of Germany, perhaps Berlin?" My accent was a dead giveaway, though I used to carry an Austrian accent. I had transitioned due to the long days in Berlin. I also understood that trying to pretend that I was Czech wasn't going to work on this soldier as he was much more qualified than I wished he was.

"Just sightseeing now that the Führer has taken over these lands, the architecture is wonderful, isn't it?" I tried to act as if I was in my own little fantasy.

"While it may be nice, why do you act the part of a fool? By birth you yourself are much better than these people, you must be confident in yourself if you want to declare yourself as German, as it is not what the basis of our power is built upon? Why should we bow down to those who are powerless in comparison to us, play fools in their land? My friend, you cannot be German if you act like this." I felt a well of anger build up inside, as though he may have been correct, factually it still pained me.

"If a mother died while giving birth to a child, an accident, is it right for the child to live?" I asked with frustration in my voice, approaching him slowly.

"What?" he asked, diverting the attention from his rifle.

"You heard me, if the mother dies, so should the child, isn't that your belief? The father must kill the child to assert his dominance? As by birth the child could only have been made by the mother in which it was killed. Therefore, it would only be right for the father, who could only watch, to kill the helpless baby. Otherwise, for what right does the father get to live by?"

"Your point?" he said, coming closer.

"My point is that you are a delirious buffoon who can't think for himself, as you are too caught up in pleasing people who you will never meet, and who would never give a damn about your existence!" As he pointed the rifle at me, I put my hands up, slicked back my hair, and asked a simple question. "What's it going to be then, soldier? Am I just another drunkard to drag off the street? Maybe a man to shoot?"

I was steady, despite the quick drumming in my chest. The rifle barrel dangled inches from my face. It showed me how brittle this pretending had become. I watched the soldier's face shift in what appeared to be the puzzle solution too complicated for him. He hesitated. The grip on the rifle tightened, still aiming with minor deviation. "You speak boldly for a man at the wrong end of a gun," he said, his voice low and careful.

"Boldness is all I have left," I said. "You know, it's really something to be hunted. It clears out the fear; what's left is desperation and defiance. A man with nothing to lose won't quail, even at death's door. Isn't that what your ilk admires the most?"

The soldier's eyes narrowed, a flicker of uncertainty within. "You test my patience, *friend*."

"Friend?" I laughed bitterly. "Is that what I am? Just a fellow German wandering these streets looking for meaning, like you? Or perhaps I'm the enemy you have been trained to hate, hiding in plain sight."

He stepped closer, bringing the rifle to my chest. "Stop your riddles and tell me who you really are."

I leaned forward slightly with my hands still up in mock surrender. "I'm exactly what you think I am: a man with a past he cannot escape and a future he cannot see. But you, you're just a cog in a machine that doesn't care if you break. So go ahead and pull the trigger if it makes you feel powerful, if it gives you purpose."

The silence grew heavy and stretched between us like summer air. For a time, I really thought that for once in his life, he would actually act and might pull the trigger to end this entire charade. But then, his eyes shifted—perhaps holding a glimmer of doubt or fear.

"You are insane," he muttered and lowered the rifle just enough to let me breathe in the air again.

"Perhaps," I said, taking a calculated step backward. "But maddened alive me."

Before he could change his mind, I turned and walked away, my heart hammering in my chest. Each step felt heavier than the last, the weight of the encounter pressing down on me like some stone. But I kept moving, blending into the crowd once more, knowing full well that this wasn't over. The soldier's hesitation gave me a glimmer of hope. If a man like him could entertain doubt, maybe there was some way out for me, too.

"I have one last test for you, 'friend'," I said, coming forward.

"It could be your last!" said the soldier putting up his rifle. In that fear, I could only say one thing,

"May I see Draco Selva?"

━━ ◆ ━━

Chapter 10

REBIRTH

May 4, 1939, Berlin, Germany

The walls again were familiar, the rotting and decrepit look pestering around, as I could only wait in the solace of hope that I could be saved by one Draco Selva. The neglect of the police station was apparent with its aged and dirty walls that were peeling plaster too. The air was heavy with the scent of damp stone and the acrid smoke. Inside an overhead bulb flickered, casting very unshapely shadows across the already dark narrow corridors. Desks jammed into corners, their surfaces cluttered with unorganized stacks of paper, coffee rings, and ashtrays spilling cigarettes. The sound of typewriter keys clacking was muffled against the background of someone's occasional barking.

It wasn't fear that gripped me now; it was probably something much steadier - a stalking resolve. This added view of a decaying place where power was thrown around without an effort would no longer hold sway over me. Of course, the oppressive aura existed, but somehow it felt weaker - like a beast I had learned to tame. It had been only a day, yet I felt a sense of confidence that may have been lacking before. It may have just been simple familiarity, but I believed it was more. I didn't feel the sense of fear that I once had, even though I was here again under false pretenses. It didn't matter to me; I could be free if I wanted to; all it took was a little push on my part.

The policemen were swarming around like ever, constantly glaring at me, and giving off crude signs of intimidation. To them, I was a defector, a nuisance set upon the world only meant for them to crush. Yet I could find it easy to be intimidated by them. The attempt at pressure mostly fell flat, especially as they were starting to fear me as well. The name of any high-ranking officer, especially with a reputation, can send any soldier into panic, and to bring it up so casually, they knew that if I wasn't bluffing, they would be in serious trouble. One scrawny-looking officer came out of the back and headed toward me, in his hand two cups with a faint trace of steam coming out of the top. He looked a little messy with his collar unfurled and heavily wrinkled, his tie almost entirely loose upon his neck, and pants creating ripples near the knees. His face, though, didn't have the same amount of distress that was apparent among his figure.

Walking at a quick stride, he came up without the scorn of malice that the others in the station had. Once there, he handed me one of the cups in his hand, which had a herbal tea blend. Although the taste was quite bland, it still made me feel warm toward him.

"So, Mr Josef?" he said, looking at some papers he had stashed away in his pocket. "How has your day been?" he said with an innocent smile.

"Nothing much, just spent my day sitting in this office. I mean it's almost morning, what could be keeping me this long? I was just a lonely dancer whose stage may have been yours?" I said rhetorically, but it seemed to hook the strange officer.

"Well, I'm sure that the citizens of Prague were quite entertained by your enumerated show. But I don't think my colleagues have an eye for the arts such as yours. Perhaps you could show them later?" Now the other policemen started to look at us, no words spoken, yet they definitely were not approving of whatever this officer wanted to do.

"Perhaps I will, but now that I've shown you, I do believe that a name is in order?"

"Well, my name is Petr Miller," he said, his tone becoming whispered.

"So you're half-Czech, that's a surprise," I said, trying to divert the attention from me. "Why then are you a soldier in this war?" The soldier stayed quiet, his brown eyes flickering as he stared; he looked as if the word he wanted to say wouldn't escape.

"My father served," he said with his head facing down, his cup of tea becoming laden beside him. I paused, watching the soldier's face as he stared into his cup. His words hung in the air, heavy and raw. My chest tightened as an all-too-familiar ache resurfaced, one I had kept buried for years.

"So did mine," I said softly, my voice barely above a whisper. I felt my fingers tighten around the edge of the table, the wood creaking faintly under the pressure. We had both known the outcome very well. The soldier's eyes flicked up to meet mine. For a moment, the air shifted—less tense, more human. He didn't say anything, but I saw it in his expression: recognition, a shared weight neither of us wanted to carry. I cleared my throat, trying to get myself together.

"Sometimes I wonder... if they'd known how it would end, would they still have 'gone'? Would they still have left us behind to live in the shadows of what they couldn't finish?" His jaw tightened, and he turned away. I couldn't say whether it was grief or anger, or both, but I knew the feeling well enough to recognize its shape.

"We were just boys when they left," I added, my voice faltering. "And now, somehow, we're expected to be men," he nodded slowly, his hands trembling as he lifted the cup to his lips. For a moment, there were no ranks, no sides, only understanding. The room seemed to go silent. It was an abrupt detour to take. The soldier, who to me looked as if he was just a boy, couldn't look straight. Those around him in disbelief that he could even talk to me, let alone share emotion with each other. It didn't seem right to be able to do such a thing in a place like this, but it didn't feel wrong. A few of the senior officers who were eyeing us from a corner came forward and boldly started to proclaim.

"Hey, Petr, what is it that we say not to do? Lay off the trash," the brutish one said.

"Yeah, what will happen if you two start to fight? You know not many are as starved as you," the tall one exclaimed.

"It will look bad on the police as a whole if they see a poor child getting mauled in the station!" said the short one, who seemed to yell extra loud, as not to be forgotten.

"Well, I won't need to worry, Officers. I don't think he will be here much longer," said Petr very calmly.

"Why is that, did you bail him out yourself?" laughed the brutish one again.

"You'll see," Petr now turned to me. "Look, Klaus, just wait here and I'm sure your visitor will arrive soon. We will just have to make preparations for him."

"Who is his 'guest' anyway, Petr?" the tall one asked.

"No need to worry," Petr said mundanely. "You won't even notice he's here. In the earliest hours of the morning, I could only sit and wait, going back unto the monotonous clicks and clacks of the police station. The tomfoolery of the officers, and worries of the assistants who tried to keep the place running smoothly. Until at around 7:36 in the morning, the door opened with a thunderous arrival, the secretary immediately perking up with a 'Heil!'" It jolted me out of my restless haze, and I sat up straighter, my heart skipping a beat. The secretary, startled but instantly alert, sprang to her feet holding out a crisp, almost mechanical. It seemed to echo in the stale air, cutting sharply through the routine monotony that had settled over the place only moments before.

I rubbed my eyes, and the haze of exhaustion lifted slightly as I instinctively ran a hand through my increasingly wild hair. It was damp with the tension of the night, slicked back in an effort to appear more presentable - or at least less defeated. For that brief moment, the memory of my fear, clinging to me just a few hours before, was nearly gone; then with a rush, it came back, thick and choking, like smoke filling the room.

There he was: Draco Selva. His walk was calm and deliberate. Exuding authority from each of his strides, he seemed to command the room's attention even without uttering a word. He was impeccably dressed in his uniform that sparkled with buttons shining under the dim morning rays filtering from the dirty windows. There was no emotion on his face, just the mask of an unyielding calm. He did not look at me, not immediately. Apparently, he had made his way toward the receptionist, his voice low and even as if he were using an undertone that allowed little room for negotiation.

"Release him to me," Selva said, as if it were all formality in the tone that controlled excess emotion. The secretary took not a second's thought. She nodded briskly, almost mechanically, and motioned.

Before I could fully grasp the significance of it all, Selva's fingers touched my shoulder, strong but not forceful. "Let's go," he said, his voice not giving anything away. Next thing I knew, his fist was grasping my jacket from behind him, and he was hefting me out through the station with a force that took me aback. The suddenness threw my heart into overdrive, a flash of panic blooming before I caught the slight edge in his movements.

The heavy wooden door shut behind us, and his demeanor changed. The composed, unshakable officer who commanded the room just moments before had disappeared. Outside, his face changed in the thin, early morning light. Anger seeped into his expression - not the ruptured kind but something simmering just underneath the surface - sharp and calculated. His eyes, cold and piercing, locked onto mine with a fury that made me instinctively shrink back.

"What the hell were you thinking?" he hissed with a voice lower than a whisper but viciously venomous as if one word were likely to open the floodgates. It was a question that I hadn't asked myself: what was I even doing? Under cover, yet I asked for my only compatriot's name; it seemed a bit backward. Unable to formulate a proper answer, I just handed him the letter I got from Lukas.

"What is this?" he said with a great deal of restraint.

"What will end any preliminary arguments?" I said, stepping back to maintain safety while Draco was looking over the letter.

"So... you have the news," he said, his anger mellowing out.

"What news? Did I miss something?" I blurted.

"No, in fact, this may even be good if you cooperate. Listen, just this morning I got a letter from Lukas; apparently, he found some good news. It seemed that Selva wasn't too open to giving details yet. 'I'm still angry at you. You idiot! How can you just request for me? You know how much trouble it is to have to explain why I'm going to meet a nobody who claimed to know me!'"

"I'm sorry... I was under gunpoint," I said a little sheepishly.

"So? You were the idiot who acted like a loony on the street! If you hadn't been so vain, you probably would have been just fine. That's your problem. You are so pretentious and egoistic I can start to imagine why you would be convicted of a crime. You can't think of how you will harm others because all you do is try to save yourself first!"

At that point, I could only stand there staring at Selva as his anger rushed at me like a dam that had just given way; there was a tightening in my chest that quickly spread and made me breathe shallowly as I tried to absorb the torrent of his frustration. My mind raced to come up with a response - something, anything that might defuse the situation, but all I could feel was a shame so profound it practically anchored me to the cobblestones beneath my feet.

"I'm sorry," I said again, this time much quieter, almost inaudible. It was all I had to offer and felt as good as useless in the face of this man's fury. Selva gave me a stormy look. If anything, that seemed to sharpen his rage. His words were freezing cold and cutting into me: "Do you even understand the kind of risk I take for you? Do you? This isn't some stupid game, Klaus. You think you're the only one who has something to lose?"

I wanted to argue, defend myself, explain how none of this had been by choice - how the weight of desperation shoved me into every bad decision I made in the last twenty-four hours. But as soon as I opened my mouth, there was nothing. Selva was right - about all of it. Recklessness, selfishness, my not being able to think further than immediate survival - it was all true. The sting of it was unbearable.

"You don't understand," I said finally, voice trembling, "how every moment feels like it may be your last. How whatever I do, I'm still a marked man, that whoever even breathes wrong at it will find a way to use it against me." Said aloud, my words trailed swiftly, with each one laced in a matching frustration that dwelled inside my heart rather than directed outward.

He took his time before responding to me. His gaze, penetrating into my existence, was searching with intense eyes. And while his anger might still be there, something seemed to have shifted in an almost imperceptible flicker of recognition in his eyes.

"And yet," he said after a long pause, in a voice that was quieter but no less firm, "here you are still breathing, still alive. And you owe that to more than just yourself. Maybe remember that next time you decide to play hero on the streets."

I tore my eyes away, unable anymore to hold them against him. For me, it felt like the sound of his words - a physical weight on me - though without denying the fact that he was not wrong.

"I'm trying," I muttered hollowly. "I really am."

An exhalation by Selva came out sharply as he passed a hand over his neatly defined coiffure. "Good," he said, his voice softer though still tinged with some anger, "because if Lukas is right and there is actually something that can be worked on, it means we need you to keep your head straight this time. Can you do that?"

I simply swiped it down and slowly took it as it crammed all my emotions into one lump in my throat. "Yes." That was all I promised or could say, but at that moment, it felt like a promise I couldn't break. Left shaking, Draco didn't skip a beat; he immediately leaped into action. "Klaus, now you as Josef Svoboda are going to be under the eyes of the police. No matter how necessary that was, this is still a consequence. That means you must either. I still haven't gotten any confirmation from Lukas, but for now just lay low. I will contact you whenever possible, but don't try to be a hero. Otherwise, I may have to kill you myself." His message was ominous but honest. I couldn't mess up anymore, not with stakes so high. Whatever was happening had to be managed before the intensity started to flare up.

"I understand, sir, but how will you reach me?" I asked, wide-eyed, everyone.

"By mail, of course," he said with a serene undertone. "Also, don't write so much in your journal. You don't want that parted from you; who knows what information you may leave inside. You know what, never mind—just don't be a liability." The thought confused me, but as we parted ways, that was all I could think about.

"Was I a liability?"

Chapter 11

MEETING

May 17, 1939, Berlin

Ever since I last talked to Draco, my desires have all changed. The longing for the outside has turned into the need for indoor solace. And the pursuit of living a peaceful life has all turned into an unraveling lie, leaving me dumbstruck on the floor. I have been able to sustain myself due to the generous funding from Draco and have been gaining weight as Ms Tereza has been insistent on feeding me until, in her words, I have "enough muscle to ride a horse," as I had previously been described as having the making of a "clothes hanger." Either way, I was able to sustain myself and am now able to spend my hours reading and writing, yet I still insist on refraining from frequent journaling. Draco may be right after all.

Almost all days turned into mundanity, except whether the sunlight pouring in through my window was pale and fleeting or warm and steady. Hours and hours spent at my small desk reading the books Draco had sent - a funny, worthwhile mix of political theory, classical literature, and even a few books on military strategy. At first, I took that as a cruel joke, maybe a way of pointing out my ignorance of the world I managed to step into. But the more I read, the more I understood that there was a method to his madness. Each book seemed to carry an unspoken lesson, a whisper of context into this larger puzzle that I now found myself entangled in.

Mostly, however, the afternoons were interrupted by Ms Tereza's noisy knocking, combined with her voice loud enough to be heard through plaster walls as she scolded me for being cooped up. Then she brought in laden trays of glorious stews, baked bread, and very much butter - just more than I thought was indecent. It would be her smile that discouraged - my shoulder in pat - always accompanies her proclamation that "A strong mind needs a strong body," leaving gobbling at every morsel as the only option. It was quite a comforting act, but doing very little to the storm inside me.

At night, I would sit by the small window of my room and watch the dimly lit streets below. The muffled sounds of footsteps, laughter, and an occasional dog barking echoed monotonously in my memory, reminding me of the world I had shut myself out of. I had thought many times about whether Draco was out there, roaming in bewildering alliances and myriads of twisty conspiracies that seemed to be his existence. His absence, paradoxically, was a strange comfort - it proved that I enjoyed the by-now protection from whatever it was that was afoot.

But safety had always been delicate, a gossamer thread stretched thin across a vast gulf of uncertainty. And there lay the letter from Lukas: folded away in a drawer of my desk, it weighed heavier than paper. I'd read it a multitude of times, learning every word by heart as well as its overtones while trying to decode what the numbers scribbled at the end actually meant. The numbers haunted me, a riddle, a shadow in the dark. I thought of writing to Draco, asking him for his view of the matter, but something held me back. Perhaps pride; perhaps the fear that his answer would only deepen my disquiet.

One of those evenings, I was turning the pages of an already-worn volume of Goethe when an idea came crashing so loudly that it made me drop the book. What if the numbers weren't meant for me to resolve? What if they were a test, an experiment he devised just to see whether I could pull this off? The thought shot ice through my veins. I really didn't know if I wanted to know the answer.

In those moments of doubt, though, the walls of my room closed in on me and converted what once had been a comforting shape into a cage. But I could not leave, not yet. Not until I figured out what role I was supposed to play in this whole unraveling conspiracy. The pain of patience was still sharp despite the knowledge that I was leading myself out of the storm of danger. It seemed unorthodox, but it still gave me a sense of diligence. I could fail, not when so much could be riding on me.

The relaxation was nice, although tedious, but this morning the whole premise changed; it started with a knock. Although I was not wholly into my reverie when this sound struck me, it was a sharp rap against the wood of my apartment door that echoed louder than would be in the silence of my little abode. I went into stillness since my hand still hovered at the edge of the book I had been reading, with its words becoming suddenly meaningless. Visitors are hardly something I expect—especially not now, not after everything.

For a moment, I just sat there as my heart thudded, looking up at the door as though it would open by itself. But when the knock came again with greater intensity, I stood up suddenly, the chair producing a small screech against the floor. My brain went wild, imagining a fresh possible scenario under which someone might be here—there was nothing good about any of them. It might be Selva, but he was hardly the type to announce himself so politely. Maybe it's Ms. Tereza, but the knock lacked the usual rhythm; she never came at this hour.

And then the chilling thought struck me: What if it was one of them from before? One of the many people who knew Draco, or Lukas, or the entire twisted net into which I had unwittingly stepped. Just the idea made the sweat collect in my palms.

"Klaus?" a voice softly called from the other side of the door. A woman's voice, familiar, yet a little dislocated.

My breath stopped dead within me. It couldn't be... but it was. The woman from an earlier chapter of my life—the stranger who had set so much of this into motion—was now standing outside my door. A fair-skinned woman stood at the threshold, dimly glowing in the muted light of the hallway, with her blonde hair neatly fixed back from a face that looked untouched by the harshness of the real world outside.

Her blue eyes had a warmth that was gentle; yet behind the brightness, one could see a flicker of sadness, or maybe an innocence too bloodless for our times. Light, melodic tones would fall from her mouth while she spoke, as each word slipped down to water like a flower petal. Instead, however, it was really her demeanor that most seemed to disarm me; a quiet grace that brought with it an almost childlike trust within the person, and that made her presence both soothing and unsettling at the same time.

"Hello... Klaus," she said again, her tone steady, low, and intimate as if fearing it would be overheard.

I froze with my hand above the doorknob. A thousand questions flared in my mind. Why was she here? How had she found me? But most urgent of all: what did she want?

At long last, I unlocked the door and opened a crack just enough to see her standing there, cloaked in the dim light of the hallway. She looked different from the last time I saw her, though I couldn't quite place how. Her expression was placid yet stern, her eyes seeking mine as though to gauge my reaction. I tried to speak, but the words couldn't come out. She gave a small smile that didn't seem to reach her eyes. "Can I come in?"

I was in doubt and turned to look behind her down the empty corridor. It felt like a trap, though I could not say how. But something in her demeanor, the quiet urgency of her request, made me step back and open the door wider.

She entered in a rush, her deliberate and precise pace, as though she had rehearsed everything to get through it perfectly. I closed the door and faced her, only to find her eyes already busy searching the room, lingering on the haphazardly stacked books on my desk, the crumpled pages of scrawled notes, with the faint smell of stew from Ms. Tereza's earlier visit.

"You've been busy," she said, her tone neutral but not unkind.

I crossed my arms, leaning against the door. "Why are you here?"

She turned to face me, her expression inscrutable. "I had to make sure you were safe."

The statement took me aback, and for a moment, I had no words but to stare at her. "Safe? From what?"

"From yourself, mostly," she said, and she sounded slightly amused. "And from the people who might take advantage of your... *situation.*"

"My situation," I repeated, the words tasting of bitterness. "You mean the situation you dragged me into? Didn't want to tell me your name, but gave mine the second they asked?"

She nodded, taking it as she had said it. "I did no such thing! But I'm here to make amends for the mess I *may have* led you into."

I was about to laugh, to scoff at the absurdity of this claim, but what stopped me was the seriousness of her tone. Instead, I asked, "How did you find me?"

"That's not important," she quickly brushed it aside. "What's important is that you're not dead, you're here, and that means there's still hope."

"Hope for what?" I questioned, raising my voice to show my frustration. "What is it that you need from me? Why now?"

She hesitated and faltered in poise for the first time. "Because things are happening faster than we anticipated, and the plans we have found... they're already at work. And you, Klaus, like it or not, are part of this."

I shook my head and stepped away from the door. "No. I'm finished. Whatever this is and wherever you're driving it, it's not something I want to be a part of."

"It isn't a game," came the sharp reply, her voice slicing like a blade through the air. "If it were, you wouldn't be alive right now.

Do you think Draco has that many strings attached to his generosity? Do you think Lukas wrote that letter without the knowledge of what it would cost him?"

That made my blood boil, and I clenched my fists tightly as I struggled to calm my anger. "I didn't ask for any of this," I said through clenched teeth.

"But you are here now, and that makes it possible for you to choose between keeping yourself locked away in this room, hiding from everything, or standing up and fighting for something more significant," she continued softly. "No."

Between us, there stretched a long silence, heavy and oppressive. I wanted not only to argue but to push her straight out of my apartment and out of my life. But deep inside, I knew she was right. The world out there was dangerous, chaotic, and even more cruel than I could have imagined. But really, this was the only world I had. After a long moment, I turned to look at her, feeling the weight of her presence pressed down upon me like a storm cloud. "What do you want me to do?" Her expression softened, a flicker of relief crossing her face. "First," she said, her voice steady, "I need you to trust me."

My shock was more than apparent, the gall one could have to ask such a question, especially after the hell I've been through these last few months, just due to a simple mistake. I had come to terms that it wasn't her fault entirely, but I still had grounds on which to be angry.

"To 'trust' you will be something I'm afraid I can't afford, but I'm sure you can find someone else to fall into this honey pot." I was letting my anger get the best of me. Why should I let my one chance of salvation go, only due to my own emotions coming in the way? Still, it couldn't be ignored, the fact that she was actively trying to push away the fact that her reckless actions have impacted my life, was where I started to get angry.

"But you must give me trust, I was not aware that we were being watched, honest to god!" she said with a plea.

"As an informer, you should," I said, looking down. "And as one... talking in the open is getting both of us nowhere." I reluctantly let her in and offered her a seat at my table. I remained standing, though.

"At least you have some brains," she said passively.

"I'm sorry?" I quickly turned my head in annoyance.

"Well Klaus, I'm glad that you have common sense. Most people in situations like these would be yelling on the street or awkwardly *running* away. You are managing to quell the situation very nicely." I couldn't tell if that was a jab or genuine, but I was glad that she herself was rational as well. She sat quite comfortably in the wooden chair, but I still wanted to maintain authority.

"Why have you come here?" I asked without pause.

"Why are we retreading ground, Klaus? All you need to know is that looking backward won't help you. All that matters is what will happen after this. Just hammering down the same question will only leave us stuck," she said without much malice.

"That doesn't matter. I may be pragmatic but you haven't given me one straight answer since I have seen you, all you have given is trouble. I don't know who you are, what you do, or even your name! Yet I'm still the hindrance for asking simple yes-or-no questions.

It doesn't matter what your plan for surviving is if all you do is keep those essential things in the dark and make mistakes by getting caught."

And now the lady's aspect changed, soft grace hardening into something sharp and unyielding. A weight darkened her pale features, and the blue of her eyes flared with an anger that cut through the air like a blade. Tension in the room thickened, coiled tighter with every second. And her voice, so often calm and composed, broke the silence with a force that made me flinch.

"You think this is my fault?" she started, her words slicing through the space between us. "That I just strolled into their hands, willingly, to put us both in jeopardy? You think this is because I'm reckless or careless? You have no idea what I've endured, Klaus. No idea what it's taken to keep you alive—to keep any of this alive."

I opened my mouth, the start of a protest forming, but it died in my throat. She wasn't finished. If anything, my reaction only seemed to spur her on, her tone climbing with every word. It wasn't just anger; it was something deeper—desperation mingled with indignation, a raw intensity that left no room for argument.

"You don't sincerely believe they need me for information, do you?" she exclaimed sharply, her voice rising in anger as she leaned forward. "That they went to all this trouble because I hold some secret they can't uncover elsewhere? They didn't capture me because I failed. They didn't capture me because I was careless. They captured me because I refused. Refused to give them what they wanted. Refused to betray the people who are counting on us. They wanted to send a message, Klaus. To me. To you. To all of us."

She would say each one of those sentences like she is dropping a hammer, every strike harder than the last. One could see this minor tremor inside her hands clutching at the edges of that chair, each knuckle locked white in its effort to anchor herself in that moment. That voice, unsteady with nothing but the rigors of being held back by a far more powerful force—rage and exhaustion and this conviction that wasn't about to budge.

"Do you know what it's like?" she pressed, her eyes locking onto mine with an intensity that made it impossible to look away. "To sit across from men who want nothing more than to break you—who believe they can break you—and to look them in the eye and refuse? To know that every second you resist is a second closer to them deciding you're no longer worth the trouble? I didn't bend, Klaus. I didn't break. And I'm still here, standing in front of you, because despite everything—despite the hell they put me through—I still believe in this. I still believe in us. I still believe that we can do something that matters."

Her voice cracked on the last word, and for a moment, the fire in her eyes softened, replaced by something far more vulnerable. Her grip on the chair loosened, but she didn't retreat. If anything, she leaned in closer, her presence filling the room like a storm cloud about to burst. Words hit like a punch, each syllable heavy with gravity I hadn't allowed myself to confront. They weren't just words - they were wounds she carried, flayed open for me to see. Each one left a mark, an indelible reminder of a truth I had been too consumed by my own anger to consider. She leaned forward in the chair, her hands holding onto its edges as if it was the only thing keeping her on the earth, her knuckles white with the strain.

"Do you know what it feels like, Klaus?" she asked, her voice cutting through the silence with a sharp edge. "To stare down men who view you as little more than an implement to be twisted, bruised, and cast aside? Men who feel they can rip everything from you—your strength, your heart—and shape you into something that suits their desires? I sat there, through their eyes, day after day, knowing what they wanted, knowing what it would cost me if I refused. And I did not give in. I did not break. Not for them. Not for their threats. Not even for their lies." Her voice quivered, but it wasn't a weakness. It was the weight of everything she had gone through, pressed against the fragile facade she had constructed. She inhaled sharply, steadying herself, and when she spoke again, her words were quieter but no less powerful.

"And now I'm here," she went on, her eyes boring into mine, "standing in front of you because despite everything— everything—I still believe in this fight. I still believe in what we're trying to do. I may have put you in the spotlight Klaus, but you always were a player whether in an article or an interview, you were always there to put fuel to the fire. You are not to blame, but it is necessary for you to atone, to help those who can't do it themselves. To validate all those trying to fix this problem, even in their own interest."

Her eyes stabbed at me, searching, probing for some hint of understanding within the walls of my mind. "You're angry with me? So be angry. You think I did things wrong? Maybe I did. Don't stand there and pretend like you're the only one to pay a cost for this. None of us wanted this place, Klaus. None of us asked for this storm. But we're in it now. And either we find the way to cross this storm, or we go under - it ends. Alone."

The air between us felt heavy, almost suffocating. Her words lingered, thick and unyielding, refusing to be ignored. I could feel my defenses cracking under their weight—not from guilt, but from the raw honesty in her voice. It wasn't the measured calm she usually carried or the quiet urgency that had brought her to my door. This was different. This was real. For the first time, I saw beyond the mask she wore—the carefully composed facade of strength and control.

The woman beneath emerged, stripped bare by the enormity of what she'd endured. A woman who had walked through hell and come out the other side, not unscathed but unbroken. A woman who, despite every reason to give up, had found the strength to sit here and demand more from me than I thought I had left to give.

And in that moment, I hated her for dragging me into this and forcing me to see what I didn't want to see. But more than that, I respected her. Because she was right, and that truth was harder to face than any of the anger I had clung to so tightly.

The silence that had followed her words was stifling, heavy with unspoken truths and emotions neither of us wanted to confront. I turned away, crossing my arms tightly across my chest, my eyes fixed on the floor as if it might somehow offer some respite. Anger burned inside me – a fierce, stubborn anger that refused to let go – but it was no longer alone. Beneath it, creeping in like a shadow, was something colder and sharper: guilt.

Her words had struck me harder than I'd expected. Each one carried the weight of her conviction, her sacrifices, and her pain—pain I hadn't allowed myself to see. I wanted to cling to my resentment, to hold onto it like a shield, but her voice lingered in my mind, cracking through the armor I'd so carefully constructed. Still, I couldn't look at her. Not yet.

Behind me, she waited. She didn't push, didn't speak again, but her presence was like a storm cloud, pressing down on the room with an unrelenting force. I could feel her eyes on me, searching for something I wasn't sure I could give.

"I don't know how to trust you," I said finally, my voice low and strained. The words felt foreign, like a confession dragged out of me against my will. "After everything that's happened—after everything I've been through because of this—I don't know how to believe in anything anymore."

Her sharp inhale cut through the silence, but she didn't intrude. Her voice was quieter now, softer, but by no means less resolute. "I don't blame you for that," she said. "I don't expect you to trust me—not completely, not yet. But I do need you to believe in this fight. In us."

I had shifted to the side a bit, looking over my shoulder. Her face was softened now, and the angular definition had smoothed into something more vulnerable. It was a look I hadn't ever seen before, and it threw me for a beat. For all her strength, for all her spunk, she was human. She wasn't some unshakable force; she was just a person trying to carry a burden that no one should ever have to carry alone.

"You want me to believe in this fight?" I asked with a bitter note in my voice, shaking my head. "How can I, when all it's brought is pain and loss? How can you?"

Her eyes didn't flinch. If anything, they steadied, became stronger. "Because the alternative is worse," she said simply.

"Because if we don't fight, they win. And if they win, everything we've lost—everything we've suffered—will mean nothing. Is that what you want, Klaus? To let them strip us of everything and walk away unscathed?" I flinched at her words, the truth in them cutting deeper than I cared to admit. My fists clenched at my sides as I struggled to hold onto the anger, the doubt, anything that might keep me from surrendering. But her voice—calm yet unyielding—chipped away at my defenses.

"I didn't come here to ask for your forgiveness," she continued. "I came here because I need you to see what I see. Understand that you are not the only one who's paid a price for this. You are angry at me? Fine. Be angry. Do not stand there and pretend you are the only one who lost something. We are all caught in this storm, Klaus. None of us asked for it, but we are here." And we swim or drown in it separately.

Like lead, her words hovered there in the air, impossible to push past. My chest squeezed in a breathless tightening as walls around me crumbled, crushed beneath the weight of her words' raw honesty. There was no seeking forgiveness, no plea for leniency, but laying open, stark, unadorned, that which is naked and ugly in me, defying me to step into that place. Neither of us said anything for a long moment. Tension hung in the air, punctuated only by the slight thrum of the city through the window. Slowly, I turned to her, my anger gone but replaced by a weariness that settled deep in my bones.

"You think this is easy for me?" I asked, my voice quieter now, almost a whisper. "You think I wanted any of this?"

"No," she said firmly, her blue eyes locking onto mine. "And neither did I. But we don't get to choose the battles we're thrust into, Klaus. We only get to choose how we fight them."

The simplicity of her words caught me more than any argument she could have made. My shoulders slumped under the weight of her gaze, words, and presence until I felt I would shatter. And yet, beneath the weariness, something flickered back to life – a spark of something I hadn't felt in what felt like an eternity.

I didn't want to admit it. I didn't want to admit that, despite everything, she was right. But the truth was undeniable. If I walked away now, if I gave up, then everything we'd endured, everything we'd lost, would have been for nothing. Breathing deeply, I went closer to her, my movement slow and purposeful. She still clutched the sides of the chair; her knuckles were white from the pressure of her grip, but she did not even jerk as I reached down and came eye to eye with her.

"All right," I said finally, my voice steady despite the storm raging inside me. "I'll give this one more chance. But if I'm going to do this, I need the truth. No more half-answers, no more secrets. I need to know what we're fighting for—and what it's going to cost."

A relief crossed her face, so brief I might have missed it if I hadn't been watching her so closely. She nodded, her expression set. "You have my word," she said softly. "No more secrets. No more lies." For the first time, the tension between us seemed to ease. The room felt lighter, the air less oppressive. It wasn't forgiveness, not yet. But it was a step. A fragile truce in a war neither of us had chosen but had no choice but to fight.

I felt the stretch of her arms, reaching out to help me up. And as I straightened, I saw something in her eyes that I hadn't noticed before – a quiet strength, tempered by vulnerability, that made me realize just how much she had endured to get to this moment. And for the first time, I felt a flicker of something I hadn't allowed myself to feel in a long time. Not trust, not yet. But the possibility of trust.

As I looked at her, unwavering and resolute, a realization struck me like a thunderbolt—perhaps, just perhaps, we could survive this storm together. Her conviction was undeniable, her strength unyielding. And for the first time, I felt the faintest stirrings of belief, not just in her, but in the possibility that we might actually succeed.

But with that thought came another realization: the fact that Selva had to be heard immediately in case we were all going to go forward with this. This was already making much of our plan useless. Its secondary goal - the one we thought impossible - was already achieved. There was no more waiting. We could go directly to the next level, but whatever that may hold for us.

"Klaus," she said, her voice smooth but carrying an edge that made me wary. She tilted her head, a sly glimmer in her eyes, as if she expected my reaction.

"Yes?".

"I've already sent everything to Selva," she said, her tone deceptively casual, but her words carried the weight of a bombshell. "He has all the information he needs to proceed. He'll arrange a meeting as soon as it's feasible."

Her calm declaration left me reeling. "What?" The word escaped my lips before I could stop it, sharp and incredulous.

"Don't be rash, Klaus," she added, rising from her chair with the measured grace of someone who had already thought ten steps ahead. "All your questions will be answered in due time."

I stood there, dumbfounded, staring after her as she walked toward the door. My mind was racing, trying to stitch together what had just occurred. She had done this all on her own, without asking, without so much as suggesting it to me. How long had she been plotting this? How could I have been left so blind?

A cold realization crept over me. This wasn't just her asserting control; this was her demonstrating that she had always been a step ahead. She hadn't needed my approval or my input, and that stung more than I cared to admit.

But the bigger question that gnawed at me, refusing to be silenced, was, "What was my role in all of this?" I thought I knew where I stood and what I was there for. It now felt as if the ground had shifted from under me, and I was on shaky footing.

"Wait," I called after her, my voice firmer than I felt. She paused, her hand on the doorframe, but didn't turn around.

"What is my part in this?" I demanded, the words spilling out before I could second-guess them. "What aren't you telling me?"

For a moment, I thought she might ignore me entirely. But then she turned her head just slightly, enough for me to catch a glimpse of her profile. Her expression was unreadable, a mask of composure that betrayed nothing.

"All in due time, Klaus," she said again, her voice soft but unrelenting. "For now, trust that Selva knows what to do. And so will you, when the time comes."

With that, she was gone, leaving me alone in the room with my thoughts – a thousand questions and no answers.

I sank back into the chair she had vacated, my mind racing. Whatever game we were playing, she held more cards than I'd realized. And while I was used to operating in the shadows, I couldn't shake the feeling that this time, I was the one being kept in the dark.

But one thing was clear: I couldn't afford to hesitate. If Selva had the information, the clock was already ticking. Whatever this next step was, it would demand everything I had to give—and perhaps more than I was ready to face.

For now, all I could do was wait. But the weight of her words lingered, heavy with the promise of revelations to come. As she got up, I was left stunned. How could I be left in the dark? And what was my bigger role in all this?

"And Klaus, the name is Victoria."

Chapter 12

GROWTH

July 6, 1939, Prague, Czechoslovakia

The air in the morning carried a really biting chill. My journal in my hands, getting rough due to my age. It's been a while since I last wrote. It seemed that the morning was really made for screening the reality of our situation, for as we walked down the streets, there was just an unbearable silence between Selva and me. The cobblestones were really threatening as I walked over them, but I suspected that it was the knocking of my own uneasiness that was causing the stumbling. The earlier tirade of Selva rang in my ears, and his frustration was completely felt, primarily because now Selva moved with purposeful calmness - a plain psychology under everything.

We entered a small café hidden within an alley, and a faded swing sign creaked tautly on rusted hinges. Selva willfully nodded one curt head in the direction of the proprietor, who locked eyes with him for a moment too long before retreating behind a counter. The smell of freshly brewed potent coffee and secrecy lay thick inside. Selva signaled me to take a seat at the corner table, so I did, sinking into the creaky chair while he unceremoniously deposited a folded letter on the table between us.

"From Lukas," he muttered.

I stared at the letter, and my heart raced as Selva lit a cigarette and leaned back, focusing his gaze on me with disdain and curiosity mixed. With a skillful touch, I unfolded the paper as if it could fall into pieces at my touch. The signature is unmistakable. Lukas's precise, deliberate script has each letter like a soldier marching in perfect formation.

"Klaus, I've found something." It isn't merely about your name anymore. "The framed charges against you were prepared by someone who has something much greater at stake than we imagined. You were never the target - you were bait."

My breath caught. The moment tragedy struck. For a split second, everything blurred as the mind raced with all sorts of possibilities to come up with a meaning. I proceeded:

"Evidence is incriminating, alibis point toward a senior official in the regime. I can't name names, but their plans surpass what we have seen. So, Poland is next, Klaus. It's not an invasion; it's just a kind of dry run. They had to confuse their operations, and you were very handy through all of that."

The quote ends rather abruptly, as if Lukas stopped mid-sentence. A whole string of numbers follows that could be coordinates or a code I cannot decode yet. I trembled a bit while placing the paper down.

Selva let out a puff of smoke, watching me intently. "Well? What have you found?"

I considered the chances of divulging too much at stake or at risk. But the flicker in Selva's eyes, almost human beneath layers of cynicism, made me do what I did.

"...it proves what I've long suspected," I started cautiously. "My arrest had nothing to do with me; it was just a diversion."

Selva's brow furrowed. "A diversion for what?"

"I am now leaking information to foreign governments that Germany is preparing for an invasion of Poland," I said, and the words cracked in my throat. "Lukas thinks that someone in high places has caused these charges against me as a means to keep eyes off their movements."

For a moment, Selva said nothing. He leaned forward and with an enemy's vicious care crushed his cigarette into the ashtray. "You are saying that someone up in Berlin used you in order to cover their tracks? And now they are quite plotting an eastward expansion, I suppose?"

I nodded, the hollow twisting in my stomach increasing, "It's more than that. Lukas... he catches something far greater. Whosoever is behind this is not just looking for a scapegoat, they want to hurt Germany. This one is just the first step to something far worse."

Selva's eyes narrowed slightly; his composure cracked. "Do you have any idea what you are saying, Klaus? If Lukas is right, this is not just about clearing your name. You are implicating people who will have killed without a second thought."

"Then why are you here?" I shot back, the words escaping before I could stop them. "If you are so afraid, why risk meeting me? Why risk helping me at all? In fact, why don't you know about this? I had heard vague rumors getting flown around, but you… you should know!"

Selva's jaw tightened, and for a fleeting moment, he looked as if he had made up his mind to walk out. Then he leaned closer and lowered his voice to a near-whisper. "I've seen it coming. The cracks in the facade. The whispers in Berlin. People disappear without explanation. This regime isn't as monolithic as it wants us to believe. And if what Lukas says is true…" He trailed off and shook his head. "Let's just say that I have my own reasons for wanting to see this through."

The air between us thickened with unspoken truths. For the first time, I saw Selva not as the hardened soldier or the reluctant ally but as a man caught in the same web of fear and deceit as I was.

"What do we do now?" I finally asked.

Selva sighed and rubbed his temples. "First, let's find Lukas. If he has found what he now says he has, he will need protection. But then…" He hesitated, glancing around as if even the walls of the café themselves might be listening. "Then we decide what line we are prepared to cross," he added. "To stop them?" I asked, my voice and the question almost a whisper. Our eyes met, his unflinching. "To survive."

Silence enveloped the café; all the loud traffic was reduced to a whisper. I looked out of the window; people moved outside in Prague and were a blurry vision in motion. The streets were beautiful but seemed like a time bomb ticking down, counting toward some inevitable edge that we had yet to see. The patrons were ever-present under the crimson sky.

"What about the numbers?" I asked, indicating the strange line at the end of the letter. "Could they lead us to Lukas?" Selva moved closer before his finger moved along the page. "Possibly coordinates. He's clever - always has been. If it's a location, it would probably be where he's hiding. Or where he's found the evidence."

"But why not say more?" I asked, frustration bubbling beneath my words. "If it's as serious as he claims, why leave it so vague?"

Selva shook his head, a bitter smile tugging at his lips. "Lukas knows the stakes. If this letter were intercepted, he would sign his death warrant. He just gives us enough to follow without giving them anything to find him."

"Then why couldn't I have the information first?" I exclaimed.

"Because Lukas knows that you are prone to emotions and would need someone to break it all down for you. Panic attacks and feverish sprints, how could you be a reporter with such consciousness?"

Starting again at the digits, I tried to make them make sense. A part of me wanted to go to town and question everything - being disappointed and demand answers from Selva, from Lukas, from the entire twisted machinery of the regime. But another part, the part which had survived this long, knew better. This is the reality we live in, lots of anger, but not resentment.

Selva crushed the cigarette with his boot and stood. "Time to go. If Lukas is right, time will be against us. Poland is not just a plan; it's happening."

I nodded, folded the letter lightly, and tucked it into my coat. The weight pressed firmly against my chest was a constant reminder of what lay ahead. As we stepped out into the alley, its chilled air nipped at my face, but I embraced it; cold, stark, and bracing to the turmoil within. Selva's pace seemed to pick up, his gaze darting momentarily to each and every shadow. "Klaus," he said without looking back, "if we do this… if we find Lukas and the evidence he's uncovered… Well, there's no turning back. We'll only be victims of fate."

"I know, why bother?" I replied, the words steadier than I felt.

"We bother so that in some way we can help those who can't, and if not ourselves," Draco said before going silent.

And with that, we disappeared into the labyrinth of Prague, two men against a tide neither of us fully understood. The everlasting vortex shielding us from the eyes watching from above, Selva knew that a plan was to be set in motion and now that I had my role set, I only had one thing left.

"I need to know where Draco is, maybe she can be the key to all this!"

"Who?" Draco asked with an expression of uncertainty.

"Victoria"

"So… she told you? Not surprised. I'm sure you were very brash with her; otherwise, I couldn't imagine you giving any suave subtlety," Draco said sarcastically.

"And I was unaware of your calling for comedy… sir. Anyhow, it is most important that we are able to locate her now that all information has been dispersed. And figure out our new plans," I said with a feverish haste.

"Klaus, there is no rush. The plan is in motion; all that's changed is that you have the full picture," Draco said without hesitation.

"What exactly is the plan?" I asked with uncertainty.

"That is not vital information for you, Klaus," he said without pause. "And don't go whining about us leaving you in the dark; it would be detrimental for you to know anyways. Before we depart, remember this, Klaus, the world is an ever-shifting place where anyone can live or die in moments; rules will always change to where you can always come out last, so instead of figuring out how to win every battle, no matter the consequences. Try learning how to listen, try to understand how we can help you, Klaus, and then maybe we can work better. But for now, just heed my advice. Don't step out of your lane, and then maybe things will be right. Klaus, no matter how much I may help, we aren't friends; we are dependants who are using each other for a shared collective goal, just be sure of that."

The words of Draco cut deep, calculated precision slicing through my frustration like a scalpel. His tone was dismissive yet deliberate, designed to sting, and it did. I clenched my fists at my sides, my breath steadying as I fought to keep my composure.

"Dependents, huh?" I said, my voice low but sharp enough to let him know that I was in no position to roll over on this one. "Funny how you put that. Because from where I sit, it appears that I am the one scurrying while you sit here pocketing all the pieces."

Draco arched an eyebrow, a hint of amusement playing at the corners of his mouth. "And yet, here you are, Klaus. Still standing. Still playing your part. The question is, are you done complaining, or should I fetch a violin to accompany your performance?"

I stepped closer, letting the tension between us thicken. "You love this, don't you? Holding the cards, keeping everyone guessing. But you don't understand something, Draco. You think keeping me in the dark protects your precious plan? Maybe it does. Or maybe it just makes me more unpredictable. And you know what unpredictability does in a game like this? It kills people."

For a moment, Draco's eyes narrowed, his smirk fading just slightly. That was something, at least. I pressed on, refusing to let the silence swallow my point.

"I don't care if you think we're not friends. Fine. I'm not here for camaraderie, and I don't need your approval. But don't you dare act like I'm just some cog in your machine. You say we're dependants, but let me remind you, Draco: dependants go both ways. You need me just as much as I need you, whether you want to admit it or not."

Draco tilted his head, studying me like a chess master sizing up an opponent's move. He took a long breath that bordered on the theatrical as he folded his arms and leaned back slightly. "You have some fire in you, Klaus. I will give you that. But fire burns out pretty quickly when it doesn't know where to direct itself. So, let me ask you, what do you want? Truly?"

I didn't blink under his gaze, though every nerve in my body screamed at me to turn and leave. "What do I want? I want clarity, Draco. I want to know that every risk I take, every step I make, isn't just for some vague promise of a goal you've kept hidden behind your back. I want to know if this is worth it."

Draco's expression changed, the faintest glimmer of something—approval, perhaps—flickering in his eyes.

"Fair enough," he said after a pause, his voice softer but no less firm. "You'll have clarity when the time is right. Not before. Not because I want to keep you guessing, but because clarity at the wrong moment can cost lives. And whether you believe it or not, Klaus, I'm trying to keep yours intact."

He took a step closer, his voice dropping to just above a whisper. "But I'll say this: what you do, it's significant. It is not small. It is not insignificant. So if you want to prove me wrong, Klaus? Then step up. Play your part. Let me see if you are greater than a little fire burning away."

Draco turned on his heel, his coat flying behind him as he made his way toward the door. "Until then," he called over his shoulder, "keep your head down and your ears open. The world may be ever-shifting, Klaus, but that doesn't mean you can't find your footing."

The door clicked shut behind him. My thoughts are a whirlwind of anger, determination, and a faint understanding that has not fully come about yet. Maybe he didn't think we were friends, and maybe he was right. He was not, however, a puppet master who manipulated the strings from behind a veil of ignorance. There was more to him than what he presented, and more to me than he was letting on.

And if I had to fight my way through every shadow he cast to prove it, so be it. Because at the end of the day, he was right, there is no reason to help each other if you have nothing to gain.

"Klaus, in one week's time you head back to Berlin. You have no reason to be here now, and it will make everything easier. Collect your items, leave little trace of your presence, and discern nothing. When you come back, you will be something of a local hero if our propaganda plays right. Lukas has been diligent in restoring your reputation, which is so necessary in this world." I was at a loss for words; the deadline was now in front of me. I should have nothing but glee, yet I couldn't feel it coming. Only a desperate pain that I wasn't worth it; the hassle was now over. No matter, at least being able to live in my own name gave me slight solace.

Upon finally parting ways, I saw Draco give me a slight smile. He had my best interest at heart, I hoped. But for now, I would have to just suffice another week, maybe just take in the view without the writing. Hopefully, my job will be back when I come. At least I can get a semblance of normality. I'll miss Eva and Ms. Tereza though; they made life enjoyable and despite the oddities, I know that they kept me sane. I'll be sure to give them something before I go. All this hope came crashing down when the thought suddenly hit me.

"Am I worth all of this?"

Chapter 13

ASSIMILATION

July, 13, 1939

The railroad stretched out before me, a fading line of metal and gravel that seemed to dissolve into the horizon. The tracks were uneven in places, their rusted edges glinting faintly under the dim glow of the early evening sky. The wooden ties, weathered and cracked from years of neglect, sat half-buried in the ballast, some tilted as though they were succumbing to the weight of time.

Between the tracks, weeds sprouted. Their tendrils snaked upwards like nature's quiet rebellion against the industry that once thrived here. A faint scent of damp earth remained, mixed with the metallic tang that hung in the air near the old steel.

Beyond the tracks, the landscape was shrouded in a misty twilight, with spots of dense shrubbery and sparse trees breaking up the landscape, creating an intermittent silhouette against the fading light. A hollow, soft sound echoed from the tracks as I shifted my weight—a haunting reminder of the journeys they had once carried.

The road home seemed to stretch up from the tracks like some solemn invitation, its straight course framed by the quiet melancholy of this abandoned railway. It was more than a road - it was a bridge between here and there, a tether to a past that seemed both far off and near. As I checked my watch and saw the hands strike 8:00, the defunct railroad seemed to echo the ticking seconds - empty, insistent, inescapable.

The train station was this ghost of all it had once been, the facade of its thick brick stained almost black with dust and soot that coated them for decades, the arch of the roof falling in spots upon rusted, creaky iron beams swaying in gentle wind, fractured glass panes in large windows allowing shafts of dimmer light to push through and cut long shadows over the stone pavement chipped as it was down below. The station clock had been frozen at a time so long past, its hands still stubbornly pointing to an hour that no longer mattered. Benches lined the platform, their wooden slats weathered and splintered with tufts of weeds sprouting defiantly through the cracks between the stones. A solitary lantern hung from a bent pole, its flickering light barely illuminating the emptiness around it. Dust and debris swirled in the air, stirred by the faint hum of the approaching locomotive.

The train itself was a beast of antiquity.

Its massive, black iron frame emerged from the mist with a low, guttural roar, like some long-forgotten leviathan summoned from the depths. The locomotive's smokestack belched thick plumes of dark smoke that curled into the night sky, carrying with it the acrid scent of burning coal. The engine's wheels, huge and threatening, shrieked against the rails as it slowed, grinding into the station with a noise like a dire portent. At the nose of the train, a headlight stood alone, piercing through the gloom, an unwavering eye searching for something or someone in the shadows. Its brass fittings glistened dully in the light, and its number "47" was faintly scrawled on one side in smudged paint.

Behind this engine rattled the battered and scarred passenger cars, showing glimpses in their windows of dim interiors: flickering shapes of restless ghosts. And then the train stopped, finally, with a hissing sound of steam that was ear-shattering. The platform seemed to catch its breath in a collective unison as the locomotive appeared to prevail, carrying, not people, but secrets. Old, silent, and heavy as night.

Once I got on board, I immediately went to the back, walking past the pristine leather cabins, and going into the rotting economy seats. With the velvet tapering off, and reclining so small it could be considered a tilted chair. I put my bag on the window and sat in the aisle in hopes that I wouldn't have any neighbors. The caked-up dirt all over the seat crevices. I can see old bags left forgotten in the overhead. As more people kept filling in, I had the relief that no one seemed to want to sit where I was. All the children rushed for the windows in the front so that they could peek over at the engine. Other single travelers like me trying to distance themselves from each other, and the rare couple bending over backward for each other, holding up the space in their own little delusions.

After five minutes, I estimated that the train was about to leave and no one was next to me yet. I saw the last few passengers struggle in, an older woman who reminded me of Ms. Tereza and a younger girl that was similar to Eva. It was hard to let them go, as their presence felt like a fleeting connection to something human amidst the mechanical groan of the train. The older woman's lined face bore a quiet dignity, her frail hands clutching a woven bag that sagged with its unknown contents. She moved slowly, her gaze fixed on the floor as though the weight of her life rested in every step. The younger girl, perhaps twelve or thirteen, had a nervous energy about her, clutching a tattered book to her chest as if it were armor against the unknown. They sought seats at the front of the carriage, a world away from my corner of isolation. And yet, as the train began its laborious pull out of the station, I couldn't help but keep looking at them. They reminded me painfully of what I was leaving behind—Ms. Tereza's quiet strength, Eva's ineradicable joie de vivre.

The rhythmic clatter of the train filled the space around me, a ceaseless metronome marking the passage of time and distance. I leaned back against the tattered seat, feeling its rough fabric snag against my coat. The world outside blurred into streaks of gray and green as the landscape rushed past in a mad dance of motion and stillness. The dim interior was strangely comfortable. Flickering gas lamps overhead cast ill-even pools of light across the faded upholstery patterns and the etched graffiti that adorned the wooden panels. A low undertone of voices rose and fell, mingling with the creak of the train's joints and the occasional cough or rustle of a newspaper.

I looked down at my hands resting on the bag in my lap. The leather strap was worn smooth from use, and the weight of its contents seemed heavier than it should have been. It wasn't just the physical burden—it was everything it represented. The secrets, the lies, the fragile threads of a plan that felt increasingly out of my control. This all echoed as a bitter reminder of my place in all this, as Draco's words had once said: "Don't step out of your lane." But what was my lane, really? A pawn in a game I barely understood, or something more?

I gritted my teeth and forced myself to disregard the doubts in my mind. The movement of the train was mesmerizing, rocking me into an unpleasant contemplation of life. Outside my window, day slowly succumbed to nightfall. A flicker of weak lights showed through on the dark horizon: this could be a sign of a new town on the way or another illusion for the never-ending ride.

The old woman settled in beside her young companion whose head was tilted, as though praying or perhaps deep in reflection. I find myself pondering her destination, where their stories started, and the journey they make now, perhaps of escape and return.

A pang of guilt hit me out of the blue. Would I ever even remember Eva, or would Ms. Tereza know that I'd gone? But after I left, would I not be all forgotten? This was suffocating, yet I made myself take a deep breath, forcing my attention back onto the metronomic heartbeat of the train.

"How am I worth it all?" I asked out loud, for it was unrequited. Yet it was still all in my mind. As the train was rushing, the grinding of the tracks soon began to fade, the sounds becoming homogenized, everyone in their seats. The tracks, like a moaning of grinding metal, smoothed into low-humming sounds, drummed a one-two-two-three-four into a sleepless sleep. It became a rocking motion toward the outside world's bluriness of darkness streaks with faint light. There was a brief movement jostle of the carriage but not fully woken until a concert of shrill whistle of the conductor's screech of brakes brought and awoke me. Few children made noise. Before I knew it, I had dozed off, waking up into a bustling Berlin. As the people started to board off, the noise began.

Berlin. It gets transformed. The train tanks to the standstill while outside the functioning window gives one a chaotic version of sporting pleasure. All shadowing buildings, shadowy light from street lamps—all these were coming to greet me, their harsh contrast marking the solitary, silent agricultural countryside from the warm, throbbing life. As the train slipped into the station, the sounds of Berlin came well and clearly. The low rumble of conversation, the sharp cries of vendors hawking newspapers and snacks, the rhythmic clatter of suitcases being dragged over uneven cobblestones—all of it rose in a crescendo that broke through the quiet cocoon of the train.

But once it finally stopped moving, the carriage came to life. Passengers stirred from their seats, taking hold of their things with a kind of hastened weariness. The children had slept most of the way and, now wide-eyed, were making excited small talk, a screeching and shrill chorus to the mumbled grumbles of adults. I got up and stretched, feeling my limbs stiff. The compartment around me was a blur of movement as people jostled past with their faces mixed in anticipation, exhaustion, and indifference. I picked up my bag from the overhead rack and followed the flow of the crowd out onto the platform.

It was enormous, an iron-and-glass cathedral seeming to stretch to infinity in all directions. An arched roof yawned upward, steel framing like some massive, dead rib's latticework across a great plain of concrete and tarmac. A grimy canopy of glass filters the sunlight spilling in overhead, fracturing it into the platform below like shards of green glass.

Everywhere, there was movement. Travelers streamed past, their footsteps echoing off the polished stone floor. The air was thick with the mingling scents of coal smoke, damp metal, and the faint aroma of freshly baked pretzels from a nearby stand. Porters in faded uniforms darted between the throngs, carrying trunks and cases with practiced ease.

Announcements boomed from overhead loudspeakers, their mechanical voices cutting through the din with harsh precision: "Train 47 from Dresden has arrived. Train 47 from Dresden has arrived." Words were almost drowned out by the clamor of other passengers disembarking. In the mess, the voices blended into the cacophony of greetings, directions, and quick farewells.

I moved through the crowd, my bag slung over one shoulder, trying to navigate the chaos. The platform was a patchwork of emotions—reunions filled with laughter and tears, solitary figures clutching tickets as they stared at the departure boards, children tugging at their parents' hands with wide-eyed wonder.

A group of soldiers in uniform stood at the far end of the station, their presence a stark reminder of the times we lived in. Their polished boots and stern faces seemed out of place amidst the lively chatter and hurried steps of the civilians around them.

As I walked into the main concourse, the scale of the station became even more intimidating. Huge columns supported the roof, their surfaces covered in intricately carved moldings that told of a lost era of magnificence. The walls were plastered with posters and notices—some were advertisements for an upcoming performance at the opera, others were slogans of patriotism scrawled out in bold, imposing letters.

For a moment, I stood there taking it all in. This was Berlin—a city alive with both ambition and conflict, beauty and brutality, hope and despair. It was light-years away from the quiet railway station I'd left behind, yet somehow felt utterly familiar.

A shiver ran down my spine as I stood there, the noise and movement and size of it all suffocating. But something else lay under that unease, a spark of determination: this city contained answers, opportunity, and possibly redemption. And all I needed to do was find them.

Taking a deep breath, I adjusted the strap of my bag and stepped forward, merging into the ever-changing tide of humanity that filled the station. Going past all the local shops and rushing travelers, I could see a horde of people heading toward the exit, where amidst the gray buildings, the black taxis hung around trying to pick up as many people as possible. Along with their yelling, the enamored crowd of families coming to pick up beloved relatives was more than necessary to me.

As I scoured the mess of faces, I tried to see the one I needed, I presumed was Lukas. Running down the street, I could hear my name, see something familiar. Not helped by the increasing amount of honking due to more people coming out. I felt that it was more tedious than anything else, but no matter what, it was still tiresome. After a couple of minutes of this, I could see a familiar Mercedes pull near the station, one not too unfamiliar from what got crashed. In the driver's seat, I saw a very happy Lukas. "Klaus!" he shouted, flapping at me with his arms like an over-caffeinated enthusiast. His voice carried above the car horns and vendors' shouts.

I threaded my way through the throng, dodging suitcases, children, and impatient travelers. The stifling air of the station gave way to the open street, where the acrid tang of exhaust fumes mingled with the faint scent of hot pretzels from a nearby vendor. Lukas stepped out of the car, brushing down his jacket and looking entirely too pleased with himself.

"Took you long enough," he said, his voice light with teasing. "I was starting to think you'd gotten lost in that crowd."

"I nearly did," I muttered, lifting my bag and shoving it into the back seat beside me before sliding into the passenger side. The leather felt cool against my back, a contrast to the stifling warmth of the station.

Lukas slid into the driver's seat, adjusting his cap with a casual ease. The engine hummed to life, its smooth purr a reminder of the precision that German engineering prided itself on. As he pulled away from the curb, the noise of the station began to recede, replaced by the steady rhythm of the city outside.

"So," Lukas began, casting me a sidelong glance, "how does it feel to be back in the capital? Miss the chaos yet?"

I shrugged indifferently, my gaze drifting to stare out of the window. The street passed Berlin in a haze of motion and color: the lines of determined but exhausted people, the vendors whooping up their respective wares amidst the reek of chestnuts roasting on a metal cart and bread still warm from a nearby bakery, the monochromatic facades above looming high enough to make anyone feel slightly anxious yet also kind of soothing, as though promising safety despite intimidation.

"It feels... familiar," I said finally, my voice low.

Lukas smirked, his hands steady on the wheel. "Familiar, huh? Well, that's one way to put it. But don't get too comfortable. Things are different now."

I glanced at him, noting the shift in his expression. The teasing grin was gone, replaced by something more serious, almost somber.

"What do you mean?"

"You will see soon enough," Lukas said, his voice tranquil but his eyes betraying a hint of unease. "Berlin has this way of revealing its truths. Just be prepared for them."

The words hung in the air, heavy with unspoken meaning. I turned back to the window, watching as the city unfolded before me. It was alive, breathing with a restless energy that I could feel in my bones. For better or worse, I was here, and whatever truths Berlin held, I would face them head-on.

As we took a turn into a quieter street, Lukas reached into his pocket and produced a small envelope, tossing it onto my lap.

"What is this?" I asked, reaching down to take it, looking at the plain surface.

"Instructions," he said bluntly. "From Draco. You are to follow them to the letter. No deviations."

At the mention of Draco, my chest tightened with the words that were still hanging in my head from our last conversation.

"Did he say anything else?" I asked, my voice barely above a whisper.

Lukas shook his head. "Just that you are expected to play your part."

I gripped the envelope tightly. The paper inside crinkled, and the weight was so disproportionate to the size; as if it carried more than just words.

As the car rolled to a stop in front of an almost indistinct-looking building, Lukas turned to me; his gaze steady. "So, welcome to Berlin again, Klaus. Hopefully I'm ready this time." Without another word, I stepped out of the car, holding onto the envelope tightly in my hand. The city loomed around me, its towering buildings and bustling streets a testament to its unyielding spirit. Yet, beneath the surface, I could feel the tension, the undercurrent of something darker.

Berlin had always been a city of contrasts, between ambition and conflict, between beauty and brutality, between hope and despair. Cruising on the roadside, I felt a little enamored being in this car again; the last time we crashed together, and I don't feel like I'll be able to walk it off, unlike last time. Lukas was much more focused on the road, refraining from his usual car quips, and watching the road very intently. I was feeling a relief unlike any other; even the gray sky gave a nostalgic sense of familiarity.

"Klaus, I know how you may be feeling, but don't stress. Even I don't know half the plan, and... in truth, neither does Draco," Lukas said, still with his eyes laser-focused on the road. He was most certainly given direction on what to say.

"Wait, why are you telling me this?" I asked after a short pause.

"Klaus… if we are to succeed—I know that you have been tossed all around lately, and it is necessary that we help. Draco may not have told you everything as he himself isn't aware of the full picture. This could be a hindrance in sight, or by intention but for now we don't know. All we know is that you are safe, you start at the paper tomorrow on Friday, just stay calm, the apartment is ready, yet I'm afraid I can't settle you in."

"Is the reason classified?" I asked snarkily. His following silence proved me right. "No matter, I still can't put into words what you have done for me, Lukas… I mean if not for you, I probably would still be in prison right now."

"Don't mention it, Klaus. If you want to repay the favor, just keep your head low and don't talk to anyone. Though charges may be disputed, rumors don't fizzle so quickly. Nobody will say anything to your face, but I know sooner or later they will come looking for answers," Lukas then smiled. "I bet you call that journalistic hunger, huh?"

"I guess so."

Once I reached the apartment, Lukas helped me out, my legs a little sore from travel. Upon reaching my apartment, I saw everything as good as it was before. The chair that had been broken was now replaced, my table fixed, and all cutlery clean. My bedroom looked decently maintained, without so much as dust on any counter. Lukas looked tall in admiration for the upkeep of my apartment.

"Well, buddy, I'll see you soon, just take some rest," he said as he was walking out.

"Sure haven't had enough of that," I said, and as he left, I stood in disbelief. I was really accustomed to the sound of the apartment after the door clicked shut for Lucas. Old, well-fitted but again wouldn't quite settle just right for comfort; silence engulfed me. Outside, the city was droning its ceaseless heart; involved, muffled by good stout walling, here, rather appeared to have been frozen in time.

I ran my fingers along the edge of the newly replaced table; smooth wood cool under my touch. So entirely restored it was unnerving, as though making good physically would somehow make good emotionally. It was not but lost behind shields of Polish and hundreds of repairs the burden of what had come, neither the apartment nor me.

I dropped my bag beside the couch and sank into the closest chair. My legs hurt from being holed up on an airline for too long, but the weariness that pressed most heavily down on me was different. It came from not knowing. Lukas flashed into my mind, with each line as a riddle wrapped in reluctance.

Draco didn't know everything? Difficult to believe. A man of that stature seemed to be pulling all the strings around him and suddenly in the dark? Wouldn't it be more that he just knew too much to share it?

Now, my gaze shifted toward the window, and I could still make out through the thin curtains the faint streetlight glow and now and then even a shadow as a body passed by. This was Berlin; it never actually slept, just watched, listened, and whispered its secrets to the brave ones who could catch its attention at that hour.

The envelope Lukas had given me now lay on the table, still unopened. I stared at it, its contents seeming to weigh heavily on the edges of my thoughts. It might well hold the promise of my next step – or downfall.

Not tonight, though.

At the moment, what I needed was sleep. Not just for my body but for my head - to give my brain a spin in the same grounding chaos of what had just happened to my life. And with a sigh, I pushed myself upright and started to tread toward the bedroom.

It was just as I had imagined it: firm, though not uncomfortable, the sheets crisp and faintly lavender-scented. I slipped under the covers; the cool fabric was soothing against my skin. My eyes traced the faint ceiling patterns while my mind wandered as fatigue finally overcame me.

Tomorrow there will be new challenges, new mysteries, and new threats. But for now, I could afford the luxury of sleep, lulled by the city in the distance whose heartbeat carried me through sleepless hordes into dreams that were uneasy.

I guess life could wait another day.

When I entered the office, it had a weary sense to it. No matter where I went, I couldn't see the people I once knew. Their faces appeared hollow, and there were shushed whispers as they walked by. Any relationship previously held was abandoned into the depths of their conscience. My former status of respect may not have existed. My office had become a decrepit mess, littered as if it came from a grotto. My name plaque had been disposed of, as had the rest of my framed stories. All that was left was the glass on the carpet and my defunct typewriter, with my name still etched on the side. As I went to pick it up, I could see the new name plaque lying barren on the floor. It was an odd name, Johann Seitz, someone whom I had most certainly not known, but who was now placed within what was supposed to be my space. I may have been gone, but my job was still there the whole time, was it not?

"Hello… Sir, are you lost?" I heard. "Because I don't know if you should be in my office without permission?" he asked in a puzzled manner. I realized that this is Johann that I needed. He looked quite young with few wrinkles and a decent glow to his skin. An intoxicating odor of tobacco and some cheap fragrance. His breath made me think he was inebriated, yet he wasn't poor in his composition, standing tall and proud amidst the mess.

"Ahhh, Mr Seitz—Isn't it? I'm glad to make your acquaintance. I'm Klaus Abel, and I've been abroad for a while, so I was surprised to see that my office seems to have changed ever since I left." The man had a persistent gleam on his smooth face. A smile so wide it was obviously fake.

"Well, as you know, there have been many changes going on around the world right now, and that has included our office right here. Don't worry, I may have taken your old office, but you'll get some replacement, and I will take it upon myself to ensure that you need Klaus."

The corridor outside Johann's—my—office stretched ahead, a narrow corridor seeming darker and less attractive than I recalled. The muted hum of typewriters and quiet voices barely carried past the heavy doors of adjacent offices, as if the building itself was a tomb. It seemed that every step I took echoed more loudly than it should have; it matched the tightness increasing inside my chest.

I tried to shake off the encounter, but the bitterness clung to me like smoke. The sight of my name scratched into the old typewriter stayed burned into my mind. That small, personal touch had survived even the upheaval of my absence, but the rest of my legacy had been swept aside like debris. Framed stories, accolades, respect—they had all been replaced by shattered glass and the smirking, false politeness of Johann Seitz.

I stopped at the end of the hall, looking back through the door into the office. The door was open, a few inches only, but I saw Johann moving around, tidying up on the desk that had been mine. He looked too comfortable, too relaxed. It wasn't where he belonged - but then neither did I anymore. As I turned away, a flood of memories came rushing back—late nights hunched over that very desk, the clatter of my typewriter as the words poured out, the thrill of seeing my name in print under a hard-won headline. This office had been more than a workspace; it had been a sanctuary, a place where I had fought for truth and carved out a name for myself in ink and sweat.

And now, it was gone, handed over to someone else without so much as a whisper of acknowledgment. The faces I passed in the hallway told the same story. People I had once worked alongside, shared drinks with, even considered allies, now avoided my gaze. Their hurried steps and murmured conversations stopped the moment I entered earshot, as though my presence was a stain they didn't want to acknowledge. Near the stairwell, I spotted Greta, a secretary who had always been kind to me.

She was sifting through a stack of mail, her brow furrowed in concentration. For a moment, I considered approaching her, asking what had happened while I was gone, but the tension in her posture made me hesitate. She hadn't looked up once, and I wasn't sure if it was because she didn't see me—or because she was trying not to. I secured a tighter grip on the strap of my bag, ready. The weight of those stares, the whispered judgments, was pressing down on me like an actual force. It was not just the office against me; it was also the people.

The stairs' cold marble steps led out into the distance, their polished surface dulled by years of hasty footfalls. I hesitated at the top, gripping the rail, staring down as if the act of getting down represented something more—an abandonment to obscurity, to anonymity. The thought was eating at me. Is that all there is? Is this what I've boiled down to? I thought.

I went back, making my way toward the other end of the corridor. There were still rooms in the office I hadn't visited yet. I did not want to leave without at least trying to reclaim a sliver of the familiarity I had lost. My eyes wandered over the framed photographs and awards along the walls, mementos of the paper's glory days. Once, I might have admired them. Now, they felt like reminders of a legacy I'd been cut out of. I found myself at the archives—a dimly lit, musty room at the far end of the hallway.

The door creaked open, and immediately the smell of old paper filled my nostrils. This was the place where the history of the paper was kept; each printed word was cataloged, boxed, and forgotten. I stepped inside and ran my fingers along the spines of the binders and stacks of yellowing newspapers. There was almost nothing in the room, a distant murmur of activity from the main office. My eyes landed on the corner of a folder, my name sprawled across the tab in a fading scrawl. I drew it out with shaking hands.

Copies of my old articles filled the folder, each headline a fragment of my past. Memories of interviews, late nights chasing leads, and the adrenaline of breaking a story came flooding back. Here, in this forgotten corner of the office, my work still existed. Forgotten by everyone else, but not erased. As I scanned the articles, the door opened. I swiveled my head, caught off guard by the sight of Johann standing there in the doorway.

His outline was silhouetted by the fluorescent lighting of the hall, and his typical smirk had given way to an expression of interest—almost wariness. "Digging through old ghosts, are we?" he asked as he stepped into the room. I straightened up, clutching the folder against my chest. "Something like that," I replied, my voice tight.

Johann sauntered closer, his polished shoes clicking against the floor. "You know, Klaus, I've read some of your work. Not bad, really. A bit dramatic at times, but you had a knack for getting to the heart of a story."

I frowned. There was something disquieting about the way he spoke, a measuring tone as if he were looking at some relic in a museum. "I didn't think you knew much about my work," I said, my voice sharper than I intended.

He shrugged, leaning casually against one of the shelves. "Oh, I like to know the history of the place I work. It's important to understand what came before, even if it's outdated."

The word hit like a slap, but I didn't flinch. "Outdated or not, those stories mattered," I said, holding up the folder. "They made a *difference*."

Johann nodded, his expression unreadable. "Perhaps. But times change, Klaus. The paper's focus has shifted. People want faster news, lighter stories. The world doesn't have the patience for deep dives anymore."

I put the folder down on the nearest shelf, my fingers running over the worn cover one last time. "Maybe the world doesn't have patience, but that doesn't mean the truth stops mattering."

For a moment, Johann said nothing. Then, with a slight tilt of his head, he replied, "We'll see if the readers agree. Here, let me take you to your new office."

As he led, I went to a place that I found as my own personal hell, a place that I had managed to avoid for as long as I have worked here: the Bullpen. Johann led me down the hall toward the bullpen with an air of practiced confidence, as if he owned this chaotic kingdom. His shoes clicked sharply on the tile, each step pounding my humiliation in. I trudged after him in silence, my jaw set hard, fingers clamped down on the strap of my bag as if that was the only thing keeping me tethered to reality. The faint, acrid smell of tobacco crept into the hallway, a prelude to the sensory onslaught waiting for me ahead. And then we were there. The bullpen.

It was worse than I remembered. Much worse.

The room stretched out before me like some cruel parody of a workplace, a sprawling mess of clutter, noise and indifference.

Desks were arranged in no discernible order, some pushed so close together that their occupants would have to navigate around each other just to stand, while others sat isolated like islands in a sea of chaos. Papers were everywhere—stacked precariously high, scattered across the floor, spilling out of cabinets whose doors hung perpetually ajar. Cigarette butts spilled from ashtrays and intermingled with half-full coffee cups, leaving ringed marks everywhere. The clean white walls turned gray and old with stains caused by the aging of time and lack of proper maintenance. The air itself was a punch to the face. It reeked of stale smoke, sour tangs of old coffee, and the musty undertones of damp paper, a smell that clung to your clothes, your hair, your skin—a smell that you couldn't shirk once you'd been here too long. It was the smell of defeat.

Just inside the doorway, Johann stopped. He turned toward me, giving me that god-awful smirk. "Here we are," he declared, opening up his arms and presenting me as if he'd opened up a show-and-tell with the Crown Jewels themselves. "Your new workspace, not exactly like the offices you're accustomed to, but surely you'll manage to find your groove."

Groove. The word hung in the air like an insult. I made myself nod, the movement stiff and unnatural, as I let my gaze sweep over the room. It was everything I had worked my entire career to avoid.

With every step into the room, dozens of eyes felt like they weighed on me. Conversations that had been boisterous moments before dropped to whispers or were completely silenced. People I'd once considered colleagues, even friends, watched me with expressions of pity and thinly veiled satisfaction. My return was no victory; it was a spectacle.

I had stopped right in the middle of the room, my bag still over my shoulder, my back to Johann. Now he stepped forward, crossing his arms, and went on smiling with an expression that seemed to have been painted on with a thick brush. "Well," he said, thumping me on the shoulder a little harder than necessary, "What do you think? Home sweet home, eh?"

Home. The word was a cruel joke. This wasn't home. This wasn't even a place I recognized. It was a battleground, a den of mediocrity and broken dreams, a space where ambition went to die.

"I think," I said slowly, carefully, "that it's going to take some getting used to."

Johann kept following me through the day, making slight jabs at my undone stature, always pestering me with the new changes. Certain people moving places, names of those recently retired. His constant following with his freakish smile made me hold back the urge to punch him. What used to be a place of solace was now turned into a barren hell, where nobody was there for me. Johann laughed, the sound grating against my ears. "Don't worry," he said, "you'll fit right in."

As he turned to leave, I had to ask him one final thing,

"Who are you, Johann?" I asked without expecting an answer. "Why are you here?"

He laughed, "I'm here so that you can fail, so that your little stunt won't go unnoticed, otherwise how can *we* as a society live, with a worm like you hiding through the crevices? You must be monitored if *he* is to be satiated."

Johann's words lingered in the air after he had sauntered out of the office, leaving behind a silence that felt heavier than the clatter of the typewriters.

"He is watching, you know."

The phrase clung to my thoughts like smoke curling into every corner of my mind, refusing to dissipate. He. Not a name, not a person—just an undefined figure whose existence mattered to just me alone. The ambiguity was maddening. Automatically, my initial instinct was to push it off, writing it off as Johann's usual dramatics, a parting shot intended to unsettle me, make me question every little thing under the sun. But something about how he said it, his deliberate pacing, the faint smirk, almost imperceptibly shifting in his tone, told me this was more than a game.

Watching his figure disappear into the hallway, the door swinging shut behind him, I looked back at the folder, my resolve hardening. I was stunned; it couldn't be over—not by a long shot. I approached what was meant to be my desk, which, in reality, was a shabby excuse for an assigned workspace - buried beneath mountain neglect. Stubs of cigarettes were spilling out of an over-brimming ashtray; crumpled papers with coffee stains on them piled into heaps that formed in a chaotic fashion; broken pens oozed dried-up ink across the surface; an utterly stale smell of mixed tobacco with something sour, resembling old food, hung in the air. Everything that desk is not is the very opposite of the former pristine, organized sanctuary I kept in my office.

The message was clear. This was not just neglect. It was the deliberate action of others who didn't care about my being back, or worse: because they resented it. The condition of the desk screamed at their indifference, their dismissal of everything I once stood for in this place. My fingers gripped the strap of my bag, anger simmering just below the surface. I would not let them see it, though - not yet.

I spent the next few hours awkwardly writing about whatever story I was sent, working with efficiency but no passion. After a few odd hours, it came the time to leave. I felt immense relief not being stuck in such a harsh environment, where every move was monitored, not by force, but by a hope that I would lose face.

By the time I reached the front entrance, my chest was tight with anger and frustration. The glass doors swung open with a creak, and I stepped out into the bustling Berlin streets. The air was cold, biting against my skin, but it carried with it the distinct scent of the city—smoke, rain-soaked pavement, and a hint of something metallic that I could never quite place.

I stood there for a moment, letting the chaos of the city wash over me. Taxis honked, street vendors called out their wares, and a steady stream of people flowed past, each one caught up in his own world. Berlin was alive in a way the office no longer was, a contradiction of vibrancy and tension that felt both overwhelming and exhilarating.

But even in the noise and commotion, I couldn't get rid of this feeling of loss. This was a city that had always represented contrasts, a delicate balance between ambition and despair, beauty and brutality. And now, I was stuck somewhere in the middle, trying to find my footing in a place that didn't feel like home anymore.

I took a deep breath and started walking. The cobblestones beneath my feet were slick from an earlier rain, and the chill in the air was enough to make me pull my coat tighter around me. The rhythm of the city began to seep into my bones, and with it came a flicker of determination.

Johann might have stolen my office, and the people inside that building may have turned their backs on me, but that wasn't the end of my story. The city loomed over me, towers and labyrinthine streets, a challenge I was more than ready to face. I didn't know where this path led, but one thing was certain: I wasn't done. Not by a long shot.

They could try to erase me, but I'd find a way to write myself back in.

Chapter 14

CURTAIN CALL

July 29, 1939, Berlin, Germany

It's been almost two weeks since I came back to Berlin, and in that time I have never felt worse. All that I had built, all the reputation that I had, all the praise I was given—came falling down. Now I can only put my head down, suffering from failure rather than a lack of challenge. No longer could I be happy with what I had because I had the lingering taste from the relative abundance once provided to me. Typing away at the desk didn't matter; I would still be in the same place.

Lukas has been out of the city since he picked me up from the train station, and I haven't had word of him since. Selva has never been easy to reach, and Victoria may as well not even be relevant by now.

It was almost as if I were floating along through the city, invisible and forgotten, as it throbbed with heat and noise, never changing. The café that used to greet me by name was now full of unfamiliar faces. The newspaper stands that no longer bore my bylines on the front page were showcasing other illustrious works such as those of Johann Seitz and names that felt foreign to me.

Here stood one corner; I stared upwards at the mighty buildings gleaming under streetlights, too much of a contrast to my fading spirit; and there under it stood unyielding and proud while I cowered under the weight of my failures. Each puff would create a silvery cloud from my mouth in the cold air, enunciating that a man is breathing but not truly living. His shoulders drooped beneath the weight of all the times he had lived when he had been someone.

Eventually, I crossed again to that park, full of benches that gave me shelter during the times of my highs and lows in my career. But that park too had changed. It was now quiet with giggles of lovebirds and only the bark of their pet far off to disturb them. I sat on the creaking bench, running my fingers through my hair, that ever-faint smell of ink and paper still lingering on my skin. So I wondered for the first time in years: Was it worth it? All those sacrifices, those sleepless nights spent working, now the friends who pushed me so far are no longer with me—what had it all added up to? A typewriter with my name deep in it, a legacy that had withered away in my absence, and this city no longer had a space for me.

The bitterness that had been sustaining me over all these weeks started to dissolve, but in its place came something colder and more hollow. I no longer hated the people with whom I had been replaced or the systems that had moved on, assuming their right to go on without me. I was angry with myself—angry for holding on to a past that no longer existed, for not knowing how to let go.

Making it to my apartment felt more foreign than ever, all gray and dull, unchanged through this endeavor. The angels are still staring at me, their eyes still blank and cold. It became nothing short of a habit to watch them as I cascaded upon the stairs. Entranced in the hope that their eyes will follow me. This pattern was consistent every day, after going up, I would go to my kitchen and start to prepare dinner, while thinking about what book to read.

Once I finished dinner and my reading, I would try my best to sleep, but couldn't ever find myself doing so. I would rather start a cleaning spree or try to write in my journal, yet the page was blank. No matter the time I spent, it was still blank, going into the early morning hours, then only exhaustion could get the better of me. All in all, this cycle repeated, with only the slightest changes.

Today when I went up, I expected the same, only to see that the one man whom I had been completely oblivious to until now was inside my apartment.

"Selva! What are you doing here?" I asked in a voice too loud. I didn't recall giving him my keys. I got so struck when I entered the apartment and found him sitting there. Selva. He lounged in my armchair, whiskey glass in hand, looking like he'd been there forever. It churned in my stomach; I couldn't account for whether it was anger or unease - both actually.

He didn't flinch, didn't even bother to look startled. Instead, he swirled the whiskey in his glass as if he owned the place, tilting his head ever so slightly as he glanced at me. "Ah, Klaus," he said, his voice smooth and calm, as though I were the intruder. "You really are late. I thought I'd have to start without you."

"Start what?" I dropped my bag onto the table, the thud punctuating my question. My anger flared, hot and sharp. "And don't dodge the question. How did you get in here?"

Selva waved a dismissive hand, as if that did not matter. "You are always concentrating on all the wrong things," he said with a faint smile that boiled my blood. "Why I am here should be the question, not how."

"That's not a reply," I stepped forward and glared. "You don't trust just barging into my life like this. I don't work for you anymore, Selva."

"Ah, but you misunderstand, my dear Klaus," he chuckled - a low, gravelly sound that grated on my nerves. "This isn't about work. This is about survival." He leaned forward slightly, fixing me with a look that made me feel like a chess piece on a board I couldn't see. "You may not have noticed, but the world is changing. And quickly. I thought I'd stop by to see how my favorite journalist is handling the storm."

I scoffed, crossing my arms. "Handling it just fine, thank you. Though I'm sure you've already heard otherwise."

"Fine?" Selva rose from the chair with an unsettling grace, the glass of whiskey now forgotten on the table beside him. He approached me, his steps slow and deliberate, his voice dropping to a tone that sent a chill down my spine. "Klaus, I've seen corpses with more life in them than you right now. Look at you - wasting away in this dingy little flat, hiding from the world like a beaten dog. That's not the Klaus Abel I knew."

His words hit me like a train. "You don't know what you're talking about."

"Don't I?" he said, stepping forward just a few feet away, boring his gaze into mine. "And I know exactly what's happened to you. You've let them win. You've allowed this city, this paper, and all these pathetic little men to push you into a corner, and now you're too afraid to take a swing."

My fists clenched tight, the heat rising in my chest. "What do you want from me, Selva? What are you really doing here?"

"I am here," he said, his voice softening but losing none of its intensity, "because you're too valuable to waste. Berlin may have forgotten you, Klaus, but I haven't. There's still work to be done. But not from behind that desk in the bullpen. No, the world is bigger than that. Like Johann taking all your prestige, your talents being wasted in the corner of the paper. You need grit, hunger, Klaus; otherwise, we won't be able to save you. My efforts will be in vain."

"What are you saying?" My voice unwittingly cracked.

"I'm saying it's time to leave this place behind," he said, his eyes glinting with something I couldn't exactly place. "Berlin is a sinking ship, Klaus. If you stay here, it'll drag you down with it. Come with me. There are bigger things at play—things you can't even begin to imagine. But if you're with me, you'll have the chance to make a real difference."

I stared at him; my mind spun with the dizzying revelations. Partly, I wanted to laugh in his face and tell him to get out and never come back. But there was a smaller, quieter part of me that hesitated. What if he was right? What if I wasted away here?

Selva put forth: "Think through it." He turned his body away and roped off his coat, which dangled down from the back of the chair. "But all in good time. The world won't wait for you to think it through."

By the door, he halted and turned back toward me with a whisper of a smile on his lips: "Oh, and Klaus," he continued, "you should lock your doors next time. Not every person walking into your life will have a good interest in you." His eyes glinted toward the newspaper on the table. "Get ready, Klaus, soon you'll have change, the monotony will stop and all your little answers may find an end, but truly consider if this is the path you want to take…the one of those who will live in pain, but push the ball forward. Or choose to live on the sidelines, in the bliss of ignorance, and get that lack of responsibility you will never find again."

And just like that, he was gone. The door clicked into silence after him, leaving me standing in my apartment with the lingering whiff of whiskey. For the first time in weeks, something curled and unsettled in me—not something I had felt in what felt like a lifetime: a flicker of purpose.

It was the last sound I expected it to make, but the door clicked shut behind him. I stood transfixed, staring into the space he'd just vacated and breathing an unsought welcome of whiskey and the well-worn leather of his coat. My mind raced on a million tangents, with each thought clawing over one another for top position, yet they brought me back again and again to the same maddening point: Selva's words.

He had entered as if the place belonged to him, and in fact, it somewhat did. Not the apartment itself, no - but my thoughts, my attention. Something had planted itself deep inside me, something that even fury or disbelieving tantrums could not shake off.

His voice reverberated in me like a resonating echo rippling through the silence.

"Berlin is a sinking ship, Klaus. If you stay here, it will take you down with it."

I sank down onto the edge of the couch, staring at the glass of whiskey left behind by him. A faint circle of condensation clung beneath it to the tabletop, giving it what felt like an odd symbolic presence. Selva had visited and moved on, leaving an indelible impression behind.

Why had I let him get to me? He always had that incredibly annoying knack of seeing straight through all those walls built around me, stripping his way behind the carefully constructed armor I hid behind. And, damn! He was right—about everything: the city, the paper, my so-called career. Buried me, just like the pressure of that glass, as if it leaves nothing at all to give.

For a moment, I stared at the glass before reaching out to it. The whiskey was still warm from his hand, and I drank it down in a single sharp gulp, definitely. It burned all the way down, but not enough to extinguish the fire he left behind. That slight flicker of something I had not felt for weeks, maybe months: purpose. Or was it anger? They were so tightly knit, I couldn't tell anymore.

My gaze had drifted to the coat rack hung close to the door where my own worn-out jacket dangled like a ghost from better days. Selva's words were heavier than the jacket itself.

"You have let them win. You have been cornered by this city, this paper, by these pathetic little men."

I hated him for saying it. Hated him for being right. But it also had a hypnotic quality to the way he said it, as if he knew

I would follow him long before I did. That sparkle in his eye as he walked away wasn't arrogance but certainty. Selva never made a move without knowing the outcome. Life was chess to him; he was always five steps ahead.

But could I trust him? The question lingered, gnawing at the edges along the rim of my mind. Selva was dangerous, not only because of his influence but also because he could alter reality according to his whims. It made you create that reality in your mind. He drew you into it and narrowed your perspective until you could see nothing else. You could not get out once you were in.

I stood and paced the room, the floorboards creaking beneath my restless steps. My apartment felt smaller now, as if it had compressed all the air, prompting the walls to close in around me. The thought of spending another night here, alone with all my doubts and failures, made my skin crawl.

I thought of the typewriter sitting on the desk, its dusty keys locked inside it. I had not written anything substantial for weeks. It was irritating that the empty, glaring pages mocked me in reflection with my own stagnation.

Selva's words rang sharper in my ears this time. "Come with me. There are bigger things at play – things you can't even begin to imagine." What bigger things? What was he up to? And why did he need me? What would I sacrifice?

Those were the questions, anyway, and they were enough to prod me into motion. I grabbed my coat from the rack, familiar worn fabric slipping easily under my fingers. My head was spinning with uncertainties, but I knew one thing for certain: I couldn't stay here. Not tonight. Not like this.

The city outside was still very much teeming with life, buzzing in all the familiar chaos. I stepped out into the night, the cool air biting into my skin, and let my feet carry me forward. Where to? I'm not sure. But for the first time in a long time, I wasn't just drifting along.

Immediately, I went to my car and rushed out to where my car was, speeding along the road. I knew I still had time. Going through the pipeline of the streets, I couldn't stop thinking, unable to repress the lust I had to go faster. It was only when I saw the bleak gray building and a surprisingly large sign that I knew I was always in the right headspace. Marching up the stairs, I could see the decrepit interior, countless people lazing around, trash all over the floor. I went to my office only to see Johann sitting there, all smug-like.

I squinted suspiciously. "What job? All you do is laze all day while the rest of us work like dogs."

"Is that not what you did, Klaus? Complain day by day about your fellow workers, who eventually started to care less and less about *you*. Thinking that you could do as you please just because people decided to deal with you? All you are is an investment in the German mind. An illness that propagates itself with all the self-righteous arrogance it wants without even for a second thinking about the bigger picture!"

You gained your position by sheer luck on petty half-bit stories. I climbed from the bottom, using any advantage to help bring me forward. I may have needed to help take you down, but not all is fair... is it now Klaus—so why do *I* deserve to be here? First consider why you should even be asking." Johann's face was red, his hair becoming a little undone. My anger quelled due to his immense presence, yet I wasn't defeated. I had only known of this man's existence for less than a month, so why should I even listen? I gave him a piercing blank stare. Unable to go forward, it looked as if Johann wouldn't give up.

"Johann… what gives you such boldfaced confidence that you feel you have a right to give such orders to me? While I may not be perfect, I can see right through you. An aristocratic, two-faced snob who is unable to think straight. You may not be highly educated, but you will certainly listen to anyone or anything. Yet I still find it peculiar that *you* would have such thoughts about me without at least looking into the waters to see how much better you fare."

A cunning smile crept across his face; it seemed that something unexpected had come to fruition for Johann. "*He* will be happy… yes, he will."

"What do you—"

"Silence, Klaus… give me silence. Because no matter what you say, *he* will always prevail," Johann started to look down. He began to shake uncontrollably, as if this "he" was an omnipotent being.

"Who is '*he*' and why should I give him so much heedance?" I asked, losing a little bit of the fear that I once had of Johann, who was quivering like a spastic in the office.

"Oh… I shouldn't say his name, but you should meet him already. He did tell me that he 'took care of you'. I should be grateful now, shouldn't I? Respect his wishes and all that jazz…" I was beginning to get the idea of who it was; confirmation was necessary though.

"Landas looking for me?" I asked with a forced indifference.

"Of course you fool, of course," Johann looked to be slowly losing it, with all his words becoming slurred, his head kept shaking as he spoke, all the while he couldn't look forward, his eyes (and therefore his body) kept jerking around in a mix of far and grandeur over Landa. Why do you believe that you just lost everything overnight? No, it was all Landa, starting a false rumor to losing your job, it was all his— I'm just a man getting what is his own from fate. Maybe I shouldn't get involved; after all, Landa is a very important man, and you… are more or less a rock in his path. Yet it confounds me how much importance he lends in your favor, as if you could be something *more*?" I stayed silent, looking at the man degrading in front of me, his true nature becoming ever more present, his case wasn't meritless, yet I still couldn't understand why he seemed to be able to have reason, in that voice of pure delusional fantasy."

"How about a truce, we set aside the differences, and give ourselves the respect we may have discarded, and let this feud end, god knows I have enough going on anyways."

"A truce," he said, gesturing with his cigar. "With Landa back in town looking for you, your days in this city could be numbered."

I shook my head in disbelief. "You're nuts if you think I'm going to join you in anything, just allow the past to wither."

Johann shrugged casually. "Suit yourself," he said, standing from my desk, tossing his cigar on the floor, and crushing it under his boots. "But when Landa's plan eventually comes to fruition - and it will - at some point, you'll regret turning down this opportunity."

He then took a pause, collected himself, and cleaned his surroundings. After about five minutes, he returned to me,

"Anything else, Klaus, now that we are on new terms with each other, at least in person." He still had a slurred undertone.

"Yes, I quit," Johann said with a look that baffled me. Without saying a word, Johann sauntered out of my office, leaving me alone with my thoughts once again. The idea of working alongside Johann made me sick to my stomach, but what was Selva planning? And why did Johann seem so certain of its success?

In the midst of all this, the management of syllogistic leave from my office was careful, leaving me alone with those thoughts again. The prospect of being seated by Johann's side made me holoskian, but what was Selva's plan? Why was Johann so sure of his success?

I needed more information. I needed to know if Draco would get the message.

The moment I stepped outside the door, an unfamiliar sense of lightness enveloped me, something strange yet oddly comforting for my experience. Everything around me was unchanged—the same streets, buildings, and city—but it was of no account. It mattered that I had changed. Feeling a happiness long awaited, I considered myself giddy.

But once I reached the open gate, all of that happiness disappeared; that brief sensation was all but a distant memory, for when I saw that gate, it was as if the walls were caving in, his demeanor friendly, yet I knew it was everything but. Hans Landa. He still stood, with the impossibly perfect posture, clothes that were so pristine you would wonder if you were in a store. A smile so fake, it had a slight charm.

It didn't seem that all was well, though; his face was becoming longer, less bright. The new rule was taking its toll on people like Landa as well. He turned to me, giving that solitary look I had seen when we first met. Underlying the facade was someone deeply disturbed, someone who wouldn't care for life or death in the moment, but those choices would weigh on his conscience. It was a spectacle in a man that was both indicative and tragic.

"Hello Klaus," he said without giving a glance. "What are the chances that we may meet again? I'm happy you got your post back after all that conspiracy nonsense." He spoke through gritted teeth and utter frustration.

Hans Landa's presence was like a phantom materializing in the dim twilight of Berlin's streets. As I approached the gate, his figure became more distinct, his impeccable posture and immaculate uniform cutting a sharp contrast against the dreary backdrop. He stood as if the world around him had no power to intrude upon his personal perfection, though something in his expression hinted at weariness even from a distance.

"Ah, Klaus," he said, his voice carrying that irritating lilt of mock politeness. "What fortuitous timing. I was just thinking about you."

"Were you?" I replied, keeping my tone neutral, though my muscles tensed instinctively. "I didn't think I was much interested to you anymore."

"Oh, no," Landa answered, broadening his smile and clasping his gloved hands behind his back. "You've always fascinated me, Klaus. A curious cat, with eyes that can creep too near a lion's den without realizing its danger."

"Must you always speak in riddles, Landa?" I asked, crossing my arms. "Or is this another game of yours?"

"Games?" His eyebrows arched theatrically, as if the suggestion offended him. "Come now, don't be so cruel. You wound me. I found our last chat enlightening. May I give you my opinion?"

"Funny, I don't recall inviting you to any of them."

He chuckled, the sound low and gravelly, and stepped closer. "Invitations are overrated. I find the best conversations happen when they're least expected. Like this one."

"So let's get to the point," I said, my patience thin. "What do you want?"

"What do I want?" Landa parroted, pretending to sound surprised. "Ah, such a direct question. I like that about you, Klaus. No frills, straight to the heart of things." He paused, his eyes glinting with something I couldn't quite read. "But perhaps the better question is, what does Berlin want from you?"

I narrowed my eyes. "If you're here to deliver a cryptic warning, save your breath. I've had enough of those to last a lifetime."

"Oh, I'm not here to warn you," he said, shaking his head. "I'm here to congratulate you."

"Congratulations!" I scoffed. "For what? Surviving another day in this city?"

"Partly, yes," he admitted, his smile twisting into something sharper. "But mostly, for being chosen. You've been given an assignment, Klaus. A very important one."

"Is that so?" I replied, folding my arms across my chest. "And what exactly have I been 'chosen' for?"

Landa's smile grew wider, his teeth flashing in the dim light. "Ah, but where's the fun in simply telling you? Let's savor the moment, shall we?"

"I'm not in the mood for your theatrics," I snapped. "Spit it out, Landa."

He let out a mock sigh, disappointed by my lack of patience. "Very well, if you insist. You've been assigned to travel to Poland. Next month, to be precise. You'll be journaling the Reich's advancements."

"I quit Landa!" I exclaimed. The whole room stopped to look at me.

"And we will promptly fix this miscalculation. Welcome back, Herr Abel! You will start your next assignment in *Poland*. Don't make me repeat myself."

Landa said all this with a predatory look; his whole purpose here was to strip me of all my self-accomplishments and worth, into just another mold for them to use.

The words hung in the air like a guillotine blade poised to drop. I stared at him, struggling to mask the unease churning in my gut. "Poland," I repeated flatly. "And what exactly am I supposed to journal there?"

"Oh, I'm sure you'll find plenty to write about," Landa said smoothly, his tone maddeningly nonchalant. "After all, history is about to be made. Don't you want to be part of it?"

"History," I echoed bitterly. "Is that what they're calling it now?"

"Call it whatever you like," Landa said with a shrug. "But you're going, Klaus. The Reich has *decided*, and we both know what that means." Giving a little chuckle at the end.

"What if I refuse?" The words slipped out before I could stop them, though I knew the answer.

Landa tilted his head, his smile never wavering. "Refuse?" he repeated, as if the concept amused him. "Klaus, you've been around long enough to know how these things work. There's no refusing. Only compliance."

"And if I don't comply?" I challenged myself, though my voice lacked conviction.

He chuckled again, a soft, mocking sound that made my skin crawl. "Oh, Klaus. You're smarter than that. Don't make me spell it out."

I clenched my jaw, the weight of his words settling over me like a shroud. "Why me?" I asked, trying to keep my voice steady.

"Why not you?" he countered, his hands spreading wide as if the answer were self-evident. "You're one of Berlin's finest, Klaus—a storyteller, a man with a discerning eye for detail. The Reich values that. You should feel honored."

"Honored," I echoed, the word heavy with sarcasm. "Yes, of course. How could I feel anything else?"

Landa's smile wavered for the briefest moment, and I sensed a flicker of something—maybe pity or regret. But just as swiftly as it emerged, it vanished. "Enjoy what time you have left here," he said, his tone softening ever so slightly. "The next chapter will be transformative."

"And what about you, Landa?" I inquired, my voice sharper than I had meant it to be. "Will you be part of this 'transformation' as well?"

His smile reappeared, yet it failed to touch his eyes. "I'll be precisely where I'm needed," he remarked with an air of mystery. "As will you."

With that, he turned on his heel and walked away, the click of his polished boots against the pavement echoing behind him. I stood there, watching him go, my fists clenched tightly at my sides, the weight of his news settling over me like a leaden sky. Poland. The invasion. It was soon to come, and I found myself being pulled into the very heart of it.

⸻ •❖• ⸻

Chapter 15

A HERO

August 13, 1939, Berlin

Time has been fleeting unlike ever before. Minutes became hours, hours became days, and before I knew it, I was already being briefed for what was to come. Lined up in front were rows of soldiers with incomprehensible swear words being thrown around. The pandemonium reached a point where I wasn't even cognisant.

"Wake up, Reporter!" I heard as I was beginning to doze off. His voice was a knife cutting through the chaos. "Do you think this is a vacation, Herr Abel?"

The general was precise; he was powerful and filled his room with the kind of authority that did not need words for orders. With a neat and perfect uniform, with all buttons polished to a mirror shine, and every bit of the posture as straight as if the weight of the world was on his shoulders and refused to bend him. His face was lined by sharp creases, etching stern composure into it; his piercing eyes were scanning everyone there, calculation mixed with a quiet intensity. Though stiff and unmoving, there was a sort of subdued energy beneath that was always in check and ready to blow open into action at any given time. I swallowed hard, and every soldier turned and looked at me. I was embarrassed. I responded, "No, sir."

His tone was almost disdainful, but he said 'good.' "If there's no room for daydreamers out there on the front lines." You're here to watch, record, and report. You'll be just as much a part of this as any of them," but make no mistake, you. The soldiers were unreadable, but their faces were too uncomfortably attentive, gesturing toward.

The weight of the officer's words fell over me as he moved on. I glanced at the men in front of me, and they were a tapestry of emotion. Others stood with rigid discipline, their eyes straight ahead, showing nothing. Some twitched their hands, and others darted their gazes around the room. Their voices were low, but their tension was clear: a few whispered quietly to one another.

One soldier caught my eye. His face wasn't old, not even much aged, but his eyes, dark and hollow, spoke of things seen too much. His jaw was set, and there was a quiet determination in the set of his jaw, but he clutched his rifle tightly, his knuckles white. My throat was tightening. They were not just soldiers, but men about to be dropped into a maelstrom, a storm out of which there would be no escape.

The officer's voice droned endlessly, listing objectives, protocols, and expectations, but my mind drifted again, to the enormity of what I was about to face. This wasn't just a war for the soldiers; it was a war for me too. I was supposed to write down their lives, difficulties, triumphs, and failures. I would write every word, and the weight of their sacrifices and the judgment of history would be with every word.

A cold fear spread through my chest. But what if I wasn't up to it? What if I didn't capture the truth? What if, in the end, my words, my observations, didn't matter?

"Abel!" My spiraling thoughts were cut through by the officer's voice again. His expression was unreadable, but he was standing closer now. "Your transport leaves at dawn."

I nodded, trying to keep my voice firm through the storm of doubt inside me. The soldiers filed out, their boots echoing against the concrete floor, and I stayed where I was. I was about to face something so big. I could only admire these men; no matter how scared they were, they carried a quiet strength. However, they could do nothing to avoid marching into the unknown, lives subject to orders and duty.

I was no soldier, yet my own duty pressed on me equally heavily. It scared me, but I knew it stirred something deep within me, something I hadn't felt in a long time. I should be able to face the storm if they could. It was too late to turn back now. For better or worse.

'It wasn't easy these past weeks, my apartment had been turned over inside and out. All that I was accustomed to was again stripped away. Contact with the outside world was useless, as I was sized up for the pain of war. Nothing I had done before could help; all that I was known for was forgotten in the minds of the men who examined me, prepping me with the reassurance of safety and respect upon arrival, how I'll be looked upon as 'a model citizen' in the eyes of the Führer.'

He was the root of all this, the years I have worked, the reputation I had built and burned, all was because of him. Why? Did I have freedom in this 'new' world as it was foretold, or am I just meant to be a slave for those to step on?"

Selva looked at me, troubled; this was days ago. "I'm proud you can at least face the music, Klaus. I understand how…" His voice trailed off, but it lacked his usual sense of control. Sitting around in my shabby, half-empty apartment, it felt as if I was killing a version of myself. I looked at Selva, and he didn't look directly at me. The image was clear as if it had happened moments ago, though it was days ago. He said he was proud that, at least, I could face the music, Klaus, his words deliberate but unsteady, with the faintest crack under his usual veneer of control. "I understand how…" His voice had faded, apparently leaving the thought unfinished, as if he, too, couldn't quite say what was there, just beneath the surface. He wasn't like that, and that made it even more unsettling.

I sat now in the dim, enclosed shell of my shabby, half-full apartment, killing a version of myself. Slowly, agonizingly, piece by piece, not all at once. This space, filled with the stuff of my own inadequacies, each passing moment seemed to chip away at the person I was, or the person I thought I was. The room was too quiet, and the kind of quiet that made it impossible to get away from your own thoughts.

When he heard of my decision, Draco seemed proud. Offering his help with what appeared to be a feverish kind of fervor, he would have come immediately. It wasn't pity, per se, but it was there, an air of inevitability, of him helping me less to show me kindness and more a duty he'd given his word to. However, none of his efforts could dislodge the idea that it was all for nothing. Why would anyone put any energy into people like me? A man who was practically useless, who had spent much of his life teetering on the verge of action but never quite jumping.

I was told I was intelligent, above average even, but what had that done to me? My so-called intellect was just a shield for me, a way to explain my inaction and failures. It was now a millstone around my neck, a fact I could not shake off that I had fallen so far short of who I could have been.

They have their own burdens to bear, heavier than anything I've had to carry — Victoria and Lukas. Always moving forward as if some unseen force was propelling him along, Lukas, with his unflinching sense of duty. Victoria, so sharp and unyielding, and carrying a sadness she never let slip past her steely exterior. I envied their strength in ways I could never emulate, but they were strong in ways I wasn't.

I know that will be the true test, and soon, I will be on my own. No one will be there to catch us if it all gets too much. The thought is sobering, and it's both dread and determination. That may be what Selva had been trying to say, in his own faltering way, that facing the music means embracing the solitude that comes with it.

But there's a strange sort of freedom in that solitude as well. A slight chance to rewrite who I am. To stop being the guy who has to be pulled out of the fire and become somebody who can stand in the fire and not flame out. It's terrifying, and it's the first glimmer of hope I've had in what feels like an eternity.

The sun continued to edge its way below the horizon, making the shadows in the room lengthen and everything turn a muted grayish light. It was fitting, somehow, a liminal space, in between day and night, as I had been in between who I used to be and who I might become.

Once more, I thought of Selva's troubled expression, Draco's fervent support, Victoria, and Lukas, and all the rest whose lives had touched mine in ways that had made me into someone I could not reverse. I didn't know if I deserved their faith in me, but it didn't matter if I did or not. What was important was what I did with it.

He was dying, and the person I was, the man who had spent so much of his life observing from the sidelines, the one who was too afraid or too uncertain to step into the fray, was dying. Perhaps that wasn't such a bad thing. Perhaps something new could be born in his place. Something braver, something stronger. Or maybe not. Maybe I would fail, as I have failed so many times before.

I was ready to find out, but for the first time. Rather than playing with the lights, step onto the stage, ready to be more than just a placid audience, but someone who can have a legacy and truly make a difference.

As I now snapped back, looking at the militia in front of me. The sound of boots stomping against packed earth in rhythmic stomp: a relentless drumbeat in my chest. A wave of disciplined chaos swept across the field at soldiers, moving in near-perfect unison. Sharp, unyielding commands sliced through the cold morning air barked. I was a spectator from the edge of it all, vast and unrelenting, and yet I couldn't shake the feeling of complicity.

The view from my perch was unobstructed, a sea of gray uniforms moving in uniform mechanical precision across the training grounds. There was the metallic clink of rifles being readjusted, the hiss of breath escaping compressed jaws, an occasional shouted correction from an officer, a sonata of control and strain. It should have been exhilarating, impressive, on such a scale. Instead, it just left a knot in my stomach, tightening with every passing moment.

I held the worn notebook in my hands, and the blank pages looked at me accusingly, casting condemnation into my emptiness. What was I supposed to capture here? The efficiency? The determination? The inevitability of it all? Words were weak, a feeble attempt to cram this massive *into* something as tiny as a page.

I wished I couldn't but from my vantage point, I could see the faces of the men below. Their eyes were full of fear, buried deep but visible if you looked closely. Resolve was a volatile cocktail that could explode at any moment, and it mingled with determination. Some of them looked at one another; they exchanged glances, words whispered between them like fragile threads. I saw others staring ahead, their faces locked in masks of steel-faced determination.

What did they see when they looked at me, a man standing apart, detached, scribbling these notes that might one day shape how this moment would be remembered? Did they hate me for being so distant? Did they envy it? Or was I just invisible, another thing in the background of their world?

I jolted back to the present with a sharp command. A soldier misstepped and reprimanded so sharply that it sounded like his misstep cut the air. I saw him snap back into line, and his movements were rigid, almost robotic. I couldn't write it down on my page.

I thought about Selva's words, spoken in their usual unnerving calm. He had said, 'Face the music, Klaus, your eyes heavy with anticipation, and some other look I just couldn't identify.' Now it lingered with me as I watched the men march forward, their steps in sync yet thickened with the weight of something I couldn't see.

The chill of the morning air seeped through my coat. I shifted uncomfortably. His enthusiasm about my assignment had been almost infectious. The enormity of what lay ahead now pressed down on me like a physical force, but I stood here. What was I supposed to do with all this? How was I supposed to make sense of it, to make it make sense, to distill it into something coherent and truthful?

The field lay before me, a staging of discipline and desperation, and I felt like an intruder in someone else's story. Yet I couldn't look away. Each one was an essential cog in a machine, replaceable. I couldn't see their faces anymore, a mass of humanity distilled to its most basic form.

My hands closed over the notebook, its pages as blank as my thoughts. The morning passed, and the afternoon, and the shadows stretched across the training grounds, and I stayed there, rooted to the spot. Unbroken rhythm of the soldiers, unbroken purpose. I felt the weight of their world and the crushing inadequacy of mine, and I watched. The whole preparation felt as if it were a fever-dream. Constantly getting tips on survival and how to hide and gather as much information as possible. I was told that this was the truth, yet I wasn't allowed to share it.

My headlights always changed into something so vague the message became a footnote. Any truth said will be constricted to where only one will be victorious. It was for salvation I did it, yet it still pained me, though I never had the strength to change to speak my voice.

"Abel! Do you have your belongings set?" I didn't care to remember the general's name or face; it was all blank.

"Yes, Sir!"

"The border will station you until the end of the month, miss no detail, and most of all, keep safe. 'Operation Case White' is a team effort after all."

"I understand and won't let you down, sir," I said with a quiver.

"I know you won't..." The rest, I couldn't remember.

⸻ ◆ ⸻

Chapter 16

STATIONARY

31 August 1939, Danzig

I stepped off the train in Danzig, the air was thick and heavy. The station was a hive of energy, a chaotic energy that felt contagious, but I couldn't tell if it was excitement or fear. Probably both. I moved through the crowd beneath me; gravel crunching under my boots, my satchel pressing against my side like a reminder of my task here—tools for documenting a story: Pens, notebooks, my typewriter.

The Free City wasn't free. Something, like smoke, was sitting in the air, clinging to tension. Civilians were hurried and uneasy, while soldiers moved purposefully through the station with their crisp uniforms and precise movements. The conversations were clipped and sharp, spoken in short barks of orders or growls of engines outside. Standing there with my leather bag and polished boots, feeling like an outsider, even more so than usual, I tried not to get swept up in the tide.

I stepped out into the streets, and there was a strange familiarity and alienation. They were still here, the cobblestones, the spires of the old churches, the neat rows of buildings. The atmosphere had changed, however. It was a bold and suffocating view of German flags hanging from windows and balconies. Soldiers and crates filled trucks that rumbled by. I watched as a boy in a uniform, not much older than I had been when I started writing, climbed onto one of the vehicles, his face pale but determined.

Weaving through the throng of people, I wandered deeper into the city. The marketplace was quiet, usually a place as noisy and alive as possible. Vendors barely looked up as I passed; stalls were half-empty. The smell of bread was faintly wafting out of a bakery door ajar. I stood there momentarily watching children playing at the bottom of the steps to a boarded-up shop. Their laughter was jarring, a fragile echo of what was normal, a city holding its breath.

I stopped short when I turned into the square near the Marienkirche. The sight froze me for a moment: Rifles in hand, soldiers stood on the steps of the church, lined up, faces a mix of discipline and something more human, anxiety, perhaps. A tight circle of officers stood across the square, talking in low voices. I couldn't hear much, but the words I heard—logistics, timing, orders—tightened the knot in my stomach. A voice came through my thoughts as I lingered. "Herr Abel?"

A young soldier was approaching me. His face was pale, but his stance was resolute; he looked barely out of school. I answered, my voice steady enough for it to pass for calm. "General requests your presence. He's in the Rathaus, room 15." He pointed toward the massive building on the edge of the square.

Following him, I nodded, and my boots struck the cobblestones in a rhythm that sounded too loud for the relatively quiet. I took in the city as we walked. The buildings had ornate and inviting facades, but now, the trappings of occupation—flags, posters, soldiers at every corner—weighed them down.

My nerves were frayed by the time that we reached the Rathaus. The square stretched from the building, with its Gothic arches casting long shadows. The soldier opened the heavy wooden door, and I stepped inside; the air was suddenly cool and still.

My eyes adjusted to the dim light, and I paused momentarily. I replayed the scenes I'd just walked through—faces, soldiers, tension in the marketplace, that oppressive weight of those flags. I was here to write what was happening and to chronicle history, but history seemed to be swallowing me whole.

This was Danzig, where something was about to become irreversible. I was here, in the tide, and I didn't know if I was documenting the story or if the story was documenting me.

In my hands, I only had a letter that I received before I left from the Minister of Propaganda, Joseph Goebbels. I had heard of him around the office, but only in passing. You'd think people spoke of him as if he could command attention just walking into a room, like a stage actor drawing in all eyes. It was surprising to find out he was smaller than I had anticipated—he was almost diminutive, and there was something about the way he carried himself that you couldn't miss. His face was often described as sharp, angular, as if his face were made for his role. But his slicked-back hair and piercing eyes only seemed to accentuate the image people painted of him.

I was told his voice was his most powerful tool - rich, resonant, and hypnotic. People who heard him speak said his words could make you feel as though you were swept up in a kind of magic, even the most skeptical person felt like they had to pay attention. They were said to be fervent, passionate speeches, speeches that could be manipulated and speeches that could persuade.

But amid this meticulously crafted image, some said they saw a suggestion of something more: a desperation, maybe, or a desire to be seen, to be validated. I wasn't sure if it was true, but I had no way of knowing. They mentioned his hand would tremble when he adjusted something as simple as his cufflink, or his gaze wouldn't be quiet in the place he wanted it to be when something didn't go his way.

I gathered that Goebbels was terrifying and tragic, a man who had sold parts of himself to the masses. People said he believed in the cause he was preaching, but I couldn't tell if it was from true conviction or the powerful pull of power.

Either way, there was no denying his ability to control, his mastery of propaganda. All of it came through in that letter, a powerful reminder that he was someone to reckon with, even from afar. I hadn't even penned the letter, as I feared what it said, until I was already on the Train to Danzig. When I opened it, it was different from what I expected.

Ministry of Public Enlightenment and Propaganda, Berlin

August 25, 1939

Herr Klaus Abel

Reichspost Correspondent

Berlin

Dear Herr Abel,

It's time for Germany to fulfill its historic destiny. Operation Case White is much more than a military campaign; it is a critical turning point for the Reich and our people. As a journalist, you are responsible for the truth of our actions, the truth as the Reich perceives it, to reach every corner of the Fatherland and beyond our borders.

You have to sell Poland's continued provocations and disregard for peaceful negotiations as the drivers of this operation. We, Germans, must make clear to the world that we act with no ambition, but out of necessity to protect the German people in the East, who are living in a state of suffering and misery for too long at the hands of Polish aggression and misrule. Your reports must reflect this truth: this is a mission of liberation and defense.

I expect your dispatches to reflect the courage, discipline, and unity of our soldiers, and the brilliance of our Wehrmacht is a story in itself. To show their determination, their claim that they believed in the Führer, and their loyalty to the cause of the Reich. The heroism of those who fight for the German people must inspire the German people. But at the same time, we should make foreign audiences understand the futility of any opposition to our strength.

It is your responsibility to document the campaign, but be careful about what you choose to include. Talk of triumph, of the restoration of order, the German people's resolve. Avoid destruction or suffering in general, and of the civilian population in particular; any unnecessary emphasis upon them. As such, let your words support the message of unity and purpose that is the impetus for our actions.

Herr Abel, in these critical days, you are the voice of the Reich, and your pen is as important as the weapons our soldiers carry. I trust your instincts and dedication to the cause, and your reports will be reviewed to ensure they fit the nation's needs. Remember always: This is a moment the world will remember, and your work will define how it is remembered.

I know you will rise to this challenge. The Fatherland depends on you.

Heil Hitler!

Yours faithfully,

Dr Joseph Goebbels

Reich Minister of Public Enlightenment and Propaganda

The language exuded confidence and dominance. Goebbels was leaving a lot to ride on this mission. It may be a turning point for our country, and that gave me hope. I clenched this letter tightly on the way to the town hall, which wasn't so grand, only benign, about half the size of ours in Berlin.

However, the building stood like a monument to the city's independence, its red-brick facade towering above. The architecture, with its Gothic intricacies, seemed to tell history stories. The tall clock tower loomed over the city, like a watchful eye keeping track of time in a place where time itself seemed to stretch and warp. The pointed arches and narrow windows made it feel like something out of a forgotten era, as if it belonged to another world entirely. I couldn't help but glance up at that towering spire, wondering how many others had stood in this spot, staring at the same clock, waiting for something to change.

It was no less impressive inside. The wood paneling and frescoes still retained their age-old elegance, the halls were full of authority. The Great Hall seemed almost too grand; as if it was out of place, out of time, out of the world. I pictured the debates, the decisions, the life-or-death issues that had been made in this very room. This was a place where the fate of Danzig had been decided, and power was wielded by those who knew what it could do.

It was haunting, though. It was a little empty now, the grandeur, the history, the sense of importance. The town hall symbolized the loss that had happened, but the city was no longer independent as it once had been. However, it held onto the past in its own way, as the present marched forward. Danzig was in stone and mortar, beautiful and powerful and far, far away at other times.

The interior was just as ancient as the exterior, with slight chafing along the walls and less-than-stark stability in the poles. I passed several identical rooms before reaching the room with 15 plastered at the top. Bits of the numbering were chipped off, so the five became like a 'c', and the one was split in two.

As I entered, the silence was broken by the general's voice, low and measured, as he motioned for me to sit. He was immediately there, overwhelming, in his own quiet way, like a storm brewing just beneath the surface of the calm. His eyes were hard but calculating, as though he was sizing me up with every passing moment. He gestured to the chair across from his desk. He said, "Sit," and there was no room for arguing. Klaus, you're here to do more than observe. You're here to report—carefully, with precision."

I didn't know what he meant, but I nodded. I was a journalist; I had covered my fair share of stories, but this was different. His fingers steepled in front of him, his eyes softened for a moment, then he leaned back slightly in his chair.

He spoke as if the weight of his words had already sunk deep into him. This city is no longer what it was, and we are no longer in control of our own fate. "But the world still watches. They always will."

Silence stretched, and he paused before going on. "Mere observation doesn't work anymore, I've had eyes on Poland." It's more than that, Klaus. You'll be our country's eyes; you'll be our ears. That information is going to be important."

I shifted in my seat to try to make sense of what he was saying. "What do you want from me, precisely?"

I locked my eyes onto his, and for the first time there was something darker behind his eyes. "If there is a white crisis, if things start to go sideways, you're going to have to be ready. Klaus, your pen is your weapon. You'll need to write, and you'll need to keep what you know close. You could get swept into the tide, along with everyone else, if you say the wrong words at the wrong time."

His words were heavy, heavy words, and each syllable was weightier than I could bear. "What if... things get out of hand?" I already had an inkling of the answer, but I asked.

The warmth seeped from the general's face just as quickly as it had appeared there. "You'll tell only what you know, but you'll have to listen. Klaus, you can't afford to get caught in the wrong narrative. You have to be a step ahead in moments of white—when fear, chaos, and uncertainty grip this city. They will be looking for someone to blame, for someone to answer for. Don't let them look at you."

The weight of his words settled over me like a thick fog. I swallowed. "And if I fail?" I wasn't asking him, more to myself.

His eyes hardened and pierced through me as if a blade. "Failure isn't an option. Not for someone in your position. It was possible that Danzig's survival depended on the truths you discovered—or the lies you didn't."

I didn't know if it was a warning or a command, but I nodded and it started to sink in the weight of responsibility. The general didn't need me to say more. Without even knowing a bit about him, I was led out and back onto the streets. My determination the same, but fear wasn't such. I was growing a pit in my heart, one where it felt like consuming everything, all that could stop it was quitting, or risk getting lost in a storm I had no path to leave. I started to palpitate in my head, my body sweating despite the cool autumn weather. I wanted only to scream, yet again words wouldn't leave.

Writhing on the floor was the only thing I could do to ensure that I wouldn't run, dropping both the letter and my bag on the floor. The buildings started to become taller, twisting in on themselves, surrounding me completely. The ships in the harbor were all sinking inwards, while the water was rushing at me.

No matter what I did, I still remained still, waiting for the inevitable waves to crash. I watched and gave a little smile. Could this all be some twisted nightmare? That irrational fear kept me in. This perpetual limbo, which all started without any rhyme or reason, may be over.

Just as it almost hit, I suddenly jolted upwards without control. I could feel something wrap around me, the buildings reverted back, and the ships were where they stood before. I looked back to see a soldier who hoisted me up, currently picking up all I dropped, and turned back to give me a hearty smile.

The soldier put my bag in my hand and the crumpled letter, his grin a remarkable contrast to the heavy atmosphere surrounding us. His voice was steady, but warm. 'You alright there, friend?' he asked. He looked at me not with judgment but with something like understanding.

My head felt heavier than ever, and I nodded. I mumbled weakly, 'I'm fine.' "That's all, just... a momentary lapse."

Shaking his head, he let out a soft chuckle. "A momentary lapse, huh? You looked like you were about to let the world swallow you whole. That happens to the best of us, you know." He crouched slightly, picked up a stray paper that had slipped from my bag, and stood, handing it over to me. "But the thing is, they don't teach you that in books or letters—you have to wade through the trenches before you can see the other side."

I just stared at him, not sure what to say. The words were calm, almost too calm, like a man who'd been around the block enough to know the burden that it carried but chose not to be crushed by it.

My gaze met him firmly, he tilted his head. 'I'm not running from the pain. I'm not pretending it's not there.' Trust me, that'll only make it worse. It's about getting through it… every agonizing, gut-wrenching moment. It's because on the other side, there is something worth it. There always is."

His words sank into the pit of my chest where fear and doubt churned like a storm, and I swallowed hard. "And what if there isn't?" My voice was quieter than I had intended, and I asked.

The soldier didn't hesitate. "Then you make it worth it. Whatever it takes. But giving up? Crushing you before you've even fought back with the weight? That's not the answer, my friend. Don't let the pain blind you to the reason you're here."

His hand clasped a firm and steady grip on my shoulder. You're stronger than you think. Even if you don't feel it now, strength isn't easy. That's from doing what you have to do, even when it seems impossible."

His words just hung in the air, heavy but strangely comforting. It was a glimmer, the faintest, not hope exactly, but resolve. A small ember, enough to keep me standing, barely burning. I muttered 'thanks', my voice still shaky, but sincere. "I… needed that."

His grin softened into something more serious, and the soldier nodded. "We all do, sometimes. "Don't forget it when things get hard," he said. He straightened and gave me a quick, almost imperceptible salute. He turned, and without another word, walked away, his boots clicking against the cobblestones.

He walked away, clutching my bag, the letter wrinkling under my grasp. His words rang in my head, in the quietest parts of my mind. Through the trenches... doing what needs to be done. It felt like truths I hadn't been ready to face but now, I couldn't turn back. I breathed deeply, squared my shoulders, and began walking forward again.

I felt a surge of relief as I kept walking along the streets, watching the boats pass and strangers all enjoying their lives. Most didn't look very rich, with torn clothes and starved bodies, yet they still managed to muster great smiles on their faces; they didn't lack anything as they themselves seemed happy as could be. The merchants weren't making many sales, yet they still spoke to people for hours, without expecting them to buy a thing. The beauty of this started to creep upon me as I watched this whole little city function even under the immense pressure present. A metropolis like Berlin couldn't imagine a future like this; however, we will still believe that we are better.

I dressed for dinner in a restaurant gazebo that faced the lake.

Not dressed for dinner, but it was only a quaint restaurant gazebo overlooking the still, mirror-like surface of the lake. The air was crisp: a hint of pine, damp earth and the reminder that autumn was fleeting. Lanterns cast a soft, warm, amber glow in the wooden structure, and the cold steel of reality should have loomed on the horizon. It was another world, a setting, detached from the madness that would come with the rising sun.

My order was simple: pierogi, delicately stuffed with some golden filling and some deep red wine. Rich, but unassuming flavors, a taste of a culture that held on to its identity, even as it hung in the balance for annihilation. The unspoken sadness each bite brought was this— that the land, so full of pride and color, was about to be destroyed by forces beyond any control of the people of the land.

I sat there, dreaming of soldiers, savoring what would be my last meal before the invasion. They were probably in the throes of their final preparations somewhere not too far from here. I saw them, beating the life out of themselves in relentless drills, their muscles straining with the weight of their equipment, faces hardened into grim determination of one who might not have another sunrise. Some were probably praying, clutching rosaries, whispering desperate words to a higher power, hoping their faith would get them through this storm ahead. Perhaps others, the more cynical of them, would have found solace in laughter, camaraderie or the numbing grip of a drink.

There were the Polish, then. An oblivious people steeped in history and resilience, unaware of the impending catastrophe that, in a few hours, will land on their feet. I wondered how innocent they would seem to be in this, the mothers tucking their children in bed, the shopkeepers closing the shutters of their stores the same way that they have hundreds of times in the past, the young couples strolling hand in hand, whispering sweet promises to one another under the warm glow of streetlights. They were unaware that their world would be irrevocably changed by morning, that their cities would soon be filled with the booming of marching boots, the roll of tanks, and the screech of air raid sirens.

I thought of it, and my chest tightened, not with guilt—I didn't think I had the luxury for such a feeling anymore—but with a cold, detached sorrow. The land they called home would be theirs no more tomorrow. The Führer would have added another line to his ever-growing journal of conquests, another conquest in an unending march toward an empire that was to encompass the continent.

The deep crimson liquid caught the lantern's light, and I swirled the wine in my glass and took a slow sip. I didn't miss the irony of enjoying the finer things: a warm meal, a picturesque setting, a moment of seeming tranquility, while the machinery of war continued to roll forward, prepared to tear apart the lives of so many innocents. That was a grotesque juxtaposition, one I wasn't sure I'd ever reconcile.

All seemed indifferent to it except the lake before me. The chaos brewing on its shores had not disturbed its surface. The most haunting part of that scene might have been that nature was so apathetic to the tragedies of men. The stars above twinkled faintly, their light passing over and over again, across and across, and on and on, across unimaginable distances. My life may have been a mess, but I found appreciation in the fact that I wouldn't be alone, that somewhere I could find solace with those who share similar fates with me, and if they could survive in such a harsh world, maybe I could too.

I reached into my journal. I haven't opened that in a while, and upon inspection, I saw a sliver of paper slipping out of the back. I turned to see where I last wrote. It was folded and quilted neatly but had a little brown streak set across it. The note only said "*to Klaus Abel*". I couldn't understand how it came in, but when I opened it, it was more than surprising.

August, 12, 1939

Klaus,

You've always been the type to overthink, to let every little thing burden you like an anchor. And now more than ever, you need to be steady. We're walking a tightrope these days, and the only way forward is one careful step at a time.

Stay calm. That's the first thing. There is no time for second-guessing, no room for panic. You're stronger than you think, although you've always been too modest to admit it. Klaus, trust that strength, and don't let the noise around drown it out.

Most importantly, remember why you're doing this. The story, the career, not even fleeting pride of being 'there to witness it all' is not the point. This is about coming home. That's the goal, Klaus: so you can make it back in one piece with your soul intact. Do whatever it takes, make whatever compromises you have to, do whatever you have to do. It's not about hanging on to ideals. It's about not letting go until you make it to the other side.

I know it's easier said than done, and especially for someone like you. If anyone can do this, it's you. Just keep your head down, do what they want, and don't get into trouble. Don't forget to breathe, and Klaus.

When this is all over, we'll be waiting for you.

—Lukas

Out of the letter came a stamp that had a picture of Sagrada Família temple from Barcelona. It was a sweet gesture made by Lukas, who probably doesn't know what is going on yet he sent a message to me anyway. I don't understand, but as I was on the lake, overlooking the crowd, I felt more than just that, I felt as if I could control if only I could stand tall.

When I went back to the barracks, I couldn't feel a thing, only listening to the indistinct chatter among the soldiers. In my hand, the letter; I stuck it in my bag and prepared the equipment for what was to ensue tomorrow. I hadn't gotten to know the men around me well, but one thing was clear: no matter what happens, I must ensure their efforts won't be in vain.

Chapter 17

HANDCUFFS

September 1, 1939, Bromberg

I lay in bed, it must be only two o'clock, "in just a few hours Poland will be ours." Is what I hear getting sung drunkenly from across the hall. Most soldiers are sound asleep waiting for when the invasion strikes. Whatever I did I couldn't let my mind stop, I didn't feel tired rather it was a nervousness that was unrequited inside me. I spent my time scribbling on spare paper, or taking the interview of some drunk soldiers.

"We will take from all that come in your way!" one said.

"No! We will only take whatever benefits us, leave the trash in—" the other spouted before passing out on the spot.

I wrote, as nothing else could be done. I could only imagine the field in which my father once passed as a soldier. Now I will walk that same path, only instead of fighting I will watch, tell the stories they may not be alive to tell. I may cower from the sides, but I hope that the bravery shown by these soldiers may be heard.

There was nothing else to be done, so I wrote. Now I will walk the same field that my father passed as a soldier. Instead, I will only watch, tell the stories they may not be alive to tell. I may cower from the sides, but I hope their bravery may be heard.

And time passed, and I could hear the voice of my late father, the stern but kind man that helped shape who I am. Its echoes were like distant cannon fire, and his lectures came back to me. He had always expected more of me, even when I screwed up. He would say, 'Klaus, strength is not just in the body, it's in the will.' He was a soldier, a man who could meet his shadow on the battlefield, and here I was not a soldier, not a man who could meet his shadow on the battlefield, but an observer, destined to write while others bled.

I remember the look on his face when I came home with a perfect mark in English, or when I showed him my work. That was back when my pen seemed to be able to win battles on its own. Now, however, as I was about to step on the same cursed soil where his life had been taken, I wondered if the ink I spilled would ever be worth one drop of his blood.

I could feel the guilt tightening around my chest with every thought. I had told myself that what I was doing, documenting the war, was remembering him. Deep down, I knew that wasn't entirely true. I was afraid, afraid of the very fight he had taken up, afraid that I could never measure up to his courage.

Then I stared at the empty page; my pen trembled in my hand. I wanted to tell the truth, to make sure the world knew what these men suffered. But I couldn't get rid of the shame. I stood at the edge of the fray but never dared to cross into it and wondered if he would look down on me now?

I held onto the hope that my words could find meaning in their sacrifice, even as I felt unworthy. I suppose if I could write their stories well enough, with the honesty and the heart my father had always admired, then perhaps I'd find a fragment of the courage he had carried to his grave. The night was unbearable. As soon as I felt I needed to leave, I saw the lights go on.

"Alright, Soldiers!" The general commanded. "Today is the day that will make you. A day when everything is different. Some of you will come to this field as boys, and some of you will leave as men. I know some of you will feel the weight of doubt pressing on your hearts. But hear me now: there is nothing great that has ever been achieved by a great man who bowed to the doubts of the world. Greatness isn't given; greatness is snatched by the ones that dare to believe. Standing unfaltering, unfazed, unflinching, committed. We aren't fighting to survive today; we're fighting for a vision, a belief that whatever happens these actions will pave the way to something better. It may not feel right now, but what's coming up may not be right either. It might ask you to sacrifice things that would truly put your soul to the test. History, however, is not written by those who waited for the world to agree with them. It is written by those who dared to stand, who decided to do what had to be done when others would not. I ask you, now look within yourselves. That spark that just won't die, that fire. When you step on that field, take it with you. Take it with you, and for each other, and for the future you will create with your bravery. It is not the end of your story; it is the beginning. What we dared to dream of is greater; the world will know that we stood, we fought, and we will know that we dared to dream of something greater."

With that, he left, and the others began changing into their uniforms. As soon as I slipped it on, it felt wrong. The fabric, new and clean and stiff and unnervingly smooth, didn't seem like it was mine. Almost too precise, too mechanical, like the uniform itself was a declaration of order I couldn't embody. I caught a glimpse of myself in the warped, propped against the barrack wall, in freshly pressed gray.

My toes still had a little bit of boot pinch, the laces were a little too taut, the soles not quite broken in. The belt cinched tighter than I wanted it to, biting into my waist, but I couldn't loosen it and felt like I was making a concession to some invisible critic. The uniform demanded a standard of me that I wasn't sure I could meet; everything must be exact, perfect as if the uniform was something that I had to live up to.

Then there was the bag. The straps were a pain; I tried to adjust them so it wouldn't dig into my shoulder. The canvas was sagging unevenly, the weight uneven. It swung unpredictably when I moved and served as an almost constant reminder that I was out of place in this role. I cursed, fumbling to find a balance, the buckles clinking louder than they should in the silence of the room.

The strap from the camera hung down my neck and cut into the back of my collar. The polished lens glinted faintly in the dim light, and that felt like a noose. In this setting, I couldn't get it out of my head that it seemed more like a weapon than a tool. Ironic wouldn't be the word for it; the camera, supposed to capture moments, felt like a silent witness to my own unease.

I shifted the weight of the strap, but the discomfort didn't go away. The camera, its cold metallic frame pressing against me as if it were warning me, was recording it all.

Preparation was going on all around the barracks outside, boots thudding on the wooden floors, voices barking orders, clatter of weapons being checked. The sound of everything seemed to be amplified, sharp and intrusive, but distant. But my heartbeat was the loudest of all. It thudded against my ribs, erratic and relentless, making out the chaos beyond the walls.

I tried to steady myself, but my breath stuck in my throat. The uniform was clean, unspoiled, but it was suffocating me, tightening with each moment. The camera, the bag, the uniform itself, all pressed down on me, as if the air had become thick.

It was an insidious and unshakable fear. Not the kind that screamed or panicked, but the quiet, gnawing kind that dug into your stomach and burrowed itself into your mind. What was I doing here? It was a journalist playing a soldier, or worse, a soldier playing a journalist.

I looked down at my hands smoothing the crisp lapels of the jacket. I was trying to project calm, but they trembled slightly. Somehow in the back of my mind, a voice whispered that this uniform wasn't mine, that it was for men with convictions that I didn't have, with purposes that I didn't understand.

And yet, here I was. Standing on the threshold of something I couldn't fully grasp, dressed and equipped. Tightening the bag's straps one last time, I took another breath, forcing my fingers to still. A silent promise to record everything, to leave nothing unseen, the camera dangled at my chest.

By the time I could even register what was going on, it was full battle force. The air, which had been so crisp, was now thick with tension. Precision-edged armies marched in unyielding lines with uniforms of stark contrast to the chaos that surrounded them. An impenetrable wall of discipline, they filed into the square piping, ready to assert their dominance; to prove that they are authority. It wasn't a thought, it wasn't a hesitation. Under a dimming sky, the cold gleamed off their weapons, as their eyes were as steel-hard with their resolve.

Once they were in place, the opposition struck. Out of their ranks came fire like storms out of a sky, guns shooting splitting air into deafening cracks ricocheting off stairs in the narrow streets. Wicked forces hit the first rounds and civilians scrambled as they tried to find places to drop into the labyrinth of colorful buildings that, only moments before, had been full of laughter and the chatter of life as usual. But now they were tombs of fear and desperation; their walls were a feeble shield against the terror without.

Life rushed down the streets, and soon they were rivers of blood. Bodies piled on bodies, their silent screams being drowned out by the chaos as their crimson stains spread across the cobblestones. There was no time to think, there was no time to mourn. It was so brutal, so overwhelming, so unrelenting, it drowned out everything else.

My hands were trembling, and my camera went up almost automatically, framing the scene before me. I became the lens, the only way I could endure to bear witness to the terrible injustices that were being done, right before my eyes. Silent cries, silent pleas for the world to see what we had become, every shot I took.

It was an endless battle of steel and fire and fury. Violence touched all corners of the city—there was no place left untouched. Artillery strikes now shook buildings that had stood proud, cracked and crumbling walls, shattered windows, their only remains a jagged mess of what had been. Smoke filled the air, stung my eyes and choked my breath, rendering much of what was happening just feet away impossible to see. The thick clouds of ash and gunpowder choked up the sky above, once a clear canvas, now lulling under the shade of gray.

The faces of the soldiers were hardened with training, shaped like instruments of war. They couldn't escape the terror of the moment. The stark difference in their movements amidst the raw chaos around them: some advanced grimly, others faltered, their faces betraying a fear they tried to hide behind their weapons. The rattle of machine gun fire never ceased in the distance, and the heavier booms of mortars shook the earth itself. Fresh shockwaves reverberated through the streets, marking the beating of a dying world.

In the meantime, the opposition fought hard, firing back as their hands shook and they clung to whatever they could, desperately unwilling to surrender. They were outmatched, outnumbered, and the hours dragged on, and they were losing ground. The violence was taking over the city; the war machine was literally swallowing it whole.

Once filled with vibrant streets, filled with civilians, now their lives cut short in the madness and motionless in their homes, between the lines.

I couldn't look away. My hands were heavy with the camera, but I couldn't stop. I wrote it all down: the destroyed homes, the injured, the chaos. I captured snug moments, pieces of history; moments that would haunt me much later when the smoke fell. I snapped picture after picture, and deep down I felt an emptiness. Was I a witness, or was I complicit? Every click of the shutter made me think, am I making things worse, bombarding the war with my lens.

The wounded cried out on the streets, mixed in with the sound of gunfire, and the smell of death clung to everything. The buildings weren't the only things crumbling; the city's spirit was broken by the weight of this violence. Once the streets were dotted with the laughter of children and the chatter of neighbors; now they were filled with blood-soaked ruins and the twisted remains of lives forever changed.

So, the soldiers pushed on, on and on, not stopping. The final pockets of resistance were wiped out, and they reached the heart of the city, the once grand plaza lying in rubble. The sounds of battle were lessening; the once deafening din of warfare reduced to the heavy silence of a city beyond repair.

Finally, the city gave up, after what felt like an eternity. But it was hollow, no pride, no joy. We tasted only bitter defeat, theirs and ours. We had won the city, but we'd lost something much greater. The city of Bromberg was chaos incarnate. The streets, once orderly and alive with the mundane rhythms of everyday life, now bore the scars of war—shattered glass crunched beneath my boots, and the acrid stench of smoke stung my nostrils. I adjusted my camera strap nervously, its weight heavier than usual against my chest. The uniform clung to me like a second skin, clean and unmarked in sharp contrast to the devastation that surrounded me.

As I stepped into the city square, I was struck by the surreal juxtaposition of the scene. Soldiers moved with precision, their gray uniforms blending into the drab, ash-smeared facades of the buildings. Civilians shuffled through the ruins, their faces etched with fear and disbelief. A mother clutched her child, her shawl pulled tightly around them both as if it could shield them from the madness.

I raised my camera instinctively, but my hands hesitated. What was I capturing? What was I preserving? The stillness of a moment before another scream, the flicker of life before another loss. Each frame felt like a betrayal, like stealing something sacred and fragile from people who had already lost so much.

The sharp crack of gunfire echoed from a nearby street, and I flinched, my grip tightening on the camera. A soldier brushed past me, his expression unreadable, starkly contrasting the chaos he left in his wake. His boots left a trail of soot and grime on the cobblestones, the remnants of destruction trailing behind him like a shadow.

I caught sight of a church spire in the distance, rising defiantly above the smoke. It was intact, miraculously untouched amid the carnage, drawing my gaze like a beacon. But as I moved closer, I saw the faces of the people huddled outside its doors—refugees seeking sanctuary, their eyes hollow, their hands clutching whatever belongings they could salvage.

"Keep moving, reporter," barked a voice behind me. I turned to see a lieutenant, his face hardened and impassive. I nodded, unable to summon a reply, and continued forward.

The streets grew narrower, the debris more oppressive. A toppled cart blocked my path, its contents—a mix of vegetables and shattered glass—spilled across the road. I stepped around it carefully, the soles of my boots slipping slightly on the uneven surface. Every sound seemed magnified—the distant rumble of artillery, the cries of the wounded, the murmur of prayers whispered into the thick, choking air.

I lifted my camera again, forcing myself to focus. Through the lens, the world looked distant, almost bearable. I framed a shot of a soldier helping an elderly man to his feet, the contrast of their uniforms and rags striking against the backdrop of the ruined city. The shutter's click was almost comforting, a mechanical reminder of my purpose here.

And yet, as I lowered the camera, the weight of it all returned. The devastation wasn't something I could frame or contain. It seeped into every corner, every crack, every breath.

Bromberg was a city transformed, its heart ripped open and laid bare. And I was a witness, an observer in a war that didn't care for observers. I adjusted my bag, the straps digging into my shoulders, and took another step forward, my boots leaving faint impressions in the soot-covered streets.

For the first time since arriving, I allowed myself a moment to feel the enormity of it all—the destruction, the suffering, the impossible task of documenting it. My fear and unease coiled tightly in my chest, but I pushed them aside and kept walking. There was no time for hesitation, not here, not now. Bromberg had already fallen, and all that remained was to let the world know.

As I went around, I got a few notions from soldiers, mostly about how the death and massacre were justified due to the overall message it sends to the world. Others contemplate the lives they took. But it was the story of one soldier in particular who amazed me; his name was Kwame Jones, a German-born African man who was somehow in our forces.

I kept my eyes on Kwame, his eyes filled with memories he had to carry. The silence was heavy in the room, like the air between us knew the truth he was about to share. He breathed deeply, as if he was ready to speak words that had haunted him all his life.

Kwame started his voice rough, almost cracking, as he said, "I didn't want to fight. I never wanted to be a part of this madness. They came for my family when they threatened to burn everything we owned, our home, our dignity, and if I didn't serve them, they let us know they would make us suffer. They would make us feel their hatred, not just me, but my mother and my sisters. They'd make us pay for nothing more than the color of my skin."

I could see it in his eyes, the pain of remembering the threat, the fear of being unable to do anything about an enemy so cruel, so relentless. The memory of those moments clenched his fists, as if making his whole body tremble. I didn't know what to say. How could I? I had led my own life as a march of duty and never felt what he was talking about.

"They used to say they would wipe us from the earth, treat us like cattle, like we were nothing. They didn't just want to take our lives — they wanted to take our souls, our identity. They would have come for us if I hadn't joined their army, if I hadn't proven my worth to them. We would have been torn apart by them. It wasn't just fear. It was terrifying."

I swallowed hard and realized then that Kwame wasn't just another soldier like me; he was fighting for something much more personal: his family, his survival.

His voice was growing quieter now, "Survival. That's what it came down to. Watching them burn our house down, seeing my sisters dragged away because of what I couldn't stop. I didn't know if joining them would save us, but if I didn't, they would be the end. They would make us disappear. I couldn't let that happen."

I had to imagine what it was like to be standing at that crossroads, between the ones you love and the enemy. Not really, there had been no choice. He kept going, though, as if he had to explain, as if his actions had to be explained to me, to someone who might understand.

His voice became steadier, more resigned. "I thought if I fought for them, I could prove to them I wasn't just some foreigner to do them in. I didn't care about your flag or your ideals. I just wanted to survive. I wanted to give my family a chance to live, not to be taken away. Maybe I could protect them, I thought, make them see I was worth something. Worth sparing."

I could feel something heavy twist in my chest. I had never known the kind of fear he was talking about, the kind of fear that makes you grab a weapon not because you're loyal or patriotic about it, but because you're desperate. I had fought for honor, for a greater cause. Kwame… he was fighting because if he didn't fight, then he lost everything.

Now his voice was barely a whisper, "I don't know if it was the right choice," Kwame said. It wasn't about ideals or honor, but it was in the end. It was about survival. I could either be their pawn or I could stand up against it; it would have been pointless. When the bullets start flying, you don't care what's right or what's wrong. Your family, the ones you love, you think about, how can you keep them safe?

I couldn't come up with the right thing to say, so I nodded. Everything he had said I could never understand; everything I had just assumed.

I repeated softly, "Survival." I softly repeated, 'Survival.' It was the first time I understood why he fought, and for the first time, I really understood it. His words felt like a hammer on my weight. Hearing such a story being told without fear or malice in his heart, it moved me. The kind of raw honesty I wanted to do something, anything, to show I understood, to acknowledge the pain he had carried all this time.

I looked at Kwame, his face serious, but not broken, and I had felt something with this feeling of sincerity that I had never had. His voice was not bitter, not resentful. He'd found peace in his choices, in his survival, even as if it didn't matter. A kind of quiet dignity in all that chaos. I opened my mouth to say thank you for sharing something that was so painful, so vulnerable. Before I could even say it, there was a sharp, searing pain in my side.

Then the world around me tilted violently and my legs gave way. I hit the cold stone floor with a thud. I gasped, air rushing out of me, vision turning to a blur of dark and light. I blinked, trying to focus, trying to understand what had just happened. I could see it—blood, my blood, spreading across my abdomen, pooling quickly on the ground.

I raised my hand to my side, and it was heavy, like moving through molasses. The pain sliced through me, like a hot knife.

I could see blood on my fingertips, slick with crimson, dripping slowly to the floor as I brought my hands up to my face. It was surreal; it was like watching someone else's life fall apart before my eyes.

I pushed myself up but my body wouldn't comply. The room spun around me. Outdoors, I could hear the sounds of battle: distant, muffled explosions, the crackle of gunfire, but it all seemed so distant, so far away, as if it were happening in another world. All that mattered was the burning agony in my side, blood soaking through my shirt, the coldness starting to creep over me.

I whispered, my voice thin and weak, but he didn't say anything. My thoughts were slow and murky in the darkness. Was he still there? Had he seen me fall?

I could hear my pulse, rapid and frantic, thrumming in my ears, and I knew, with a sickening clarity, that I was bleeding out. It was like a thunderclap, and I realized what Kwame had meant for the first time. Survival. He had fought for it with everything he had, and now, here I was, clinging to my own life, knowing that the simple truth was all too clear: not everyone survives.

I was shallow breathing, the world slipping away in each passing second. The cold stone under me got further and further away, and I wondered if I would even get out of this room. Was I going to die like this, all alone? I had no idea.

Someone was calling my name. I thought it was Kwame, but it was far away and muffled. It was a blur of his face moving in and out of focus.

Was he coming to help me? Or had he already left, his mind on something else? I wanted to call out, to tell him I understood, to thank him, but the words stuck in my throat. Instead, I could only close my eyes, the edges of the room fading into darkness.

At that moment, I realized what Kwame had been fighting for. He had fought not just for his family, but for the chance to breathe, to live, to see another day. And now, as I lay there, the blood staining the floor beneath me, I understood the raw desperation that came with that desire to survive.

The world around me faded to a dull, aching quiet, and all I could focus on was the fight for my own survival, the pain of that fight, and the cold certainty that the world was much more fragile than I had ever believed. Was he coming to help me? Or had he already gone, his mind elsewhere? I wanted to yell out, to tell him I knew, to thank him, but the words clogged my throat. I could only close my eyes, the edges of the room fading into darkness and I couldn't do anything else.

I knew what all these people had been fighting for at that moment. Fighting not for their family, but to breathe, to live, to see another day. That desire to survive, the raw desperation, I could feel it now as I lay there, the blood staining the floor below me.

All I could see was the fight for my own survival, the pain of that fight, and the cold certainty that the world was much more fragile than I would have ever thought.

Chapter 18

RETRIBUTION

September 10, 1939, Berlin, Germany

I lay in and out of consciousness for days after the near-fatal incident. My wounds are healing but ever-present. I couldn't feel my legs, nor arms, yet I could still be mobile in time. It had swallowed all inside it, from the darkness to the time and the very life itself. All that was left to me was to hang on to that throb within, and that felt damped too. It was like I had turned into a ghost; my body was keeping me tied to this place, and my mind was slowly moving away from it. Each flicker of the fluorescent lights above shot a jolt to my senses, pulling me back from the edge, and then the cold void of the room enveloped me once again.

The walls, bare and white, closed in on me like a prison. There was no warmth here, no color, no sound but the dull hum of machines keeping me tethered to some semblance of life. Sterilized air made the breath labored; a push in the chest. Even sucking in air became a torture. Pervasive and relentless, antiseptic smell and clung to my skin as I went shallowly inside myself. Suffocating. Unrelenting. It seemed that this place had decided it was about to wipe out every fiber of who I was.

I couldn't tell if it was night or day. It was as if the sun outside shone for no reason because here, it did not matter. The cold white walls reflected nothing of warmth or time. It was always the same—always still. I would open my eyes, trying to focus on something, anything, but nothing ever seemed to change. The machines beeped at intervals. Nurses shuffled in and out with now-muffled, distanced voices, yet all of it felt miles away from the real-life world I had once known.

At times, the pain would flare up again, sharp and hot, but even that faded into the background. No matter how hard I tried to focus on it, no matter how many times I moved my hand to touch the wound, I couldn't get away from the overwhelming blankness around me.

I could hear murmurs in the hallway, voices that seemed to belong to other patients, other victims of this war. Sometimes I would wonder if they were still alive or if they, too, had been lost to the same numbness that had claimed me. Were they even real, or were they just echoes in my mind, ghosts of the world outside this place?

It spread like ink in water through my thoughts, getting into all the cracks and crevices of my mind. I wondered whether I would ever come out of this place with the blots on the body healing up, but whether those inside me would ever fade. But then again, what did it even mean to heal here? It was as if the hospital became some kind of limbo where time didn't matter anymore, and people were kept alive but not allowed to truly live.

Every so often, a nurse would come in, checking my vitals, adjusting the IV, but their eyes never lingered long enough for me to catch a glimpse of any kind of empathy. They were just doing their job, moving through their routines like automatons, unable or unwilling to see the human beneath the bloodstained sheets.

So back went to my head in time, way before the attack—before all of it was falling apart. I thought of the streets and the people; I thought of the world from which I am now so disconnected, wondering whether, in fact, I would be able to connect with it all once again. Could I go back to the old life, or would this place, this vacancy, be everything for me hereafter?

The only thing I was sure of was the slow, steady beat of my heart, reminding me that, no matter what happened, I was still here. I was still alive, though I had no idea for how much longer. It was as if some cruel joke had been played on me, leaving me in this place from which there seemed no escape, no respite, where all that one could cling to was the fight within him, an endless struggle not to let the darkness take over him.

Apparently, I got caught off guard by some patriotic Polish who happened to be handy with his firearms—he was killed on the spot. The days went by slowly, the wounds would heal with time, but my fear was left unable to be quelled. It became so immense I stopped everything but to eat, reading was all but forgotten, and I hadn't heard words from the outside world. All news was being withheld from the public, and right now I was one of them.

It was the stillness that left me unkempt. I tried to recall all I knew and tried to put it somewhere. I looked, my journal on the side of the golden buckle, shining. Once in my hand, I saw underneath the newspaper of the day. It was about our invasion in Bromberg. In it, I saw some of the pictures I took, that of the city with our flags all hoisted over it. I went to the pages; it was all different. No interview came through, only just some jabber about how Poland will be better because of this, but all the pain we caused, all hidden, erased from the eyes of the public, only for those who know.

I was still in my bed, paining from all sides, yet it didn't matter what I knew, I couldn't speak. I had my journal in hand, but it didn't matter. For all I know whatever is written may be false, it all matters who wields that pen. In a fit, I ripped the paper to shreds because no matter what I did to survive, it wouldn't truly matter. No matter how I wrote it, it would all be covered up. As in the end, all I did never mattered.

The sun came over me, basking my face with a warm layer of protection from the cold floor beneath. I looked over at the gray buildings of Berlin; though the smoke was heavy, they started to look cleaner, more blue. All the pain I may have felt, the fear I faced, I still saw them, still the buildings all facing as they should. I heard the occasional nurse come around the side, but nobody looked in.

I got out of bed, I saw my white gown turning a dark pink, legs quivering, but still able to support me. I went to the window and allowed myself to enjoy the glorious sunlight, for just one more day.

⚊ ◆ ● ◆ ⚊